Dave Zeltserman lives in the Boston area with his wife, Judy. After working for over twenty years as a software engineer, he now spends his time writing novels. Serpent's Tail also publishes his "man out of prison" noir trilogy: *Killer*, *Pariah* and *Small Crimes*.

Praise for *Pariah*

"A doozy of a doom-laden crime story that not only makes merry with the justice system but also satirizes the publishing industry" *Washington Post*, Best Books of 2009

"Darkly enjoyable... clear, crisp prose; his fearless portrait of amorality; and his smart plotting... what a fine addition to the local literary scene he's become" *Boston Globe*

"*Pariah* is a terrific blast" *Metro*

"*Pariah* is sure to catapult Zeltserman head and shoulders above other Boston authors. This is not only a great crime book, but a gripping read that will crossover to allow greater exposure for this rising talent" Bruce Grossman, *Bookgasm*

"Sheer astounding writing" Ken Bruen

"With this book Zeltserman entrenches his position as the ranking neo-noirist, putting a contemporary spin on a tradition that goes way back to Thompson and James M. Cain. If you like your fiction dark, lean and u......................... has to be at the top of your list" Roger S......

"It's the kind of book that is going to spoil whatever I read next, as it's going to be found wanting compared to this" *The Bookbag*

Praise for *Small Crimes*

"There's a new name to add to the pantheon of the sons and daughters of Cain: Dave Zeltserman" *NPR's Top 5 Crime and Mystery Novels of 2008*

"Zeltserman's breakthrough third crime novel deserves comparison with the best of James Ellroy" *Publisher's Weekly*

"A Jim Thompson mentality on a Norman Rockwell setting... *Small Crimes* is a strong piece of work, lean and spare, but muscular where a noir novel should be, with a strong central character who we alternately admire and despise" *Boston Globe*

"*Small Crimes* is one of the finest dark suspense novels I've read in the past few years" Ed Gorman

"Zeltserman creates an intense atmospheric maze for readers to observe Denton's twisting and turning between his rocks and hard places. Denton is one of the best realised characters I have read in this genre, and the powerfully noir-ish, uncompromising plot, which truly keeps one guessing from page to page, culminates with a genuinely astonishing finale" *Sunday Express*

"*Small Crimes* proves a deft entry in the tradition that goes back to Jim Thompson's *The Killer Inside Me*, James M. Cain's *The Postman Always Rings Twice* and Charles Willeford's *High Priest of California* - small masterpieces celebrating the psychopath as a grinning archetype, as American as apple pie" *Sun-Sentinel*

OUTSOURCED

Dave Zeltserman

A complete catalogue record for this book can
be obtained from the British Library on request

First published in 2010 by Serpent's Tail,
an imprint of Profile Books Ltd
3A Exmouth House
Pine Street
London ECIR OJH
website: www.serpentstail.com

ISBN 978 1 84668 732 7

Designed and typeset by folio at Neuadd Bwll. Llanwrtyd Wells

Printed in the UK by CPI Bookmarque, Croydon, CR0 4TD

10 9 8 7 6 5 4 3 2 1

Outsourced is dedicated to all the software engineers I've worked with over the years. And maybe even to a couple of my old managers.

1

The bar was mostly empty, which was typical for a Wednesday at two in the afternoon. Dan Wilson had the bartender pour him a Guinness Draft and a Harpoon IPA, and brought the beers back to a table in the corner where his companion, Shrinivas Kumar, sat waiting.

Dan, a large affable man with close-cropped hair that was far grayer than it should've been given his forty-eight years, handed the Harpoon IPA to Shrinivas – or Shrini, as he liked to be called – and took a seat across from him. As usual, Dan's mouth was twisted into a slight grin. Dark circles under his eyes betrayed his typical good humor, however.

Shrini was fourteen years younger than Dan. He had a medium build, olive-color skin, and a serious demeanor. He dressed neatly and wore a musk-scented cologne. Shrini grew up in a northern region of India, near New Delhi, before moving to the States to attend college at the University of Florida. Majoring in computer science, he had moved to Massachusetts after graduation where he worked steadily as a software engineer until a year and a half ago. That was when the small software company he and Dan worked for had shut its doors. Since then he'd had one short-term contract job lasting four months, but nothing else. He took his wallet out.

"How much do I owe you for the beer?"

"Shrini, come on, buddy, put your wallet away. You get the next round, okay?"

"In that case, cheers," Shrini offered, lifting his glass.

"Just like old times, huh?" Dan said, a sadness in his eyes countering his grin.

Both men drank quietly, both deep in their own thoughts. Shrini started to say something then closed his mouth, his body tensing as he looked around to make sure no one was within earshot.

"You are meeting your friend, Joel, this afternoon?" Shrini asked, his voice low.

"That's right. I got a two-hour drive up to the boondocks of New Hampshire. Goddamn redneck bastard. His house is in the middle of nowhere. The damn place is like a military compound."

"You are sure you can trust him?"

"We worked together for eleven years. I can trust him." Dan paused to sip his beer. "Joel and I have kept in touch the last seven. He's a good guy, good heart. A little abrasive maybe, but a good guy."

"And you think he will want to do this?"

"I'd have to think so. He was laid off two years ago and hasn't worked since. I know he never made any big money and with three divorces I'm sure he didn't save shit. At this point, he's probably spending down his 401K like the rest of us."

"That is still a big leap to being willing to do this."

"I know the guy. He'll want to come onboard. And what the fuck else is he going to do? A fifty-five-year-old software engineer out of work for two years? Maybe go back to school for bioengineering? At his age? Or how about becoming a real-estate agent? How many real-estate agents do we need?"

Dan had worked himself up with his speech. He drank the little Guinness he had left and wiped the back of his hand across his mouth. When he looked up, he noticed his companion frowning deeply.

"Shrini, buddy, what's wrong?"

"I don't like this. This is very big what we're doing, and I don't know your friend. I know people in India I could bring here—"

"You got to be kidding me," Dan said, raising an eyebrow. Then, muttering under his breath so it was barely audible, "I'm not bringing in people from overseas. With the way things are today, the FBI would be on us in a heartbeat."

"Please, hear me out—"

"Shrini, you've got to trust me on this. Joel is exactly what we need. Politically, the guy is far right to the point of being nuts and his religion now is the goddamn second amendment. He's got all the guns we need, and I guarantee you none of them are traceable."

Shrini, very low, "There are other places we can get guns."

"Yeah, there are. But not without putting us at risk. And there's more to it than that. When you meet Joel, you'll think he looks like nothing. Five foot six, a hundred and fifty pounds maybe. But he works out every day, and bumping into him is like bumping into a brick wall. And he's definitely got the balls for this, maybe more than the two of us."

"Dude, I got the balls to do this."

"I know you do, buddy, and I trust you. I wouldn't be here

talking with you if I didn't. Let me tell you more about Joel. He was kind of a fuck-up in college, dropped out in the middle of his freshman year so he could go to Israel and enlist in their army. This was nineteen seventy-three. He ended up fighting in the Yom Kippur War. You could never tell by looking at him, but this guy is as hard as nails."

Shrini was frowning again. "How did he end up back in the United States working as a software engineer?"

"After his army service, he married an Israeli woman and then moved back to the States. For a number of years he sold bathroom accessories to department stores. I guess he got sick of that and went to school at night and got a degree in computer science. His first job as an engineer was in my group at Vixox Systems. We drank a shitload of beers together when he went through his first divorce."

Dan lowered his gaze to his empty beer mug, and started pushing it back and forth between his hands. Shrini chewed on his lower lip as he sat silently.

"You're not having second thoughts, are you, Shrini?" Dan asked after a while. "Because if you are, that's okay. We can walk away from this anytime."

"Don't worry about me. I'm very serious. I'm doing this."

"You look so damn worried. We've worked out all the details. This is going to work fine. And don't worry about Joel."

"I won't worry about your friend. I've been working with you long enough to trust your judgment."

"Then why do you look so constipated?"

"Fuck you."

"Come on, talk to me."

"I keep thinking about Gordon. Whether we are making a mistake."

"We've talked about this."

"But he is so strange."

"I've known Gordon almost twenty years. Yeah, he's a little different, but he's more eccentric than strange. But, you know, we need him. This won't work without him."

Shrini showed a slight smile. "I think you worked out the plan so we would have to need him. So you could help Gordon out one more time."

"Yeah, that's my mission in life, to help out my misfit friends. Gordon, Joel… you."

Shrini responded by flipping Dan the bird, a good-natured smile breaking over his face. The smile faded as the moment passed. "You are sure we can trust him?"

"No question. I'm willing to bet my life on it, aren't I?"

"You mean both our lives."

Dan looked back at his empty mug. "We can trust him."

"So we are really doing this," Shrini said.

"Yep, we're really doing this." Then very low, barely loud enough for Shrini to hear, "We're going to be robbing a fucking bank."

Shrini finished his Harpoon. "I'll buy us another round."

"I better not." Dan sighed. "I've got to head off to the boondocks of New Hampshire."

Dan wore dark shades as he drove, and even so, had to squint against the glare from the sun. It was a struggle keeping his eyes open. Seven months earlier an ophthalmologist had told him that he had retinitis pigmentosa. According to the doctor, he'd probably had it since his mid-thirties. At least it explained the problems he was having with bright sunlight and driving at night. He knew things were getting worse. Over the past couple of years he felt as if he'd been losing a portion of his peripheral vision and recently he'd been having trouble focusing on small print. He hadn't told anyone yet about his condition, especially his wife, Carol. That was the last thing she needed to hear now.

He thought about Carol. His being out of work had been especially rough on her. This morning, though, she surprised him. It was as if the clock had been set back and nothing in the world was wrong. Before Carol left for work, she came over to him and sat in his lap and gave him a long passionate kiss. It had been months since she had done that, and the tenderness in her eyes nearly floored him. She was so damned beautiful at that moment that he felt himself physically aching.

Whatever he had to do for Carol, for his children, he was going to do. Even if it meant robbing a bank...

Although he had been able to put up a good front for Shrini, the idea of the bank robbery terrified him. Except for pocketing a candy bar from a drug store when he was a kid, he had never stolen anything – never broken the law, never resorted to violence, never really even been in much of a fight since eighth grade, and here he was planning a bank robbery. Actually, he had *planned a bank robbery*. He and Shrini had already worked out the details. Now it was simply a matter of putting it all in motion.

The plan seemed to have taken on a life of its own, carrying Dan and Shrini along with it. Neither of them were capable of backing down. Both probably wanted to, at least Dan did. At least he would have if it weren't for the fact that his retinas were deteriorating. When he lost his job, he also lost his long-term disability insurance. Without that insurance he was screwed. Unless he followed through with the robbery, he would be sentencing his family to a life on welfare. Robbing that bank was going to require nerve and somehow he was going to have to find a way to muster that nerve within himself.

In the meantime he would have to keep from getting overwhelmed by the whole thing. Focus on one step at a time. He tried telling himself that. He broke out laughing. The problem was he was a damned good software engineer and was always searching for mistakes in his logic. Now he was doing the same, playing out the worst-case scenarios in his mind. He tried to slow down his thoughts, tried to simply concentrate on the road. A knotting in his stomach almost doubled him over. His hands ached as he gripped the wheel. He had to get himself under control before he arrived at Joel's house, otherwise the plan was dead. Joel had the uncanny ability to smell fear on people.

God, he wished he had brought an extra shirt with him. The one he was wearing was already wet with perspiration. He was going to have to stop off at a mall along the way. He couldn't meet Joel feeling the way he did, especially with a shirt drenched in sweat. Somehow he was going to have to muster up some sort of confidence, some nerve.

2

Gordon Carmichael sucked in his gut as he studied himself in the bathroom mirror. At fifty-eight he still had a full head of thick blond hair, and as far as he could tell, not a single gray hair in the mix. He moved his face from side to side as he examined his skin for wrinkles. Satisfied, he took a step back. He pushed his bottom lip out, raised his chin, and patted the flesh under his jaw. If it weren't for those damned jowls he could pass for his early forties. He pushed the flesh back with his hand, seeing what he would look like without them. Mid-thirties, maybe. If he could only afford the surgery to take care of them there was no reason why he wouldn't be able to pass for a much younger man.

He gave himself one more look in the mirror before turning away. He had already shaved five years off his resumé and was going to need to shave a few more off to get his age under fifty. Forty-seven seemed as good a target as any, jowls or not!

Gordon sighed. He made his way out of the bathroom, through a cramped bedroom, and to a third room that served as a combination dining room, living room and computer room. There wasn't much to his condo – only four hundred and twenty square feet. At one point he had it paid off. During his three years of being out of work he had taken all the equity he could out of the place. He had tried making his monthly living expenses by trading stock put and call options, but a bad few months had cut his savings down to under five thousand dollars. Now he had a stack of home equity loan bills that were past due and last week received his first foreclosure notice. If things didn't turn around soon he was in deep shit. He sat down in front of his computer, brought his resumé up and gave it a facelift by changing some of the dates while slicing four more years off his tenure at Vixox Systems. He felt a twinge of regret as he looked over his cosmetically updated resumé. One of the few accomplishments that meant anything to him was his twenty-one years at Vixox. Now, after two adjustments, those twenty-one years had been reduced to ten. For some reason, the thought of that made him feel a bit empty inside.

He posted his updated resumé on several high-tech job sites. Before turning off the computer, he checked his email and saw he had something new from Elena. The letter simply stated that she could no longer contact him because she was marrying someone from Oregon. Even though the letter was only two short sentences he had to read it several times before it registered. When its meaning finally hit home, he sat frozen for a long moment, wanting nothing more than to put his fist through the computer screen.

"That's it!" he yelled to his empty condo. "I'm out of here!"

He grabbed his car keys and made it to his front door before stopping. What he wanted to do was get in his car and drive until he hit the Jersey shore. Not that he knew anyone there or even liked being in Jersey, but it was far enough away that he could distance himself from his problems. As he was about to head out he remembered he had agreed to meet Dan the next day for a few beers. He thought about blowing Dan off but decided it wasn't in his best interest. So the Jersey shore was out, at least for the time being.

Still, he had to get out of there. For the hell of it he decided to visit Peyton. The two of them had been friends for over twenty years, even longer than he had been friends with Dan. At the peak of the tech market craziness – right before the tech crash of '01 – Peyton had struck it rich. The startup where he was working had been bought for a ridiculous amount of money and Peyton had cashed out at the top, clearing almost eight million dollars.

Gordon drove to Peyton's house, if you could call it a house. To Gordon it seemed more like a collection of ill-fitting structures. Like some sort of three-dimensional jigsaw puzzle gone awry. Peyton had owned what was for the most part a small shack before becoming a multi-millionaire and, instead of moving into a larger home, had instead added one extension after the next. The original dwelling was no longer recognizable and the monstrosity that was left in its place didn't fit in with the simple farmhouses making up the rest of the street.

Gordon felt somewhat uneasy as he pulled up to the house. The last couple of years he had been seeing Peyton less and less. No real reason, other than that he was beginning to feel like a leech when around his old friend. He parked in the driveway and, after ringing the buzzer a few times, Peyton answered the door wearing a robe.

"Hey, hey, what's up, man?" Peyton asked.

"Not much. I was driving by and thought maybe we could go out for a couple of beers?"

"Hey, you know I'd like to, but, well…" Peyton hesitated, flashing a sheepish grin. "The kids are out of the house and I'm entertaining my wife right now, if you catch my drift."

"Oh jeez, sorry I interrupted you."

"No sweat, man. Maybe next week I'll get us tickets for a Sox game. Maybe I'll even be able to pick up a couple of Green Monster seats. Sound cool?"

"Sure, sounds like fun. Uh, I wanted to tell you about an email I got from Elena."

"Now's not really a great time, but next week, okay, Gordon?"

"Uh, sure, next week. Um, I've been thinking more about that restaurant idea."

"Yeah, man, so have I. Probably not the best idea to mix business with friendship, you know what I mean? But we'll talk about that next week. Cool, man?"

"Sure, uh, cool. And give my best to Wendy."

"Don't worry, I'll do that and in a few minutes I'll also be giving her my best."

"Oh, uh, just one more thing, Pey—"

"I got to go, man. Next week, okay?" Peyton said as he closed the door.

Gordon stood frozen for a moment, feeling red-faced, his hands shaking. "*Stupid idiot,*" he whispered to himself. "*Why'd you have to bring up that restaurant now? Stupid!*"

Even though there were no neighbors around, Gordon couldn't help feeling self-conscious, as if people were watching him and seeing how much of a fool he had made of himself. With a sick grin stuck on his face, he lumbered back to his car.

Once inside, he smacked himself on the side of his head with an open palm.

"Stupid!" he swore to himself. "Well, that's it. I'm not going home now!"

It was only three in the afternoon. Too early for dinner, but he could drive to Lowell and pick up some takeout Cambodian that he could eat later. For him Lowell was an oasis, one of the few places nearby where he could get good ethnic food. When high tech was booming, most of the companies settled within a rural area about thirty miles northwest of Boston. Not a bad area if you were into horseback riding, or maybe raising a family, but it sucked as far as eating out went. Lowell, though, was only a twenty-minute ride.

Traffic was light, and Gordon got to Lowell in less than fifteen minutes. He decided to bypass his usual Cambodian restaurant. The last few times they had skimped on the portions, and besides, he didn't like the vibes he was picking up there. Instead he pulled up to a newer restaurant that he had noticed a few months back.

A young Asian girl sat bored behind the cash register. As Gordon approached, she glanced up and gave him a slight smile.

"Very hot weather we've been having," Gordon said.

"Yes it is," she said softly. "Very hot, muggy."

"No air conditioning in here?" Gordon asked.

"No, not now. Later we'll turn it on."

"I guess it's too early for dinner and too late for lunch. Normally I get takeout at a Cambodian restaurant a few blocks from here, but I noticed that you had opened last time I drove by."

"Thank you. I am sure you will like our food."

"I certainly hope so. What do you recommend?"

"Everything is good here. The shrimp is very good."

Gordon looked at the menu. "I notice your shrimp dishes are your most expensive," he said.

"They're very good," she said, her slight smile weakening.

"Well, in that case, why don't I order this shrimp dish, the one with peanuts and spicy lemon grass sauce."

"I will have the kitchen rush your order," she said. "No more than five minutes."

Gordon watched as she walked towards the kitchen. The girl was tiny, slender, with long black hair reaching almost all the way down her back. The tight green skirt she wore outlined her hips and legs. He felt a drying in his mouth as he watched her walk away. When she came back, she smiled politely at him before turning to the magazine in front of her.

"Are you Cambodian?" Gordon asked.

"Yes, of course."

"Well, it's not so obvious. You could be Vietnamese. I do know Vietnamese who work in Cambodian restaurants."

"I am Cambodian."

"What happened in Cambodia under Pol Pot was simply awful," Gordon said. "People wearing eyeglasses shot for being intellectuals. Can you imagine that?"

"I only know what I have read. That was well before my time."

"I'm sorry, of course. I have to say your English is very good. How long have you been in this country?"

"I was born here."

"Really? I wasn't trying to imply anything. Only that your English is really quite good. Much better than what I hear at other Cambodian restaurants that I go to."

"I guess I should thank you."

"Can I ask you a personal question?" Gordon said. She looked a bit flustered as she turned towards him, her smile now completely gone.

Gordon put his hands on his hips and stuck his chin out as he posed for her. "How old would you guess I am?" he asked.

"I – I don't know. I will be right back."

She turned and hurried away. Gordon dropped his pose. He felt like getting the hell out of there, but he had already ordered his food. A couple of minutes later a Cambodian man wearing a suit came out of the kitchen. He headed straight towards Gordon. When he got to him, he handed Gordon a takeout bag.

"Food today is free," he said. "I am the owner. Please do not come back here."

"Why not?"

"You were making the girl working here very uncomfortable."

"How was I doing that?" Gordon asked. "Jeez, all I was trying to do was be friendly."

"That is not what she said."

"What did she say? That I was hitting on her? Come on, I was only trying to make conversation while waiting for my food."

"Please leave here."

"Because I asked her to guess my age? Jeez almighty. I only asked her that because I wanted to know if she thought I could pass for under fifty."

"Your age? I will guess your age. You are dirty old man. That is my guess for your age. Now please do not come back here."

Gordon stared into the other man's eyes. He resisted his initial impulse to punch the man in the face. Instead, he dropped the bag, stepped on it, then turned and left the restaurant.

3

Carol Wilson felt like crying. The firm's senior law partner, Tom Harrold, had scheduled a meeting with the paralegal group for three thirty, and she couldn't stop worrying that she was going to lose her job. The lawyers weren't that friendly to begin with, and the last week they had been more brusque than usual. One of them, Bob Thorton, couldn't even look her in the eye when he gave her her last assignment. And then there was Charlie Bishop. He did all the computer work for the law firm, and the last few days he had been giving Carol and the rest of the paralegals an almost apologetic smile.

She picked up one of the liability cases that she needed to read, but she couldn't concentrate on it and after a while the words just started blurring together. She felt a hand on her shoulder and looked up to see Nancy Goldberg standing next to her.

"We've got that meeting in a few minutes," Nancy said. "Let's go get some coffee."

"I don't think that would look good. Why don't we wait until three-thirty and get some on the way?"

"It doesn't matter."

"Have you heard anything?"

"Why don't we get some coffee?"

Carol felt light-headed as she stood up. She had to lean against her chair for a moment before she trusted herself to move. At forty-four, she was still very attractive. Slender and petite, with shoulder-length blond hair, and girl-next-door type features. The stress of the last year, though, had started showing around her eyes and mouth, making her look somewhat worn out. When Dan lost his job a year and a half ago, she had started looking for work. Before having kids she had been a paralegal for seven years. Finding a job was harder for her than she'd expected, with firms clearly wanting younger paralegals, and it took her five months to find this position. Nancy, while only twenty-six, was a five-year veteran, having worked at the law firm since college.

The light-headedness passed. She caught up with Nancy, and the two of them walked silently to the break room. Nancy poured two cups of coffee and handed one of them to Carol.

"What did you hear?" Carol asked.

Nancy took a sip of her coffee. The muscles along her jaw hardened as she faced her co-worker. "That they've added a bunch of new email accounts," she said. "Charlie Bishop told me an hour ago."

"What do you think that means?"

"It's not good."

"Oh, God." Carol had to sit down. "I can't lose this job now."

"Maybe I'm wrong. Anyway, I'm sure you'll find another one

if you need to. Me, I've decided to join the bastards and go to law school."

"Why would adding new email accounts mean they're going to get rid of us?"

"Maybe I'm wrong," Nancy said without much conviction.

Carol had to bite her tongue to keep from crying.

"I'm sorry, Carol. I didn't want to upset you, I guess I wanted to give you some advance warning. Or maybe I'm just in a lousy mood. Anyway, I'm probably reading stuff into things."

The two of them sipped their coffee. To Carol it was tasteless.

"We'd better get to that meeting," Nancy said.

The rest of the paralegal staff were already waiting in the conference room. Most of them looked concerned, a couple of them bored. Tom Harrold, short, balding, sixtyish, with a round head and small, almost baby-like ears, stood by his chair at the head of the table with his hands clasped behind his back. He peered through thick glasses at Nancy and Carol as they made their way to their seats. Tapping his foot impatiently, he waited for them both to sit down before checking his watch. Then he looked back up at his audience and cleared his throat.

"I called this meeting to dispel any rumors that we are planning a layoff," he said. "Nobody here is going to lose their job."

He waited for a reaction. There were a couple of sighs. Another paralegal a few years younger than Carol, Charlotte Henry, clapped her hands. Carol found herself breaking into a smile. Out of the corner of her eye she caught Nancy smirking.

"We are, however, going to take advantage of a unique opportunity," Harrold continued. "Many of you may or may not know this, but India has a similar jurisprudence to us. We are in the process of hiring legal assistants in that country—"

"At one fifth of the cost," Nancy whispered to Carol.

"...who can research issues for us at night. What this means—"

"We will be your cutting your hours so we can pay ourselves bigger bonuses," Nancy said under her breath.

"...is that all of the lawyers here at this firm, including myself, will be able to work more effectively. Issues raised late in the day will be able to be researched and resolved by morning. This will result, initially anyway, in a smaller workload for all of you and, unfortunately, we will have to ask for a reduction in hours."

Nancy burst out with a short laugh.

"Excuse me, miss, do you have a question?" Harrold asked, glaring.

"No, sorry, just choked on something."

"Drink some water then," Harrold said. He glared at Nancy for another few moments before turning his attention back to the rest of the paralegals.

"As I was saying," he said. "This may result in a hardship for some of you. We apologize for that, but our hope is that this will increase our productivity and, most likely, this reduction will only be temporary. I will have my secretary notify each of you by the end of the week as to your new hours. That is all."

Carol looked around the room and saw a mix of different emotions on her colleagues' faces. Some were relieved, some crestfallen. She felt a little of both. With Dan out of work they weren't making ends meet as it was. She didn't know how they could possibly manage with less money. As she was getting out of her chair, Nancy leaned over and whispered, "Temporary is right. If their outsourcing experiment works out, we're all out on the street."

Harrold had walked up to them. He stood staring at Nancy, his small mouth working as if he were chewing gum.

"Miss, what is your name?" he demanded.

She turned to face him, somewhat taken aback. "Nancy Goldberg. I've been here five years."

"Well, Miss Goldberg, do you have any expectation of being here another five years?"

Reluctantly, she nodded.

"This is a law office, Miss Goldberg. We expect a more professional attitude. Understood?"

She stood blankly for a moment, then a funny look came over her face. "I'm sorry. I guess you want me to smile while I'm being screwed. But you know, if I'm going to do that I might as well work in a whorehouse – at least I'll be in a more professional environment. Don't even bother saying it, I quit."

She gave Carol a weak smile as she walked away. Harrold watched her for a moment, his body stiff, his small ears turning a bright pink. He noticed Carol and shifted to face her. "Do you have anything you'd like to add?" he asked, his voice strained.

Carol shook her head.

"And we expect you to be punctual for all meetings. Three minutes late is as bad as thirty. Understood?"

"Yes, sir."

When Carol got back to her desk she started to cry. She couldn't help herself. Still sobbing, she picked up one of the liability cases and forced herself to read through it, being careful to keep the paperwork from getting wet.

4

Dan arrived at Bristol, New Hampshire a little after four thirty and still had a fifteen-minute drive over a dirt road to get to Joel's sprawling ranch, which looked more like army barracks than a home. The building was an eyesore. Not that it mattered. Not too many people were ever going to look at it. Joel's nearest neighbor lived six miles away.

Dan walked up to the front door and rang the bell. Joel bragged to him once that he had a steel reinforced front door installed and that no one, especially not the Feds, were ever going to kick it down. Within seconds of ringing the bell, the door opened and Joel popped out.

"Well, well, look who drove up all the way from *Taxachusetts*," he said, a big shit-eating grin in place. "You're twenty minutes late."

"Nice to see you, too. If you didn't live so far up in the boondocks—"

"Fuck you, don't give me your excuses, and I'm happy right

where I am. You can have your *Taxachusetts* with all that liberal scum." Joel scrunched his face into an exaggerated display of disgust as he sniffed the air. "What's that stench? Ah, yes, the smell of liberal scum all over you."

He broke into a short laugh and held out his hand. "So how are you doing, pal?"

"Could be better." Dan took the hand and felt like he was being squeezed in a vise.

Joel Kasner stood like a rooster with his chest puffed out. With big ears, small glassy eyes, and hair that was mostly thinning, he resembled an animated cartoon character more than anything else. He pointed to the briefcase Dan was carrying. "What you got there?" he asked. "All the money you're going to be losing to me in backgammon?"

"I'll show you later. So how things going?"

"How do you think? They suck. How 'bout you?"

"Probably suck even worse."

"Yeah, I know," Joel said, his shit-eating grin fading. "It's got to be hard. I feel for you, pal. At least in my case I've got my expenses under control and I don't have kids living at home like you. Mine are all over eighteen and I don't have to support their lazy asses anymore. Come on in, I've got the 'gammon board set up. Time to take some money off you."

Dan followed Joel into the house. The place looked like it had been decorated from garage sales. None of the furniture matched, and the individual pieces looked worn and tired. A couple of gun magazines lay scattered on the sofa.

"You beat off with those?" Dan asked, pointing at the magazines.

"Fuck you. Let's get the game going."

A backgammon board was set up on a small Formica table

in the kitchen. Joel opened the refrigerator and took out two bottles of Bud. "You want one?" he asked.

"Sure."

"A buck," Joel demanded, his hand held out.

"You're gonna charge me for that?"

"Why not? That's what it cost me. And you could've brought your own beer, asshole."

Dan swallowed back a crack he wanted to make on what Joel could do with his beer, instead reminded himself what he was there for, handed Joel a dollar and took one of the bottles. They both sat at the table, each rolling a die to determine who would make the first move. Midway through the game Joel missed a roll he needed. He stared up at the ceiling and shook his fist. "*Motherfucking cunt*," he swore. "You can't give me one goddamn roll, can you?"

"Those are the breaks, Joel."

"Fuck you and roll."

Two rolls later, Joel hit a one in thirty-six shot that gave him an edge in the game. He leaned back in his chair, satisfied. "So what are we playing for, five bucks a point?"

"I don't think so. A quarter as always. And if you're feeling so goddamn confident give me the doubling cube, okay?"

"Maybe I will." Joel's hard smirk softened for a moment. "So level with me, how's the job search going?"

"Not good." Dan paused, his stare moving towards a corner of the room. When he looked back at Joel, he was grinning, but it was a lifeless grin. "My whole career there were always engineers older than me. Now when I interview there's no one older than thirty-five. They spend their time grilling me over design patterns that didn't even exist five years ago, and look at my twenty-six years' experience as a joke because it was done in what they consider obsolete programming languages. These pricks are making me feel washed up at forty-eight. Who the fuck knows, maybe I am."

"Defeatist talk, pal. Me, I'm halfway through my JAVA certification program, and I promise you when I'm done I'll be working again."

Dan started to say something, instead closed his mouth. They sat quietly and finished out the game. As they were setting up the board for the next one, Joel looked at his friend, a weariness in his eyes. "So how bad are things for you?" he asked.

"Bad," Dan said. "I've already spent down my 401K, and what Carol's bringing in just isn't enough."

"It's your own fault! Who told you to buy a McMansion when you did? Chrissakes, I remember when you bought that house I asked you why the fuck anyone would need a thirty-eight hundred square foot home. Just sell the damn thing."

"Easier said than done."

"Then go back to school like I'm doing," Joel said. "With all your project leadership experience, you get JAVA certified and you'll be golden."

Dan bit his tongue, almost telling him that it wouldn't do any good, that by the time he finished any certification program he'd be blind. Instead he gave his friend a hard grin. "You're living in a fantasy world, Joel," he said. "You can have all the JAVA certificates you want, nobody's going to hire you. Why hire a fifty-five-year-old guy when they can get a kid out of college who's cheaper and who they're more comfortable with?"

"Bullshit," Joel looked away, his mouth weakening. "What the fuck else am I supposed to do? Just give up like you're doing?"

"Who says I'm giving up? Maybe I've got something in the works. Could be something for you too."

"Like what?"

"I might have a proposition for you."

"You're looking to start a company?"

"In a way."

"Don't be so fucking coy. Any investors lined up?"

"Joel, I'm not trying to be coy."

"Okay, fine, speed it up, though, pal. Testing, coding, whatever you need I'll do it for you."

"It's not like that." Dan took a deep breath and exhaled slowly. "I didn't tell you this, but I had a three-month contract that finished a month ago."

"Why the fuck didn't you bring me in?"

"They farmed out the development to India. If I could've brought you in, I would've."

"So what does this have to do with your proposition?"

"I'll get to that. The contract was with a bank. They hired me to architect a new security system for them. When a silent alarm is hit, they want it to go through a computer system that will simultaneously call the local police, FBI, and a private security service that they're using. It will also trigger-lock their vault and several other doors. Because of this system they got rid of their on-site security guards."

"Okay, so?"

"Their old system had the silent alarm tied directly to the local police. Now you've got a computer in the middle."

"So… if the computer goes down, the silent alarm doesn't work."

"That's right."

"Is there a backup?"

"Yeah, if the computer goes down the alarm signal switches

over to a backup system. Both systems are on battery backup power supplies."

"Pretty stupid if you ask me. They should've maintained the direct line."

"No kidding. Now this is where it gets interesting. The Indian contract house they used did a shitty job. I inspected the code and it's a mess. The system is supposed to go through a two-point-eight-second self-test at random intervals to verify everything's working fine. They screwed up, and instead it goes through a twenty-eight-minute self-test."

"So they wrote crappy code. So what? You want to point it out to the bank and have them hire us to fix it?"

"Not exactly. I modified the code a little myself. Now when it goes through its self-test the silent alarm signal is disabled."

"Can that get back to you?"

"Why would it?"

"Why? Because you architected the system, putz!"

"So what? As far as the bank is concerned, I never even breathed near the software. I made my changes to look like bad code, just like all the other crap those Indian contractors delivered. And I left no fingerprints."

"Again, so what?"

Dan paused for a moment, a sickish grin breaking over his face. "The algorithm the Indian contractors came up with to calculate random time intervals isn't random," he said. "It's predictable. In fact, I can tell you exactly when in a week that bank's alarm system is going to be disabled. For twenty-eight minutes."

Joel's eyes narrowed as he stared at Dan. "Don't even say it," he warned.

"I've got every detail worked out, Joel. This is something we can do."

"Schmuck!" Joel exploded, showing teeth. "I told you not to say it! You're going to be a bank robber now, is that it? Here's some advice, forget your own little fantasy and let's play some more 'gammon."

"Joel, we can do this. And we fucking deserve to do this." Dan wet his lips, edged closer to his friend. "You know how many years I worked eighty-hour weeks at startups trying to make some real money, only to see them all go out of business? I know you did the same. This is our chance to cash in."

"You're out of your mind."

"Just hear me out."

"Stand up."

"What?"

"I said stand up."

Dan held his hands up to signal what the fuck, pushed his chair back, and started to stand. He only made it halfway up when Joel popped out of his chair and hit him with a hard jab under his left eye. The punch stunned him. He staggered back a few steps before catching his balance. Grabbing his cheek, he could feel that it had already started to swell.

"What the fuck!"

"Hey, schmuck, you're a bank robber right? You should be prepared for shit like that."

"You asshole."

"*I'm* the asshole? You come here trying to convince me to join you in a bank robbery? Look at you, you're not even prepared to take a punch and you're going to rob a bank?"

"Try it again."

"I don't think so. You're ready for it now. But that's the

thing, you try doing something stupid like what you're thinking and anything can happen. And as you just showed, you don't have the instincts to handle what might come your way. Let me get you some ice."

Joel filled a plastic bag with ice from the freezer and returned to the table. Dan sat back down and stewed silently as he took the bag and held it against his cheek. Thoughts of how dire his situation had become kept him frozen in his chair.

"So did I knock some sense into you?"

"You could've pulled your punch. I think you broke something."

"Quit your whining. I didn't break anything. And quit daydreaming about robbing banks. You're a software engineer, remember?"

Shifting his eyes upward to meet Joel's, Dan shook his head. "No, I'm not," he said. "Neither are you. Maybe we used to be, but we're not any more. And they've locked the doors shut on us."

"Go ahead and believe that all you want. I don't." Joel absent-mindedly moved his hand to his jaw and started massaging it.

"You know damn well it's true. Any JAVA certificate you get might as well be printed on toilet paper for all the good it's going to do you."

"If you really believe that, go back to school for something else!"

Again Dan had to bite his tongue to keep from yelling out: *What good would that do? I'm going blind!* Instead, very calmly, he said, "For what? Even if I had the money for that, which I don't, tell me what I can get a degree in where they'll hire me out of school when I'm in my fifties."

"This is fucking ridiculous."

"Joel, you've worked on projects with me. Have I ever screwed up?"

"This is not the same thing."

"I beg to differ. How about hearing me out and then making up your mind?"

Joel opened his mouth to argue but instead blew out a lungful of air. He leaned back in his chair, his hands clasped behind his head. Very softly, "Go ahead."

Dan took the ice away from his face and placed it on the table. He opened his briefcase and methodically went over his plan. As Joel listened his attitude shifted from reluctant humoring to a grudging respect. At the end a glint of interest shone in his eyes, his tongue darting across his lips as he thought it over. "I have to admit it could work," he said. "You sure as fuck did your homework. Everything you told me is on the level?"

"Yep."

Joel leaned further back in his chair, his eyes glazing while he rubbed a thumb across his lips. He sat like that for a minute mulling over what Dan had told him, and all at once straightened in his seat, his eyes hard on Dan, his face flushing a deep red. "You stupid schmuck," he swore, his voice barely a rasp. "You're planning to bring Gordon into this, aren't you? Are you out of your mind?"

"This won't work without Gordon. Just like it won't work without you."

"Are you crazy? It won't work with Gordon period! The guy can't keep his mouth shut for five minutes." Joel brought his hand to his mouth and began pulling at his bottom lip. "I think the guy's a borderline psycho."

"Gordon's fine. Trust me, okay?"

"Have you talked to him about this yet?"

"No—"

"Well, don't!"

"You think I would've worked with Gordon off and on for almost twenty years if I couldn't trust him? The guy served a tour in Vietnam. He knows how to handle himself. And the plan doesn't work without him. You can see that, can't you?"

"If he's involved you can count me out. I'm sure as hell not betting my life on that loon!"

"Calm down, okay? Gordon will be fine. He's a smart guy. And I need four people in the bank for this to work. All we need is ten minutes. That's it. And I have no problem betting my life that Gordon can keep quiet for ten minutes."

"What about after? With the way he talks?"

"He'll never say a word to anyone about this. Have you ever heard him say anything of substance about what went on in Vietnam?"

Joel thought about it and shook his head slowly. "I still don't like it," he complained. A glint came into his eyes. "You mentioned four people for this job. Who's the fourth?"

"A friend of mine. We've been working together for the last five years. You don't know him. He's Indian. As soon as the job's done, he's heading to India. Which is perfect for us."

"How much of this does he know?"

"As much as I do. We've been planning this together for the last six weeks. And, yeah, I trust him. Any more questions?"

"I still don't like the idea of Gordon being involved."

"He'll say the same when I tell him about you."

"I haven't committed to anything yet! And he can say whatever he wants. It doesn't change the fact that he's at least one can short of a six-pack."

"Joel, why don't we play another couple of games of 'gammon and not talk about this. Just let it sink in, see how you feel."

"All right, fine."

They played in silence after that. After losing three straight games due to poor play, Joel threw his dice into the adjoining dining room. "*Motherfucking cunt* dice," he yelled. He took a deep breath and let it out noisily through his mouth.

"You're really serious about this, aren't you?" he asked.

"Serious enough that I've been practicing stealing cars."

"I can't believe we're talking about this," Joel said. "If we try to rob that bank and something goes wrong, your life's over, pal. Me, I don't have a wife, I don't give a shit about my kids, and I can handle living out my life in prison. You'd be throwing your family away, and I hate to tell you this, but you wouldn't last a year in prison. I'm not trying to insult you, Dan, but the simple fact is you're not tough enough to survive there."

"Nothing's going to go wrong."

"What if something does?"

"Then we're fucked. Yeah, sure, anything can happen. But we're guaranteed to be fucked if we don't try this."

"Does Carol know any of this?"

"No."

"Is she going to?"

"No. Never. How about it, Joel, are you in?"

Joel shook his head slowly for a moment, grimacing. "I'll think about it," he said after a while.

5

Shrini flexed his right arm as he sneaked a look at himself in one of the gym's mirrors. He worked out regularly and took a great deal of pride in his appearance. Now, though, there was more to it than that. With the bank robbery only one week away he had to prepare himself, get as strong as possible.

He caught another quick look in the mirror as he pushed a hand against his stomach, feeling the flatness of it. Satisfied, he moved to one of the open benches and slid forty-five- and twenty-five-pound plates on to each end of the bar. With the bar weighing forty-five pounds, that put the weight at one hundred and eighty-five pounds. He sat down on the end of the bench and then lay back, adjusting his position so he could properly grip the bar. Sucking in his breath, he pulled the bar from the rack and let it bounce off his chest once as he proceeded to do twelve quick repetitions before dropping the bar back on to the rack.

As soon as he finished the set, he sat back up and wiped a towel along his forehead and neck. He stood up and replaced the twenty-five-pound plates with forty-five-pound ones, bringing the weight to two hundred and twenty-five pounds. He sat back on the bench and shook his arms, trying to psych himself up for his next set. As he sat there, his thoughts drifted to the robbery and to his plans for afterwards.

An adrenaline rush hit him every time he thought about the robbery. While he needed the money, maybe even more important to him was the chance to prove himself. If he could do this, he knew he'd be capable of doing anything. He had no doubt that they were going to be successful. He and Dan had worked out every detail and their plan made too much sense for it not to work. Afterwards, when he had his share of the money, he would transfer it to a Swiss account and later to an account in an Indian bank. When he moved back to India, he would use the money to start his own software contracting company. He had enough contacts to know he'd be able to line up business. With a touch of bitterness he reflected on how the same people who had been so reluctant to hire him in the States would be more than happy to throw money at him to build software for them in India.

He noticed a girl at a quad machine nearby smiling at him. She was cute, maybe in her early twenties with light brown hair, and, as her Lycra workout clothes revealed, a slender, athletic body. He smiled back at her. What he was going to miss more than anything about living in the States were the girls. All different colors, shapes and varieties. He was always running into girls here who viewed him as something exotic, and he was only too happy to show them how exotic he could be. His parents had arranged for him to marry Amrita once he moved back to India. He remembered her from high school as a plump and not very attractive girl. Always a sour look stuck on her face. *Nectar* my ass, he thought, reflecting on the meaning of her name. Maybe the nectar of some spoiled fruit. That was who he was going to be stuck with for the rest of his life.

Well, he still had some time left in the States. He got up and walked over to the girl who had smiled at him.

"Excuse me," he said. "I need someone to spot me for another set of bench presses. Maybe you would be willing to help me?"

"I'd like to. I don't know if I'm strong enough."

"You won't have to lift much. When I'm on my last rep, you'll only have to pull the bar with a couple of pounds of force. Believe me, you'll be able to do it with one hand. Maybe even one finger."

"Maybe *you'd* be able to do it with one finger," she said, laughing. "I'll need both hands."

"You will be surprised how easy it is."

As she stood up, Shrini introduced himself. She told him her name was Sonia.

"Sonia? That means *golden* in Hindi. And you certainly are golden."

She laughed. "Are you looking for someone to spot you or to hit on?"

"No," Shrini said, smiling broadly. "Even if you were some smelly guy I would've asked for help. Believe me."

"Sure you would."

"Yes, of course. I wouldn't lie to someone so golden. Come on, help me out."

Shrini led the way back to the bench and showed Sonia where to stand.

"All you need to do is wait until I ask for help. Then use one hand to guide the bar back to the rack. I'll do most of the work, you will only have to help a little."

"I hope so," she said, laughing. "This looks heavy."

He made a face. "This? Two hundred and twenty-five pounds? That is only sixty pounds more than I weigh."

After positioning himself back on the bench, Shrini firmly gripped the bar and jerked it off the rack. With each repetition he cheated a bit, letting the bar bounce off his chest with each explosion of breath. Usually, he only did a set of six repetitions with that weight. Having Sonia watching him, he went past that. On his eleventh press both arms started shaking and the bar started to sink towards his chest. Sonia reached to help him.

"No, no, not yet," Shrini forced out, his face red.

With a grunt, and arching his back, he got the bar moving back up and was able to push it back on to the rack.

"That looked difficult," Sonia said.

Shrini quickly sat back up. Exaggerating a look of dismay, "That? That was nothing."

"It was nice meeting you, Shrini." She hesitated for a few seconds, then, "I guess I'd better let you get back to your workout."

"I enjoyed meeting you too." Shrini held out his hand, and smiled a bit inside noticing she seemed reluctant to let go of him. "Of course, the least I can do for your help is to buy you a drink later."

"Sure, I'd like that." She blushed slightly. "I have to admit, I've noticed you here the last few times I've worked out."

"I noticed you too," Shrini said as he tried to remember if he had ever seen her before. He found himself smiling a bit more on the inside when he noticed the subtle change in her expression, the way her smile became that much more bold. Yes, he was going to miss this country. But he was going to enjoy it while he still could.

*

Viktor Petrenko ignored the heaviness in his arms as he threw two left jabs and a right uppercut. The two jabs hit the heavy bag solidly, the uppercut lifted the bag half a foot. He stepped back and threw the same combination, making sure to concentrate on his footwork and the acceleration of his body as he let loose with the uppercut. He had been at the bag for over forty minutes, maintaining the same pace as he threw his combinations. Almost all of his punches hit solidly. The few that didn't brought a thin brutal smile to his otherwise vacant expression.

He had been boxing most of his life. When he was eleven he was enrolled in the Soviet youth boxing program. While punishing and powerful, by age eighteen it had been determined that he lacked the speed to be an elite boxer and he was dropped.

Boxing had been his one true passion. There was something exhilarating about connecting a punch to your opponent's ribs and feeling his body lift from the ground as his breath was simultaneously pushed out of his lungs. Later, when Petrenko became a chief interrogator for the KGB, he was able to experience that feeling many times but it was never quite the same. Now he had to settle for punching a heavy bag. At least most days.

There was a knock on the door and Yuri Tolkov walked into the boxing studio that Petrenko had set up in his home's basement. Petrenko ignored him and continued to hit the bag for another ten minutes before straightening up and removing the leather wraps from his hands. With pale, almost translucent blue eyes, he examined the hard calluses that had built up over his knuckles throughout the years. He grabbed a towel off a hook, wiped some of the sweat from his arms and neck, and sat at a small table in the corner where a bottle of Pravda Vodka was chilling in an ice bucket. After pouring himself a glass, he acknowledged Yuri.

"So?" he asked.

Yuri approached, stopping four feet away from Petrenko. "I spoke again with the Arabs. They have agreed to let us appraise the diamonds."

"I don't like this. How did they get my name?"

Yuri shrugged. "They claim they got it from Ekhardt."

"Ekhardt? That German bastard. What's he doing giving those Arabs my name?"

Yuri shrugged.

"I don't like it. This could be a sting operation. Perhaps FBI?"

"I don't think so." Yuri smiled, showing off badly discolored teeth. "I checked. One of the Arabs is on the FBI's ten-most-wanted list."

Petrenko considered that for a moment. "These diamonds are supposed to be uncut, correct?"

Yuri nodded.

"Then we will have them appraised."

Yuri turned to walk away, then hesitated. "Why don't we simply steal them?" he asked.

"These Arabs might have more they want to sell us." Petrenko showed a thin smile, the type of look you might see on a rattlesnake before it strikes. "Don't worry, we'll steal them with our price."

Yuri had his hand on the doorknob when Petrenko stopped him.

"Remember," Petrenko said. "Tomorrow morning we have business at that market. Bring Sergei also."

Yuri nodded and left the room, closing the door quietly behind him. Petrenko poured himself another glass of vodka and sipped it slowly.

6

During most of the ride back from New Hampshire, Dan found himself seething over Joel punching him in the face. The guy was a hothead; he knew that about his friend, and here he was planning a bank robbery with the guy? The thing was, Dan was an only child, and over the years Joel had taken on the role of an older brother, at least in some ways. If you're going to tell an older brother something he thinks is crazy, he's going to do whatever it takes to snap you out of it, right? That's what Dan needed to convince himself of anyway – as well as remembering that, when push came to shove, he could count on Joel. By the time he arrived home, he had pretty much accomplished both.

After leaving the car in the driveway, Dan walked into his house through the side door and found Carol sitting alone in the kitchen. From the redness around her eyes and nose it was obvious that she had been crying.

"You're home late," she said.

"Sorry, I was talking some stuff over with Joel."

"You weren't just drinking beer and playing backgammon?"

"No. I had one Bud. That's it. We were trying to work out some business ideas."

"You come up with any?"

"Too early to tell. We'll see."

"What happened to your cheek?"

Dan grimaced as he lightly touched the swollen area around his cheek. "I slipped getting into my car and smacked my face against the door, if you can believe it."

Her eyes shifted away from him. "There's some macaroni and cheese in the oven," she said.

"Thanks. I'll have some in a little while. Where are the kids?"

"Susie's upstairs. Gary is sleeping over at a friend's house."

"Which friend?"

"Brandon."

He nodded. "I'll see Susie and be right back."

"Take your time."

Dan hesitated before turning away from her. He wanted to say something, but there was nothing he could think of that could possibly provide any comfort. *Don't worry about a thing, honey, I'll be robbing a bank soon and we'll be on easy street then.* He felt sick inside. As he made his way up the stairs, he forced a smile, preparing himself to see his daughter.

After knocking on Susie's door, he waited for her to yell out *What?* in that overly exasperated voice of hers before he walked in. She was lying on the bed plugged into her iPod. He sat down on the edge next to her and kissed her forehead. She ignored him for a moment, then removed the plugs from her ears.

"Hi, Daddy," she said without much enthusiasm.

"Hi, Princess. I just wanted to say hello. See how you're doing."

"I'm okay," she murmured sullenly.

He felt his smile strain as he looked at her. She had been such a beautiful baby, but as she grew older that changed and it became obvious that physically she was going to take after him. Instead of being blessed with Carol's delicate features and lithe, near perfect body, she had inherited his bone structure and body type. Broad shoulders, wide hips, thick neck. It didn't seem fair for a twelve-year-old girl to have to be short-changed like that. Susie's genetic makeup was one more thing for him to feel guilty about.

"Do anything fun today?" he asked.

"There was nothing to do. Everyone I know is at camp."

"You'll go next year."

"Whatever." She peeked at him as her mouth pushed into a hurt look. "Mom said we're going to have to move," she said.

"No, honey, that's not true."

"Why did Mom say it then?"

"Your mom is very tired, that's all."

"If we moved, where would we move to?"

"Honey, please don't worry about this. We're not moving. I promise."

"I don't want to lose my friends."

"You won't have to. Honey, you've got a promise from me, okay?"

She nodded, but didn't look convinced as she pushed the plugs back into her ears. Dan sat for a moment, then patted her head and left the room. When he went back downstairs to the kitchen, Carol stared straight past him as if she were catatonic. He ignored her, grabbed a plate, and spooned out some macaroni and cheese. Instead of joining her at the table he pulled a barstool up to the counter. He took a few bites of the food before he could taste it. Not that there was much to taste anyway.

"Nancy quit today," Carol said.

Dan looked up from his plate. "Who?"

"Nancy Goldberg. Probably my only friend at work."

"I'm sorry. Why'd she quit?"

"They're cutting our hours. They're starting to outsource some of the paralegal work to India."

"You're kidding."

Carol shook her head.

"People in India can do that type of work? They know Massachusetts law?"

"Apparently so."

"How is that possible?"

"Law books and court decisions can be put on compact discs and studied anywhere."

"What are they cutting your hours to?"

"They'll let me know by the end of the week. Nancy thinks this is just an experiment. That they're waiting to see if the Indian paralegals work out before getting rid of us."

Dan got off the barstool and moved to the table, taking the chair next to his wife. He took hold of her hand. "Whatever happens, don't worry. We're going to be okay."

She reacted as if she had been slapped. Incredulous, she asked, "How can you possibly think that?"

"You just have to trust me."

"No, Dan, I don't think so. What I do think is that you have to face reality. We have no money, we can't pay our bills and we're starting to get calls from collection agencies."

"That's going to be over soon."

"How?"

"I'm working on some ideas. Just trust me, it'll work out."

She fell back into a catatonic stare, then all of a sudden hit the table hard with her open palm. The noise made Dan jump in his skin.

"Damn it! I'm not going to just sit here and trust you! We're going to lose our house! We're going to lose everything we have and be penniless, can't you see that?"

He stared at her for a long moment before shaking his head. "We'll get through this," he said at last.

"No we won't. We don't have the money to live the way we're living. Dan, I know you don't want to hear this, but we have to sell the house."

"We're not selling the house. And you had no right worrying Susie about it!"

"She's a smart kid, so's Gary. They both see what's going on."

"Why don't we just drop this, okay?"

"How are we going to pay the mortgage?"

"We'll find a way."

"No, we won't. We need to sell this house and move someplace we can afford."

"What's the point?" Dan said. "We're mortgaged up to the hilt. With property values dropping, if we sell now we won't get a dime out of this place. We'd probably even have to bring money to the closing. So why not just stay where we are? Worst case, we get foreclosed on. If that happens we can move someplace cheaper."

She opened her mouth to argue with him, but seemed to get stuck. Slowly, her mouth closed as resignation set in. Then, under her breath but loud enough for him to hear, "Maybe you could get a job."

"What do you think I've been trying to do?"

"It doesn't have to be in software."

"What do you want me to do? Wash dishes? How about bagging groceries?"

"At least you'd be bringing in some money. It's not as if I enjoy working in that law office."

As he stared at her he felt himself slipping over the edge. Whatever control he had was gone. At first all he could hear was the blood pounding in his head. After a while he could hear the words that were pouring out of him.

"You got some fucking nerve. Twenty-five years as a software engineer. Last thirteen years you sit on your ass while I'm out there working like a dog. Sometimes putting in sixteen-hour days, seven days a week. And you have the fucking nerve to complain after working for a little over one year. Goddamn you!"

As quickly as the rage had hit him it was gone. Drained, he collapsed back into the chair, dropping his face into his hands.

"I'm so sorry," he said.

He could hear Carol sobbing next to him.

"Darling, I didn't even know what I was saying. I guess we're both on edge, huh? Can you just forget the last few minutes?"

He reached over to touch her shoulder. She moved quickly, knocking his hand away.

"Don't you dare touch me," she said, still sobbing, hard lines etching her neck.

Dan sank back into the chair. For a long while all he could do was watch her as she sobbed. Eventually her crying subsided.

"How many times do I have to apologize?" he asked.

"Just leave me alone."

"You know I didn't mean any of those things." He looked away from her. "I love you."

A good minute passed as she sat still, an internal struggle tightening the muscles around her mouth. "I love you too," she finally said. "But I'm not like you. I can't just flip a switch and have everything be okay. I need time to process my feelings."

"What do you want me to do?"

"Just leave me alone right now."

"All right, sure, if that's what you want."

Dan pushed himself out of his chair. He got to the kitchen's entranceway before Carol called out to him.

"I know some of the things I said to you weren't fair," she said. "I know you worked hard for a lot of years while I stayed home with the kids. And I know that you just had that three-month contract, and that you're trying. But I'm scared right now. I don't have your sense of optimism. And I just don't see how we're going to make it."

He started to open his mouth but she raised a finger, warning him. "Don't say everything's going to be okay. Please! I'll scream if you say that!"

He wavered, then lifted his hands in a sign of surrender and left the room.

The fight with Carol wiped him out. There was so much blame, so much disappointment simmering inside her. Deep down he knew he still loved his wife, but it was getting so damn hard to be in the same room with her. That would change after he got his cut from the bank robbery. Of course, that was if the robbery was still on. Joel hadn't made his decision yet and there was still Gordon to talk to. If either of them turned it down, the robbery was dead and finished.

He turned on the set and was surprised to see the ten o'clock news had already started. He remembered he owed Shrini a call.

No one answered. He started to leave a message when Shrini picked up.

"Hey, man," Dan said, "sorry about the time. I should've called you earlier."

"No problem," Shrini said in an exaggeratedly serious tone. "I've been tied up most of the night working on my cardiovascular."

Dan heard a girl giggling in the background. "You got company. Damn, I'm really sorry about bothering you now."

"No problem, dude, we're taking a break. A well-deserved break, believe me." There was some more giggling and Shrini left the phone for a moment. When he came back, he said, "Give me a one-word answer, yes or no, so I am not held in suspense all night."

"The word would have to be *maybe*. I'll call you tomorrow."

"Okay, dude, tomorrow."

Dan sat back in the chair and watched the news for a few minutes, then flipped through the channels until he came to a new reality show called *Bank Job*. He sat transfixed, not believing what he was watching. The point of the show seemed to be to have the participants plan a bank robbery. The robbery would be staged after two months of planning in a building that used to be a real bank. Everyone would be in on it. There would be no real bullets or anything, but if the members were successful they would get to keep the million dollars that was going to be placed in the vault. Dan just started cracking up. He couldn't help himself. At some point Carol came in. She looked exhausted as she stood in the doorway.

"What's so funny?" she asked.

"Nothing," Dan said, wiping tears from his eyes. "Just this stupid reality show."

"If it's stupid, why don't you turn it off?"

"I will, I just need to veg for a few minutes."

"I'm going to bed now," she said. "Would you like to join me?"

"In a little while. I need some more time to clear my head."

"I'll meet you upstairs. Could you turn the set down? It's really loud."

The volume was barely audible, but he lowered it anyway. He wasn't sure whether she was becoming hypersensitive to noise or if she was just busting his balls, but they'd been having too many fights as it was.

"I'll see you soon," he said. She nodded and left the room.

The eleven o'clock news came on. After that, Dan flipped between the different late night talk shows. Later he found *The French Connection* on one of the movie channels. Sometime during the movie he drifted off.

7

The phone woke him the next morning. Groggy, his neck stiff, he realized that he had slept the night on the recliner. He heard Susie answer the phone and then yell out to him.

He pushed himself out of the recliner, his back stiffer than his neck. Hobbling like an old man, he found Susie in the kitchen.

"It's for you," Susie said, handing him the handset, her eyes rolled slightly upward to make sure he knew how trying it was having to answer the phone for him.

Joel was on the line. "You took your sweet time," he complained.

"You woke me up."

"Woke you up? It's nine thirty, pal. Look, I'm in Nashua right now. Meet me at ten in the north end of the mall parking lot."

"Nashua's a half hour away. I need to take a shower, brush my teeth—"

"I'm at a payphone, I don't have time for your nonsense. Your breath don't smell fresh enough for me, guess what, I don't care. You meet me at the mall parking lot at ten, understand?"

Joel hung up, not bothering to wait for an answer.

Dan placed the handset back on its base. He checked to make sure he had his car keys and wallet on him, and left the house.

Dan spotted Joel leaning against his red Ford Escort. He pulled up and Joel got into the passenger seat.

"First of all, you're full of shit," Joel said.

"Nice to see you too."

"I mean it. If you wanted a software job bad enough then you would've found one."

"Yeah?"

"Yeah, there are people our age still working in the field," Joel argued, his mouth compressing into a tight oval.

"Not as many as there used to be. And that's only because they're already in their positions. Let's see them get through today's interview screening."

"You're still full of shit."

Dan laughed sourly. "You're sounding a lot like my wife."

"Yeah, well, she's a smart girl. Even if she married a schmuck like you."

"Then why aren't I working?"

"Because you're burnt out." Joel's eyes narrowed to thin slits as he appraised his friend. "And more than that, you're pissed off. After everything you've done in the industry you're now at the mercy of these condescending smug little pricks interviewing you. But if you really wanted a job you could retrain yourself and get one."

"You're wrong."

"You're lying to me again."

A numbness had set into Dan's forehead, almost as if ice had been pushed into his skull. "Why'd you waste my time having me drive here?" he asked, his words sounding hollow in his head. "Why didn't you just tell me over the phone that you don't want to do this?"

"Who said anything like that?" Joel hesitated as he pulled at his bottom lip, pinching it with his thumb and forefinger. "I'm just being honest with myself, that's all. Something you should try. I don't look at this as my only way out. But I got to tell you, I'm sick of writing software. And there are certain things about your plan that appeal to me."

"So you're telling me you're in?"

"Maybe. I got conditions. Number one, my buddy Eric Hoffer be included."

"Eric Hoffer?"

"You met him at my second wedding."

Dan had a vague recollection of a mostly bald stocky man with small pig-like eyes. "That's your friend who got arrested," he said.

"Yeah, that's right. He got screwed in a setup. Did four months for a bullshit charge."

"Something about attempted rape?"

"No, nothing like that." Joel showed a thin smile as he shook his head. "Lewd and lascivious behavior. The idiot had a hooker in his car. He had already unzipped when the hooker spots a police cruiser pulling up alongside them and tries to save her own butt by yelling rape. That little incident cost Eric his wife, family and job, not to mention his time in county lockup. He's been out three years since then and still hasn't bounced back. He needs this."

"Sorry, Joel, but we don't need five people for this robbery."

"Says who?"

"I already worked out the details—"

"Yeah, you're an expert all of a sudden in robbing banks? You've got Gordon and your Indian buddy along, huh? Fuck that. If I'm doing this, I'm doing this with someone I can trust. Someone I know who'll back me up."

"Your friend, Eric, he's been arrested. They've got his fingerprints on record."

"So? We'll be wearing gloves, won't we? And your plan has us in disguise, right?"

Dan started massaging his forehead, trying to rub the numbness out. "I don't like this," he muttered.

"Yeah, well, guess what, I don't like having that loon Gordon involved, but I'm willing to trust you that you can control him for ten minutes. Besides, my guns can be traced, Eric's can't. We need him. This is non-negotiable. So what's it going to be? Are we doing this or are we calling it quits right now?"

Dan found himself asking why having untraceable guns mattered, even though it was obvious to him. In case a gun was left at the robbery, which could happen if one of them were shot. Or other ways too. Joel just stared at him as if he were an idiot.

"Why do you think?" Joel finally said.

Dan nodded. He didn't bother asking why they couldn't just file the serial numbers off the guns, since that answer was obvious also. In case Joel ever had to account for the guns that he had registered. "All right, fine," he said. "Your friend Eric is in. Have you talked to him yet?"

"Not yet, but he'll want to do this."

"Hold off until I talk to Gordon."

"When's that going to be?"

"This afternoon."

"Okay, but don't call me at home. And don't call my cell phone. I'll call you later from a payphone. Any communication – you, me, anyone else involved in this – will be through anonymous email accounts. I don't want there being any phone records over the next week connecting us."

"Going a little overboard, aren't we?"

"No. Fuck no. This is a deal breaker too."

Dan shrugged. "Fine. Anyway, it makes sense. No reason not to be as careful as we can. I'll set up an account later today. Try calling me tonight from a payphone and I'll have an email address ready for you."

"What do you know?" Joel smiled and punched Dan in the shoulder. "We're going to do this, huh?"

"We'll see what Gordon says."

Joel made a face. "I still don't like you dragging that clown into this. Working with him for eleven years at Vixox was more than enough for me." Joel took a deep breath, shrugging. "But I have to admit, you did put together a brilliant fucking plan. I spent all night last night trying to poke a hole in it, and couldn't."

"Thanks." Dan glanced at his dashboard clock and started feeling antsy. He had two hours before he was supposed to meet with Gordon and he still wanted to stop off at home so he could shower and clean up. "Are we done now?"

"Yeah, for now. Assuming we're still on, I want all of us to meet at my place tomorrow to go over the details. Plan on noon."

Dan nodded as the two of them shook hands.

As Joel was getting out of the car, he looked back and showed a reflective smile. "You realize if we go ahead with this, that's it as far as the two of us are concerned. Afterwards, no more 'gammon, no more meeting for beers. We'll be dead to one another."

Dan started laughing. "No problem there, Joel. Whether we rob this bank or not, I don't plan on seeing much of you in the future anyway."

Joel froze for a moment. Slowly a sneer twisted his lips. "Same here, pal," he said.

Detective Alex Resnick took the call that the owner of the Kiev Market had been beat unconscious and the store ransacked. His partner, Walt Maguire, was oblivious, his feet up on his desk as he talked over the phone with his girlfriend. Resnick tapped him on the shoulder and gave him a signal that they had to go. Maguire nodded, made several attempts to end the conversation gracefully, then muttered, "I'll call you later," as he hung up the receiver.

"What's the story?" he asked.

"Owner of that Russian grocery store on State Street got beat up."

"Any witnesses?"

"Don't know yet."

Resnick drove. He was a sixteen-year veteran of the Lynn police force and a detective for seven. His partner, Maguire, was just a kid of twenty-eight and had only made detective a month earlier. As far as Resnick was concerned, Maguire still had baby fat. With the siren on they got to the grocery store in seven minutes. Three police cruisers and an ambulance were already there. About a dozen people crowded the sidewalk trying to get a look inside the store. As Resnick pulled up behind one of the cruisers, he could see the store's front window had been smashed and a cash register lay among the broken glass on the sidewalk.

Maguire left the car and walked over to the cash register. He put gloves on, let out a few breaths and then lifted the register to his waist before lowering it back to the sidewalk.

"This mother's heavy," he told Resnick. "Must be some antique lined with lead or something. Got to be at least eighty pounds." There were four patrolmen standing outside the store looking bored. Maguire turned to the closest one. "You want to help me bring this back inside?"

The cop made a face. "If I want to go on disability, maybe. Thanks, but I'll throw my back out moving my own furniture."

Resnick walked over to the same cop. "What can you tell me?" he asked.

"The owner was knocked unconscious. Paramedics are inside with him now. It looks like he'll be okay. Whoever did this smashed up the place pretty good."

"Any witnesses?"

The cop shook his head. "The wife was there. She claims he tripped and hit his head."

"Okay, stay where you are and keep the public out." Resnick turned to the other patrolmen. "Why don't you guys check the crowd, then the stores nearby. See if anyone's willing to talk to us."

Resnick sighed. At five foot ten and one hundred and seventy-five pounds, he was three inches shorter and forty pounds lighter than his partner. He hoisted the cash register on to his shoulder and headed towards the entrance.

"What are you doing?" Maguire asked as he rushed to open the door for him. "I would've helped. And you're compromising any possible fingerprints."

"There weren't going to be any fingerprints."

Resnick carried the register to the counter and placed it where a dust outline showed it had originally been. Off to the side an elderly man lay on the floor while two paramedics worked on him. The man's wife stood nearby crying. Resnick took a quick look around. A freezer in the back had been smashed up, probably with a tire iron. Top shelves were pulled out, bottom ones kicked in. The place was a mess.

Resnick moved closer to the store owner and could see that his forehead was wrapped heavily in gauze and that blood had trickled down from his ear. He asked the paramedics how the man was doing. One of them looked up at him briefly before turning back to the store owner. "Signs are beginning to stabilize," he said. "He's pretty much out of it. Took a nasty blow to the head."

"But he'll be okay?"

"It looks that way."

Maguire had pulled the wife aside and was asking her what happened.

"My husband fell down," she said, still crying.

"You're saying he hit his head when he fell."

"Yes. He fell. Over there." She pointed towards the doorway.

"Then why's there blood on the edge of the counter?"

Resnick moved in front of Maguire, blocking him from the wife. "I am very sorry about this, Mrs. Wiseman," Resnick said.

Mrs. Wiseman's eyes were mostly shut as she cried. "Do I know you?" she asked, trying to open her eyes enough to focus on him.

"I shop here sometimes," Resnick said. "You have very good smoked whitefish."

Mrs. Wiseman nodded slightly as recognition seeped in. She was a small woman, not much at all to her. "I've seen you, yes," she said. Her head turned to the side as she watched the paramedics lift her husband on to a portable gurney.

"You probably want to go with your husband to the hospital. We can talk with you later." Resnick handed her a card. "How am I to go with him?" she asked. "How can I leave the store like this?"

"I'll have the hospital call you then." Resnick took a heavy breath. "Mrs. Wiseman, this is not Russia. People like Viktor Petrenko are not protected here. If you tell me he did this, I will arrest him, and I promise you he will go to prison."

Mrs. Wiseman seemed to shrink inwards as she watched the paramedics move her husband out to a waiting ambulance. She pushed her mouth shut, her eyes helplessly looking over the damage that was done. Then she met Resnick's stare and shook her head. "No," she said weakly, "my husband fell."

Resnick nodded and placed a hand on her shoulder before walking over to the counter. He found a yellow pages directory, called a glass repair shop and arranged for them to replace the store front window within the hour. Taking another deep breath, he moved to one of the aisles and started doing what he could with the shelves, then stacked the food back on to them.

"What's going on?" Maguire asked.

"Go check if anything came of the canvassing," Resnick said. "Give me a half hour, okay?"

"This is ridiculous. Let the old lady hire a cleaning service. And who's Viktor Petrenko?"

Resnick ignored him and continued methodically restacking the food that had been dumped on the floor. Maguire watched for a moment then, cursing to himself, joined his partner.

*

"I can't believe you had us do that," Maguire complained.

Resnick gave his partner a hard stare. "You would leave that old lady alone with the store like that?"

"That's not our job." Maguire tried to meet his partner's stare but had to look away. "Besides, I don't like being lied to. She's going to tell me straight-faced that her husband fell when it's clear as day that someone slammed his head against that counter?"

"She had no choice."

"Bullshit. And who the hell's Viktor Petrenko?"

Resnick gave his partner a sad look before turning to talk to one of the cops who had been canvassing for witnesses. "Anything?" he asked. The cop shook his head. "No one saw a thing. At least that's what they're saying."

"I'd like you to go to Lynn Memorial and take a statement from the husband when he wakes up. Okay?"

"Sure, but I'll be wasting my time. He's not going to tell us anything."

"Yeah, I know, but we need to get his statement. Why don't you wait until those repairmen are done with the window, then you can take the wife along with you."

"Sure."

Resnick clapped him on the shoulder before turning towards the Buick he was driving. He unlocked the car. Maguire got in the passenger side.

"You going to tell me what's going on?" Maguire asked.

Resnick waited until he secured his seatbelt. Then, "Petrenko, among other things, runs an extortion ring in the North Shore, targeting Russian immigrants. He did this."

"Why didn't you push the wife some more? She looked like she was ready to start talking."

Resnick shrugged.

"I mean, Jesus," Maguire continued, "what's wrong with these people? If she talks to us we can arrest the bastard."

"Then he'd have her killed. Not just her, but her husband and any children they might have."

"That's bullshit. We could protect her."

A shadow fell over Resnick's eyes. "No we couldn't," he said. When Resnick got to Essex Street, he took a right, heading away from the station house.

"Where are we going?"

"I guess we have no choice but to introduce you to Petrenko. For all the good it's going to do." Resnick drove in silence after that, a darkness clouding his face. Maguire watched him for a minute then looked straight ahead, trying not to let his partner's mood affect him. Out of the corner of his eye he noticed a thin smile crack his partner's face.

"What?" Maguire asked.

"I was just thinking of something. When you meet Petrenko, make a comment that you think he's Jewish."

"Why? Is he Jewish?"

"No."

"Then what's the point?"

Resnick's smile stretched half an inch. "Humor me, okay?"

"Fine. I'll humor you. What did you mean when you told that lady that people like Petrenko are not protected here?"

"Pretty much what I said." Resnick's thin smile disappeared. "Petrenko used to be KGB. In the Soviet Union, that sadistic son of a bitch could pretty much do as he pleased. The Russian community here know his reputation and are terrified of him."

"How'd someone like that get into the United States?"

"By invitation. Petrenko showed up in Lynn fifteen years ago, right after my rookie year. He started off as a collector, beating the crap out of deadbeat gamblers. I tried putting the arm on him and was stopped cold. I looked into it and it turned out to be someone from the State Department. Petrenko made some sort of deal with them."

"You're kidding."

"I wish I were."

"Is he still being protected?"

"Not by them, at least I don't think so. But Petrenko's smart and living a charmed life. So far I haven't been able to get anything on hime to stick."

"What's the worst he's done?"

"Probably a couple of dozen murders."

"Shit! You're joking, right?"

"I wish I were." Resnick showed a pained expression as he pulled up next to an auto body shop. "Petrenko's in there waiting for us."

"How do you know that?"

"Unfortunately, I know how that son of a bitch thinks." Resnick paused for a moment. "Be careful in there. We want to get to him, but don't let him get to you. He's got very good lawyers. You do anything he can sue you over, he will."

The body shop, a dirt-stained one-story concrete structure, had both its front and side windows covered with cardboard. Inside the place was lit up by rows of fluorescent lights. The middle bay had two guys attaching a bumper to a Cadillac. Three other guys stood around smoking cigarettes. As the two detectives entered by a side door, all five of the men looked at them for a moment before turning back to what they were doing. Resnick ignored them, knocked on a closed office door, then opened it. Viktor Petrenko was alone in the office sitting behind a desk. He frowned at the interruption.

"Yes?" he asked, his eyes deader than a mannequin's.

"I need you to answer some questions," Resnick said.

"You, I know," Petrenko said, staring deadpan at Resnick. Then looking at Maguire, "I don't know you."

Maguire stared back, trying to figure out where he had seen eyes like that before. Maybe inside the reptile house at the zoo. He matter-of-factly flashed his identification in Petrenko's direction before slipping it back into his wallet.

Resnick said to Petrenko, "The owner of the Kiev Market, a seventy-two-year old man about half your size, was brutally beaten, his store trashed."

"That is too bad."

"What happened, Viktor? Were they short this month, or did Mr. Wiseman try standing up to you?"

"Are you accusing me of this?"

"Why would I do something like that?"

"I have no idea. But if you are, I will need to call my lawyers."

"You don't need to do anything. Not if you can tell me where you were at ten o'clock this morning."

A thin smile pushed on to Petrenko's lips. "I was here, of course."

"Can anyone corroborate that?" Resnick asked without much enthusiasm.

"Of course." Petrenko stood up, walked to the office door, opened it and yelled something out in Russian. One of the three men smoking cigarettes looked back at Petrenko, tossed his cigarette to the floor and trudged into the office. The man looked more Neanderthal than human with his thick brow and a mass of black hair that left almost none of his forehead visible. Slouching forward, he ignored the presence of the two detectives and focused his stare in the general direction of Petrenko.

"Ask him," Petrenko demanded of Resnick.

"Go ahead, beat it," Resnick told the semi-Neanderthal.

The man gave Petrenko a questioning look and then started stammering that Petrenko had been in his office all morning.

"I said beat it."

The man waited until Petrenko gave him a nod before leaving the office.

"Do you think any of those men working here will say anything different?" Petrenko asked. "So unless you have someone who will say otherwise, I suggest you stop this harassment."

An angry laugh exploded from Maguire.

"Did I say something amusing?" Petrenko asked him.

"You're a goddamn coward, Viktor, beating an old man like that. Someone who could be your own father."

"No, he could not be my father."

"Why not?" Maguire winked in the direction of his partner. "You're both Russian, right? You're both Jewish, right?"

Petrenko flinched. Muscles bunched along his shoulders as he took a small step towards Maguire. "I am no *zhid*," he forced out, his color paling to a milk white. Resnick held his breath, his hand moving to his service revolver. Petrenko stopped, almost as if waking from a dream. Unclenching his fist, he sat down behind his desk.

"No offense," Petrenko said to Resnick, a thin smile back in place.

Resnick gave his partner a signal to leave the office. Then, to

Petrenko, "You want to call me a *zhid* or anything else, go right ahead. I look at you as nothing more than a rabid animal that needs to be put down, and one of these days I'm hoping to get my chance."

"Is that a threat, Detective?"

"No threat. Simply a statement of fact. I'm going to be spending a lot of time on State Street looking after these Russian store owners. I hope I get a chance to see you down there."

Once they were back in their car, Maguire turned to Resnick. "What the hell was that about?"

"I took a long shot that we could bait Petrenko into assaulting you. Almost worked."

"Thanks," Maguire said, his face reddening. "I appreciate the thought."

"You might have taken a punch, but in the long run it would have been worth it to put that psycho away, or better yet, have an excuse to put a bullet in his ear."

"Nice of you to volunteer me for something like that."

"I had no choice. He would've ignored any comment coming from me."

Maguire sat stewing for a minute. Shaking his head, he asked, "Why did he go mental over me calling him Jewish?"

"In Russia, only gentiles are considered true Russians, Jews are considered something else. A lot of these so-called pure Russians like Petrenko are as anti-Semitic as they come." Resnick paused, a darkness muddling his features. "To him, the money he extorts from these store owners is nothing, just loose change. He does it because he feels it's his duty to exercise an iron fist over them."

Resnick found an open parking spot in front of one of the

divey bars that lined Washington Street and pulled into it. "Lunch time," he said.

"I don't think they serve food here."

"We'll see."

Once inside Resnick ordered a double shot of bourbon and, after downing that, ordered another.

"I don't feel comfortable drinking on the job," Maguire said.

"Don't then. This is just my version of a three-martini lunch. Something I need after dealing with Viktor Petrenko."

Maguire rubbed a hand across his jaw as he watched his partner drink down his second shot and signal the bartender for a third. "Something that's been bothering me. What's the sense of trashing the store? How can Petrenko expect those people to be able to keep making their payments if their business is shut down?"

"They have no choice about making their payments, they'll just have to find a way. And as far as smashing up the store, when the insurance check comes in it will go right into Petrenko's pockets."

The bartender refilled the shot glass. "That's all you're getting," he told Resnick. Resnick nodded and took the bourbon in one gulp. Giving the car keys to Maguire, he held his hand out palm down and saw that for the first time since Petrenko had moved on his partner his hand had stopped shaking.

8

Holy shit. I'm going to be robbing that damn bank.

Even after all of his planning, the bank robbery had never seemed real to Dan. At some level, he must've been hoping that Joel would turn him down, that he would have an excuse to back out. Now that Joel was in, the robbery was no longer a vague concept. They were going to do it. *He was going to do it.* When the realization had first hit him it left him numb. Driving back from New Hampshire, he could barely pay attention to the road. It was as if he were on autopilot, moving without any thought or awareness. Kind of like he was stoned on some powerful shit. He remembered stopping off at home. His hair was wet so he probably took a shower, and he had a fuzzy recollection of talking with both his children, but that was all. On his way to Gordon's he must've stopped off for a pizza and a six-pack of Guinness because as he pulled into the complex he noticed the items on the front seat next to him.

Gordon was waiting in the parking lot, his belly pushing out of a worn tie-dye T-shirt, his shorts barely containing his body. He met Dan at the car.

"Hey, Dan, I thought I'd catch a few rays while waiting. So what do you want to do, eat at one of the picnic tables or go inside?"

"Why don't we go inside?"

Gordon took the six-pack, and as they walked, Dan tried to act casually. He tapped his friend on the stomach. "Putting on a little weight there, huh, buddy?"

Gordon showed a sheepish smile. "Yeah, I need to get new clothes. My back's been kind of iffy, my knees also, so I can't really run any more. Without the exercise I'm gaining weight like crazy. I'm becoming a regular fatso. Have you heard from anyone?"

"Not really, but we'll talk inside."

As they walked Gordon asked about Shrini and other mutual friends, but Dan couldn't keep his train of thought long enough to answer. When they got to Gordon's apartment, a panic overtook him. At first he couldn't breathe, almost as if a fist were squeezing his heart. He knew he was sweating profusely. The room started to tilt sideways on him. Somehow he made his way to a chair and collapsed on it, praying that he'd stay conscious and not pass out. Time seemed to skip ahead as he watched Gordon talking a mile a minute, the animated motion of his mouth disconnected from the noise that was coming from him, his voice becoming nothing more than a buzz running through Dan's head.

Almost as if a switch had been thrown, a calm came over him. With a clarity of thought, he accepted that the robbery was going to happen. More than that he had somehow become at peace with the idea. The buzzing in his head was replaced by a coolness. The world seemed to slow down on him. He asked Gordon if he could use the bathroom.

"Uh, sure, but what do you think?"

"I don't know. Ask me again when I get back."

"Jeez, haven't you even heard what I've been saying?"

Dan signaled with a hand for him to wait then walked slowly to the bathroom, his legs too rubbery to move at a normal pace. Inside, he turned the cold water on full and splashed it on his face for a full minute before looking up at the mirror. His skin was pale and clammy, with no color whatsoever in his lips. He was pretty sure he had only suffered a panic attack and that it had nothing to do with his heart. Still, he couldn't keep from showing a sick grin as he thought about Gordon being so wrapped up in his own world that he hadn't even noticed what must've looked like a full-blown heart attack.

The only towel in the bathroom appeared to have been rubbed with mud. Dan used his damp shirt to dry off his face. When he went back out to meet Gordon, three slices of pizza were gone and two empty Guinness bottles lay on the floor. Gordon finished off the slice he was working on and rubbed a hand across his face, leaving a streak of grease in its place.

"Jeez, Dan, I was telling you before about Elena. Remember a few months ago I flew her to Cancun? I got an email from her yesterday. She's blowing me off for some guy in Oregon. I think she met him while we were in Cancun."

"Gordon, I'm not in the mood to talk about this."

"Well, excuse me, then." Gordon leaned back in his chair, an indignant look pushing on to his face. "All I wanted was your opinion. After all, I just got dumped."

"Okay, I'm sorry. Go ahead, what did you want to ask me?"

"Well, what do you think I should do?"

"I'm confused. I thought you've been telling me for the last couple of months you don't even like her."

"That's not the point. I was the one to spend the money flying her from Moscow to Cancun, why should some guy from Oregon benefit from that? Besides, I wouldn't quite say that I don't like her. Her English is very good."

"You spent a week with her in the same room and didn't even sleep together. Didn't you tell me she slept on the sofa every night?"

"That was only because I snore. And after I woke up that first morning and found her on the sofa, what was I going to do?"

"What are you trying to tell me, Gordon? That you'd like to marry her?"

"Well, no, but I paid for that trip. I mean, come on, how would you feel? That guy in Oregon should at least pay me back."

"I don't know what to tell you."

"Well, you can see how I'd feel the way I do." Gordon took a slice of the pizza, chewed it half-heartedly. "I'm thinking I should forget about Russian women. This month's catalog has a very pretty twenty-eight-year-old from São Paulo. She's a dental hygienist so she's got to be somewhat educated. I could always arrange for us to meet in Rio, and then I could tell my parents we met while on vacation. The only problem is I'm not sure of her English."

"Yeah, that could be a problem."

"You're being sarcastic now," Gordon said, his hurt look reappearing. "But it is a problem. If her English isn't good then people will be suspicious about how we met."

Dan gave Gordon a hard look, trying to make up his mind. The guy was an oddball, no question about it, and he could understand Joel's reluctance to have him involved. But on the other hand, there was no question he was bright and looked at things from a unique perspective and that could come in handy. And even though Gordon liked to talk, Dan couldn't think of one thing of substance he had ever said. There were things locked away in that head that were never going to come out.

Dan said, "I'm robbing a bank. You want to join me?"

"Nah, I'd rather be a contestant on one of those other shows."

"What?"

"You know, like *Big Brother* or *Amazing Race*. I tried watching *Bank Job* last night and it didn't really do much for me."

"Gordon, I'm talking about robbing a real bank."

"Sure you are."

"I'm serious."

"Jeez, Dan, I couldn't do something like that. What would my parents think if I was caught?"

"Gordon, I'm not joking. Shrini's in on it."

"Really?"

"So's Joel."

"No kidding?" Gordon pushed his chair back and started tapping his chin with his thumb. His eyes focused on a spot on the ceiling. "The weasel, huh?"

"That's right."

Gordon lowered his gaze to Dan's face. His features had changed, becoming grimmer, harder, and it took Dan by surprise. He had never seen Gordon like that.

"You're not pulling some weird joke on me?" Gordon asked.

Dan shook his head.

"Shrini and the Weasel. Wow. Well, guess what? You can count me in."

"Do you want to know the details?"

"No, you know me. I'm not a big picture guy. All I want to know is my piece. Let me just focus on that."

Dan nodded, fully expecting that answer, just as he had fully expected Gordon to go along with the robbery. He couldn't help thinking how the line from that old Dylan song, *There are many here among us who feel that life is but a joke*, fit Gordon perfectly.

"Instead of robbing a bank," Gordon said slowly, his gaze moving away from Dan, "I've been thinking about something lately that would be easier and probably far more profitable. We could take one of Peyton's kids."

"Gordon, let's pretend I don't know what you're talking about."

"Sure you do, you know, kidnapping, ransom. We could probably squeeze several million from Peyton."

"You're not serious."

"Why not? If you're going to propose robbing a bank, why not this instead? It would be a lot easier."

"How in the world could it possibly work? Peyton's kids know us. They'd identify us once we let them go."

"Well, you can't make an omelet without breaking a few eggs."

"Gordon, come on."

"You can't tell me Peyton wouldn't deserve it." Gordon paused for a moment, choking back emotion. "He's been dangling that restaurant in front of me for three years now – ever since I was laid off. That was all his idea, investing in an open-pit Texas-style barbecue for me to run. He came to me with it. And he's been bringing it up for three years. Yesterday for the first time I tried asking him about it, and all of a sudden he doesn't want to do business with a friend. Can you believe that, Dan? He's sitting on eight million dollars and all of a sudden he doesn't want to invest sixty thousand dollars to do business with a friend."

"Let's drop this, okay?"

"Sure, we can drop it, but I'll tell you, I'd have no problem kidnapping one of his kids. Probably even enjoy taking care of that brat of his, Petulia."

"I don't want to hear this. We're not hurting anyone, especially not a kid. For God's sakes, we've known Peyton for years."

"Sure, whatever, I was just throwing out an idea. What do you want me to do for this robbery?"

"Turn on your computer and I'll show you."

Gordon obliged. After the computer came on, Dan did a search on the Internet and brought up a color photo of a member of the Boston mafia named Raymond Lombardo. "I'm hoping all those years you've spent doing makeup for community theatre can finally be of some use. Can you make me look like him?" Dan asked.

"Depends. You need to be more specific."

"What do you mean?"

"Do you have to look like him from a distance, from up close, or good enough to fool his mother? Stuff like that. How much do you need to look like him?"

"Enough so that he's identified by video from a security camera."

"How tall is he?"

"My height."

Gordon squinted at the photo, appraising it. "He looks heavier than you."

"Yeah, he is. About sixty pounds."

"I think I can do it," Gordon said, nodding to himself. "I'm going to have to add some padding, make you look heavier. What are you going to be wearing?"

"Work overalls."

"Okay, no problem there. You'll need a wig and facial hair. I should be able to build you a thicker jaw and nose. Maybe have you wear dark glasses to hide your eyes. Sure, I can do it."

"I don't need the dark glasses. I've already got cosmetic contact lenses to change my eye color. I'll also be wearing a ski mask and taking it off so I can be captured by a security camera."

"Well, that's going to be a problem."

"Why?"

"I can't use putty. Otherwise, when you take the mask off it could bend your nose. That would give the police a good chuckle." Gordon scratched his head as he thought. "I could use a rubber compound," he said slowly. "That should work. When are we doing this?"

"Six days."

"Not giving me much notice, are you? Well, if I can put together the makeup for Phantom of the Opera over a weekend, I can do this."

"You really like this theatre stuff, huh?"

"I hate it. Absolutely can't stand it."

"I don't understand. You've been doing this for years."

Gordon gave a slight smile that could've been lifted directly from the Mona Lisa. "Since college, actually. That was when I started this simply to piss my father off, and you know, I don't think I could've picked a better way. Joining the theatrical club was respectable enough that I had my mother bragging to all their friends about how I was involved in theatre, and my father just had to sit and listen and pretend he was fine with it. I keep doing this community theatre stuff so I can talk about it when I see them over Christmas."

"You've been doing this all these years just to get at your old man?"

"As good a reason as any. You haven't told me, do you want me just to do the makeup or am I going to be involved in the robbery? You know I did a tour in Vietnam."

"I need you for the robbery. We're going to meet at Joel's house tomorrow to go over the details. I'll pick you up at ten."

"Will I have a gun?"

"Yeah."

Gordon folded his arms, nodding. "Okay then."

Yuri Tolkov pulled the Mercedes into the driveway of a small cape-style house on a dead-end street in Melrose. Petrenko sat in the passenger seat and an older soft-looking man sat in the back. Yuri checked the address against a piece of paper he had, then indicated to Petrenko that they had the right house. All three men left the car, Yuri and Petrenko leading the way to the front door. The older man carried a leather bag as he trailed behind, walking as if he had pebbles in his shoes.

"There will be three Arabs, right?" Petrenko asked.

"That was the agreement."

After they knocked on the door, a window curtain was pushed aside and a man with an angry scowl opened up and signaled impatiently for them to step inside. He was in his early twenties, thin as a rail, and had a sub-compact Glock 9mm pistol shoved in his waistband. Sitting on a sofa were two other Arabs. One was a heavyset man with a thick beard trimmed close to his face, the other was also rail-thin, angry-looking and with features that looked sharp enough to cut paper. All three Arabs were wearing leisure suits.

Yuri told Petrenko in Russian that the angry looking man on the sofa was the one on the FBI's ten-most-wanted list and went by the name Abbas.

Anger flushed Abbas's face when he heard the Russian. "The agreement was we speak English only," he said, his eyes simmering. "Another word in Russian and the hell with you!"

Petrenko showed a humorless thin smile. "Relax," he said, "my employee was just being polite. All he said was that it smells like the inside of a shoe in here. I have to agree with him. Not only that, it is like an oven. Could you open a window or turn on an air conditioner?"

Abbas stared dumbly at Petrenko for a moment and then barked out a command in Arabic to the man who had escorted them in. With his scowl deepening, the man moved over to one of the windows and opened it a crack.

"We have ten diamonds for you to appraise," Abbas said, his face still mottled with anger. "Eighty others just like these are being held in a safe place."

Petrenko, unblinking, dropped his smile. "We can agree on a price, but later we will have to appraise all the diamonds and make adjustments as necessary."

"You won't have to make any adjustments, but we do not have to argue this now." Abbas slipped a hand into an inside jacket pocket and pulled out a small silk bag. He extended the bag to Petrenko who didn't bother moving. Instead, the older man with the leather bag took the diamonds and was escorted to a table where he could examine them. He took a portable xenon lamp, a small scale, a Schneider loupe, and bottles of different solutions from his bag, then hunched over the diamonds, examining and weighing each one. When he was done, he hobbled over to Petrenko and in Russian told him the ten diamonds were of high quality and worth one hundred and fifty thousand dollars.

"English! We agreed English only!" Abbas screamed. He barked out a string of commands in Arabic. The Arab standing near Petrenko reached for his Glock. Petrenko feigned a jab with his right hand and almost instantaneously rabbit-punched the man in the chest with his left, his fist moving as a blur. The punch knocked the Arab off his feet. As he hit the floor, his Glock bounced out of his waistband and landed a few feet from him. Before he could reach for it, Petrenko stepped on his hand and picked the gun up himself. The heavyset Arab started for his inside jacket pocket but stopped as he realized Yuri had the edge of an eight-inch switchblade against his throat.

Petrenko removed the magazine from the Glock and handed the empty gun to Abbas. "If I wanted to kill you and steal your diamonds I could do so easily," he said. "I do not wish to do that, though. I am hoping you and your friends will stop acting like children and that this can be the first of many business transactions between the two of us."

Abbas was shaking with a combination of fear and rage. "We had a deal! Only English!"

"He doesn't speak English, only Russian," Petrenko said, waving a hand towards the jeweler. "All he said to me was that the clarity of the diamonds is sub par and they are only worth twenty thousand dollars."

"That's right, each diamond is worth twenty thousand dollars!"

"No, twenty thousand dollars for all ten. Because I want

future business deals between us, I will pay you sixty percent of what all ninety diamonds are worth. A hundred and eight thousand dollars."

"They are worth twenty times that!"

"No they are not." Petrenko stopped for a moment to rub the area above both temples. "And quit shouting. You are giving me a headache. So do we have a deal?"

Abbas was close to epileptic, both too furious and scared to do anything but move his lips in some sort of internal dialogue. He looked helplessly at his two companions. The one next to him still had a knife edge held against his throat, the other was sitting on the floor holding his injured hand.

"You can turn me down if you want to," Petrenko added. "There will be no hard feelings on my part. If you want, try to find someone who will pay more. You can always take a trip to the New York Jewelry District and see if anyone there will do business with you."

Abbas tried answering, but couldn't get the words out. Finally, after his third attempt, he sputtered, "You will kill us if I turn you down."

"No, I don't think so. You don't want to do business, fine, we leave. But I don't think you're going to find a better price."

Yuri backed away. The heavyset Arab had turned somewhat green, and was rubbing his throat where the blade had left an indentation. Abbas looked at him and then his companion still sitting on the floor. He licked his lips. "I will think about your offer," he said sourly.

Petrenko shrugged. "You know how to reach me. Don't think too long, though." He then turned and left the house. The jeweler hobbled out next. After that, Yuri closed his knife and walked backwards out of the house.

Once in the car Yuri turned to Petrenko. "You sure you don't want to go back in there and take those diamonds? Five minutes we're done."

Petrenko shook his head. "If we're patient they will sell us all of their diamonds. And more in the future. We're offering only a fraction of what they were looking for. They will need to make up the difference by bringing in more diamonds to sell us. For them, diamonds are easy to smuggle into this country, cash is not." He paused as he made a fist and rubbed a thumb over his knuckles, feeling the hard calluses that covered them. "Besides," he added, "if I went back in there I would want much more than five minutes."

9

After his messy divorce, Captain Kenneth Hadley jumped from the Somerville to the Lynn police force when the opening presented itself. All he did, though, was trade one problem for another. Maybe he no longer had his ex-wife stumbling into his station screaming her accusations at him whenever she damn well pleased, but the job was no better. Just as in Somerville, he had to deal with the same urban crimes – car thefts, break-ins, drugs, youth gangs – but in Lynn he now had to deal with Russian mobsters. And, as in Somerville, he now suspected that he had an officer drinking on the job. When Resnick had stepped into his office, Hadley detected a strong whiff of bourbon on his breath. Couldn't the guy at least have had the decency to chew on a few mints before reporting back to the station? Resnick, though, seemed coherent, with no change in his typical bulldog manner and the same burning intensity. Hadley decided to let the matter drop. The guy was his best detective and there was nothing to indicate that this was anything more than an isolated incident. Still, he felt exhausted listening to Resnick complain about Viktor Petrenko and he was pretty sure the alcohol had something to do with loosening his detective up.

"There's got to be something we can do," Resnick was going on. "We can't just let this son of a bitch terrorize our neighborhoods and business owners. I know he's using his auto-body shop as a chop shop. Let me sit on it until we can get something on him, or better yet, let me follow him around, put some pressure on him."

Hadley looked at his watch. They'd been arguing this for ten minutes now. "Alex, with all the state cutbacks in funding we're shorthanded as it is. I can't lose you for God-knows-how-long on some wild goose chase. Besides, the victim stated from the hospital that it was an accident and his wife was more than happy to corroborate him, claiming he tripped."

"They're both afraid."

"I have to go with what they say—"

"The store just magically got trashed. Maybe the air conditioner was on too strong and blew an eighty-pound cash register out the front window."

Hadley lifted his palms up in a sign of futility. "Unless these people are willing to come forward my hands are tied." He edged closer to his detective, lowering his voice in a conspiratorial tone. "Look at it from my point of view: one way we've got an open case that needs manpower assigned to it. The other way, the way it currently stands, the case is closed. As it is we already have far too many open cases."

"Ken, that's a lousy way to look at it. Besides, we put Petrenko away and we're going to end up with a lower caseload down the road. Damn it, there's got to be something we can do."

"There is something you can do," Hadley said. "Take the rest of the day off. You're looking a bit under the weather."

"I'm fine."

"No you're not. I can't have police officers drinking on the job. Not that I'm accusing you of anything. As far as I'm concerned, you're just a little worn out and can use a few hours off."

Resnick stared into Hadley's pale blue eyes before turning away, nodding. "I've never touched the stuff before while on duty. Something about Petrenko, I don't know... I'll put in extra hours tomorrow to make up for this," he said.

"Not necessary. You've put in more than enough extra hours since I've been here. Try not to get under the weather like this again, okay?"

"You've got my word."

As Resnick walked out of Hadley's office, he acknowledged Maguire's questioning look with a shrug. "I've been told I'm feeling under the weather," Resnick informed his partner. "I'm taking the rest of the day off. Be here bright and early tomorrow morning."

"Lesson learned," Maguire said, a smart-alecky grin tightening on his face. "Booze up on the job and get some time off."

"Not a good lesson to have taught you. I apologize."

As Resnick walked away, Maguire tried telling him that he was only yanking his chain. Resnick waved a hand, letting his partner know not to worry about it.

Alex Resnick met his ex-wife while in college. She was a beautiful redhead from Long Island with a peaches and cream complexion and the most dazzling green eyes he had ever seen. At the time he was a political science major and was expecting to go to law school after graduation. On a whim he took the

Lynn police entrance exam and posted a perfect score. His dad tried like hell to talk him out of joining the force.

"Alex," his dad told him, "why do something like this? You can make a real life for yourself as a lawyer. Don't make this mistake. If you need money, I'll find a way to help you."

"Pop," Resnick said, "Jewish lawyers are a dime a dozen. How many Jewish cops do you know? Besides, you need someone who can help you fix all these parking tickets you're racking up."

His dad drove a cab for a living and the last thing Resnick wanted was for his dad to take on more shifts to try to help him out. So while his dad pleaded with him not to throw his life away, Resnick patiently argued that the police work would be good experience for a future career as a lawyer and in a few years he would go back to school at night and earn a law degree. Nothing his dad could say changed the fact that he was anxious to make a living so he could marry Carrie. He was crazy about her and more than anything wanted her to be his wife.

Eighteen months after they were married, Carrie gave birth to their son. Brian was one of those one-in-a-million type babies. He almost never cried and always seemed to break out smiling whenever Resnick picked him up. As much as Resnick loved his wife, he found that his feelings towards his boy were stronger than he could've ever imagined. Leaving him each morning to go to work was like ripping out a small piece of his heart. When Brian was two they discovered that he had a heart defect and needed a valve replaced with an artificial plastic one. The surgery was touch and go for a while, but his boy did okay.

Three years later the four packs of cigarettes Resnick's dad smoked each day caught up with him and he died of lung cancer after a tough nine-month battle. Resnick's mom died a week later – supposedly of a stroke. Her death, while maybe somewhat of a shock, didn't really come as much of a surprise to Resnick. He knew his parents loved each other dearly and he could never imagine one of them surviving without the other. He was still reeling from the death of both parents when six weeks later he found out his son's plastic heart valve was leaking and needed to be replaced. This time Brian didn't survive the surgery.

According to Carrie, Resnick emotionally abandoned her then. He didn't believe she was right, but he also didn't see any point in arguing with her. He just couldn't live within his own skin. It was that simple. He couldn't sleep, he couldn't sit still. There was so much pressure inside his chest – and the only way he felt he could breathe freely was if he kept moving. He started putting in extra shifts and taking any detail work he could, sometimes working twenty-four hours straight. Exhaustion helped. When he was exhausted he could sometimes fall into unconsciousness when he closed his eyes. The worst – the absolute worst of it – were the few times when he did dream. Brian was always with him in those dreams, and he'd have to wake up realizing all over again that he had lost his boy.

Two years later Carrie told Resnick that the day Brian had his first heart surgery was the day he lost his sense of humor. Maybe even his own heart.

Resnick stared at her dumbly. "I don't know how to respond to that."

"That's what I mean, Alex. The man I married would have thought of something to say to make me laugh. Even if it was something very sad."

"My wife, the eternal optimist."

"That wasn't even close." She paused, the color draining from her, leaving her skin a pale white. "I've cried every day since we lost Brian. Sometimes for hours at a stretch. I don't think you've cried once. I don't think I've seen a single tear from you. You keep running from it, Alex, you won't let your grief catch up to you. Unless you let yourself grieve, I don't think we can fix things between us."

Resnick didn't disagree with her, but he couldn't sit still either. He saw too much of Brian in her as she sat across from him, a pleading in her eyes as she waited for him to say something. He got up and left their modest two-bedroom house. He just couldn't do anything else.

That was about it for their marriage. They didn't talk much after that. There didn't seem to be any animosity or hard feelings. For the most part his feelings for Carrie hadn't changed since that moment when he first saw her on campus, but there was distance between them. A distance that he knew he created. Maybe she reminded him too much of his boy. Whatever it was he wouldn't let her close the gap and after a while she gave up trying. They divorced shortly after the three-year anniversary of Brian's death. A few years later Carrie remarried.

After Resnick got in his car he headed towards the studio apartment he had been living in since his divorce. Halfway home he had a change of heart, turned and drove to Lynn Memorial. Once he arrived at the hospital he talked with the doctor who had examined Mr. Wiseman when he was brought in. Along with a concussion, the old man had a fracture running along the front part of his skull and had also suffered some muscle damage in his neck. They were going to be holding him in intensive care for a few days for observation.

Resnick found Wiseman alone in his room. The old man's

head was bandaged, a thick brace around his neck. He stared glassy-eyed at the detective until a glimmer of recognition showed.

"You're the police officer who shops in our store," he said slowly, evenly, his voice a hoarse whisper. "I remember you. My wife told me how you helped today. Thank you."

"I thought I'd see your wife here."

"Why do I need her here weeping?" he asked. "I sent her back to the store. Let her weep there."

"I read the statement you gave the other officer."

"I tripped," he said stubbornly.

"We both know that's not true, Mr. Wiseman."

He shrugged as much as his neck brace would allow. "Old men trip sometimes."

"It's not right what Viktor Petrenko did to you. It's not right what he has been doing to hundreds of other people like you. I need someone to talk to me so I can send that piece of garbage to prison."

"If it were just me…" The old man's voice broke off and his lips started to quiver. He looked away. When he could talk, he said, "My wife, Anna, we've been married fifty-two years. No, I am sorry, all I can say is that I tripped."

Resnick laid a card with his contact information on the night stand next to the bed. "If you have a change of heart and are willing to tell me what happened, call me."

The old man looked back at Resnick, his half-closed eyes holding steady on the detective. "Would you be able to protect my Anna?"

Resnick couldn't answer him.

"That's what I thought," Wiseman said, letting his eyes

close. "All I can tell you is that I tripped. Excuse me, please, I am very tired."

Resnick stood watching the old man as he tried to think of something more to say. Eventually he gave up.

10

After leaving Gordon, Dan stopped off at Shrini's apartment hoping to catch him at home and got lucky when Shrini buzzed him in.

"Hey, dude," Shrini said, greeting him at the door. "I'm surprised to see you. I thought you were going to call."

Dan closed the door behind him and told Shrini to get out the bottle of tequila that he knew his friend was keeping. "We're celebrating, man. The two of us are going to be bank robbers. The next Butch Cassidy and Sundance Kid."

"All right, dude!" Shrini clapped. "Although I hope we have better luck than those two!"

Dan took a seat as Shrini searched for the tequila and a couple of clean glasses. He was amazed at how calm he felt. Almost as if he had had some kind of breakdown at Gordon's and was now just numb to the whole idea of the robbery. Whatever it was, he was grateful for it.

Shrini had brought out the tequila, along with a lime and

some salt. He poured the two of them shots. "So your friend, Joel, is going to be joining us?" Shrini asked.

"That's right. Gordon's on board also." Dan cut a slice of lime, sucked it, and then swallowed down the shot, feeling the warmth explode in his stomach. He poured himself another one. "We do have a change in plan. Joel insisted that a friend of his be included."

"You must be joking."

"Sorry, man, I had no choice. This guy is going to be getting us untraceable guns. If I didn't agree, Joel was out. Which meant the robbery was out."

"Do you know this person?"

"I met him once years ago. Kind of a shifty individual."

"I don't like this."

"I don't either, but Joel insisted on it, both for the guns and that he have someone backing him up that he can trust. I can't blame him."

"No. This is unacceptable. We could have gotten guns elsewhere. We can't be adding people that we don't know. There is too much at stake."

"I don't like this either, but this is where we're at. Look, we'll all meet tomorrow to go over the plan. You'll get a chance to meet Joel, we'll both get a chance to meet his friend. If either of us feel uncomfortable we'll call it quits."

Shrini made a face as if he had swallowed something bitter. "This is just not right, dude."

"I hear you, I really do. But what harm can it do just meeting tomorrow, see how we feel?"

"Okay, we'll meet. But this truly pisses me off..." Shrini seemed to lose his train of thought as he stared at his friend.

"Dude," he said, grinning sourly. "You've got a shiner. What happened, someone punch you out?"

"One of your many girlfriends. She asked if I'd take a message for you and this is what she gave me."

"Very funny. So what happened?"

"Nothing worth talking about. I'll pick you up tomorrow a little before ten, then we'll swing over, pick Gordon up and drive up to New Hampshire."

"We're meeting in New Hampshire? Where, at your friend Joel's house?"

"Yeah, his place is secluded, as good a place as any for us to meet. You okay with that?"

"I guess so."

"Okay, I'll see you tomorrow then."

"What's the hurry? We still have over three quarters of a bottle left."

"Sorry, buddy, I've some things I need to do, you know, to prepare for next week."

"I wouldn't waste my time if I were you. I'm seriously thinking of backing out. Believe me, I'm not happy with your friend trying to take over."

"Shrini, again, I don't blame you. But just think it over. Ten minutes, that's all it's going to take us. We'll be in and out of that bank so damn fast. Joel bringing his friend along isn't going to change that."

"But we don't know him. We don't know if he'll talk afterwards."

"You're right. We don't know him. But Joel does. And he's not going to do anything that could fuck himself."

Dan took another shot of tequila, felt it burn down his throat, then clapped Shrini on the back before leaving. Walking to his car he felt exhausted, bone-weary. He sat behind the wheel and closed his eyes for a few seconds' rest. When he opened them again it was dark outside and he felt like he had swallowed a handful of sawdust. He had to sit for a minute before his eyes could adjust to the night. According to the clock in his car it was nine twenty-three.

He expected hell from Carol when he arrived home. Or maybe a freezer burn. Instead, he was surprised to see concern in her eyes as she met him at the door. Even more surprising, she showed him a weak smile.

"I was worried about you," she told him as she took hold of his hand.

"This is embarrassing," he said. "I stopped off to see Shrini and when I got back to my car I fell asleep. Just plain crashed. I didn't wake up until ten minutes ago."

She put her palm up against his forehead, trying to feel if he had a fever. "Are you okay?" she asked.

"I think so. I haven't been sleeping well the last couple of months. I guess it all finally caught up with me." He let out a short laugh. "I'm surprised no one in Shrini's complex called the police on me. I was out of it for a good seven hours."

"I have some good news," Carol said. "You got a call for a possible job."

Dan's voice cracked when he tried asking who had called. He cleared his throat and tried again, this time getting his words out.

"I have his name written down. He's going to try calling tomorrow morning at eight. Why don't I make you something for dinner? How about some scrambled eggs with ham?"

"Sure." Dan followed Carol into the kitchen and took a seat at the counter. He found the paper where Carol had written down the guy's name. Martin Phillips. Dan didn't know him. "Did he say anything about the job?"

"Only that they're looking for a software security expert. You're certainly that." She wrinkled her nose for a second. "I almost forgot. Joel called around nine. He seemed upset that you weren't home and said he's going to try again at ten."

According to the kitchen clock it was nine forty. He sat back and watched as his wife prepared the scrambled eggs. By the time she finished, it was seven minutes to ten. He shoveled the food down, wanting to make sure he was alone in the den when Joel called.

"You must've been starving," Carol remarked.

He grunted something out in acknowledgment. He was just getting up from the table when the phone rang. He stopped Carol from answering it, telling her that he would take the call in the den.

"I tried calling at nine," Joel complained after Dan picked up. "Where the fuck were you?"

"Sorry about that. I had things to do."

"Bullshit. You know what a pain in the ass it was having to drive out two times to a payphone? Fourteen miles each way, schmuck!"

"I'll tell you what. You can bitch and moan all you want when I see you tomorrow. We'll set up email accounts then also."

Joel's voice changed, becoming somewhat reserved. "We're on then, huh?"

"You tell me. What did your pervert buddy say?"

"Fuck you. Be here at twelve sharp, understand?"

Joel hung up. Dan stood frozen for a moment before putting the receiver down. When he looked up he saw Carol standing in the doorway watching him.

"Why so secretive?" she asked.

"What? No, nothing, just typical Joel stuff, that's all. Have you been standing there long?"

"No, not long. I wanted to ask you on my way upstairs if you would like to go to bed early tonight. It's been a long time since we've gone to bed early together."

"Sure. That would be nice. I just want to stop off first and see the kids."

"They're both in their rooms." She hesitated, an odd expression on her face as she studied him. "Did Joel do that to your face?"

"What are you talking about? I told you yesterday I slipped getting into my car. Believe it or not, that's what happened."

"Dan, is anything wrong?"

"No, of course not." He forced himself to maintain eye contact. A hotness flushed his face. "Why do you ask?"

"You looked so angry when you hung up the phone. Or maybe intense. I don't know, I never saw you like that before."

"Nothing more than this out-of-work bullshit. And you know how Joel can be. He was going on some rant about the liberal scum in Massachusetts. I guess I wasn't in the mood for it."

"He called twice just to talk about that?"

"Not exactly. He had a question about a possible job lead."

"Why was he calling from a payphone?"

"Was he?"

"According to the caller ID."

"Really? Maybe he was at the mall."

"But he has a cell phone. I know that he usually calls from a cell phone because of the caller ID."

"This is Joel we're talking about. You'd have to ask him. I'm going to go see the kids and then meet you upstairs."

As he walked past her he could hear the blood pounding in his head. He had to steady himself against the wall for a moment before he could trust himself to move. He knew Carol was staring at him from behind – he could feel it on the back of his neck. What he didn't know was whether she suspected something or was just digging. Probably just digging. He tried to remember whether he said anything damning during his phone conversation that she could've overheard. Jesus, why'd he have to hurry off to the den like that? He knew Carol well enough to know that it wouldn't take much to get her curious.

Standing outside his son's bedroom door, he took a deep breath as he composed himself, then knocked and walked into the room. Gary was lying on the bed watching a baseball game. He turned and smiled sadly. "Hi, Dad," he said. "Red Sox are losing. Lugo just popped up with the bases loaded and two outs."

Dan pulled up a chair next to the bed. Gary was ten and physically took after Carol. Small for his age, thin, blond hair, almost feminine good-looking features. Even so, he was a good athlete, playing shortstop for his baseball team. While Dan hoped that Gary would catch up in size, with his good looks and easy-going manner he had no doubt that when his son grew older he was going to do well with the girls no matter what his height ended up being.

He tousled his son's hair. "I can't believe how spoiled you kids are getting. Two World Championships in four years. You can't expect them to win them all."

Gary grinned widely, said, "Sure I can!"

Dan smiled at his son. "Shouldn't you be going to bed soon?"

"They're in the eighth inning. Can't I wait until the end of the game?"

"What's the score?"

"Nine to two," Gary said dejectedly. "But they can still catch up. Let me watch the rest, please?"

"Okay, but right afterwards you go to bed, promise?"

"Promise. Thanks, Dad."

Dan kissed his son on the forehead. Before leaving, he looked back and watched the concentration on his son's face as he lay on the bed, eyes glued to the ball game. It touched him that his son could be so passionate about something as simple as a baseball game. With a note of regret, he realized it had been a long time since he had felt anything like that.

Susie must've been listening for him because as he was closing Gary's door she opened hers. She tried to look uninterested as she walked out of her room plugged into her iPod. She stopped and gave him a sullen stare before taking the earplugs out and muttering hello.

"Hi, Princess," Dan said. "I was just about to knock on your door and see how you were doing."

"I guess I saved you the trouble," she said, her bottom lip pushing out, fortifying her sullen appearance. She hesitated for a moment, then asked, "Can you take Julie and me to the beach tomorrow?"

"I can't, darling. I have to meet with some people tomorrow."

"Mom says you have an interview at eight in the morning. We could leave later."

"I'm sorry, but I have to meet with some people after that. Maybe Saturday?"

"Whatever," she said. Her mouth seemed to shrink as she stared straight ahead. "Julie and I can always take a bus to Salisbury beach."

"I don't think so. I don't want you taking a bus all the way up there by yourselves."

"How would you stop me? You won't be home. You're never home. Even though you're not working you're never home."

She stared at Dan, her eyes challenging him to argue with her, and then she turned on her heels and rushed back into her room, closing the door hard behind her.

He sighed and rubbed his eyes. Earlier, he would've been eaten up by guilt over having to turn his daughter down so he could plan a bank robbery. Now he just felt nothing inside. He had finally gotten used to the idea of what he was going to be doing. There was no longer any fear, just numbness. More than that, though, he felt committed to it. He had robbed that bank so many times in his mind that he was now anxious to do it in real life. The thought struck him – if he was offered a job, then what? He forced the thought out of his head. He'd cross that bridge when he came to it.

He showered quickly and brushed his teeth before going into the bedroom. Carol was waiting for him, lying on the bed wearing one of his old T-shirts as a nightgown. He got in next to her. She moved closer to him, moving her thigh so it was on top of his, her mouth searching for his mouth, her breath hot, her hands touching his chest. Then her hands moved lower. He tried playing along, but he couldn't shake the numbness he was feeling. It was almost as if she were trying to get a rise out of a dead man. After a while she gave up. She pushed away from him and turned over on her side.

"Goodnight," she said, her voice flat.

"I'm sorry, Carol, I guess I just have too much on my mind."

"It's been weeks since we've even tried doing this."

"I'm sorry—"

"Forget it. Let's not talk about it. I'll make sure you're up early for your interview. Goodnight."

Dan closed his eyes. Still nothing but numbness. Not quite peace, but also not the torment he had been routinely suffering each night. No thoughts racing through his mind. No images of the robbery gone bad playing out in his head, no imaginary police sirens, no shootouts, no bloody bodies. Just an emptiness filling him up. After a while not even that.

Carol woke him the next morning. Even after passing out for seven hours in that parking lot, he had still slept soundly through the night. With all the stress he had been under he figured his body needed the extra sleep.

He offered to make breakfast, but Carol insisted on doing it. While he sat at the kitchen table and watched her, he couldn't help wishing he had time for another shot with her in the bedroom. She looked fresh, relaxed, her hair pulled back in a ponytail, her skirt making her hips look so damn slender. When she brought him a cup of coffee, she let her fingers linger on his hand for a long moment. Her smile was as pretty as any he had seen in years.

"Good luck with the interview," she said. "I have to head off to work, but call me. Let me know how it goes."

He nodded and told her he would. She gave him a quick kiss and squeezed his hand. He watched as she left, thinking to himself for the first time in a long time how beautiful she was. It was only seven fifteen. He sipped his coffee. When his cup was empty, he got up and poured himself another one.

At eight o'clock the phone rang. When he answered it a man introduced himself as Martin Phillips. He told Dan he was vice president of Software Development for a new startup that was forming and that he had found Dan's resumé online and was intrigued by all of his software security experience. He hesitated for a moment, then remarked how he couldn't tell from Dan's resumé how much JAVA programming development experience he had.

"I've been learning it on my own," Dan said.

There was another hesitation from Martin Phillips, then with his voice significantly less cheery than it had been, he said, "So you don't have five or more years of actual work experience with it?"

For a moment Dan could feel the blood boiling inside him. He heard himself tell Phillips to go fuck himself. There was a momentary silence before the line went dead. Dan stared at the handset, a bare-fanged grimace tightening over his face. Then, as his facial muscles relaxed, he called Carol, reaching her at her desk. He told her the phone interview went well and that he had a second interview scheduled for the following week.

11

Yuri reported to Petrenko that the Arabs had contacted him. "They cried, but eventually agreed to your price," he said.

Petrenko cracked his knuckles, a glimpse of satisfaction flashing over his dead eyes. "Didn't I tell you so?" he asked.

"You were right. We will be stealing those diamonds at that price. Ten cents on the dollar." Yuri paused, showing extensive denture work as he smiled. "Maybe we should still consider stealing those diamonds with guns. Afterwards trade that dead Arab to the FBI for one hundred thousand dollars' reward money."

"Not enough. Our Arab friends were expecting maybe half a million dollars for those diamonds. Which means they need to smuggle more into this country to raise the money they need. We could end up taking millions from them. No, Yuri, we will stroke this golden goose a while longer."

"Why wouldn't they simply sell them in Europe for a better price?"

Petrenko shook his head as if talking to a child. "How

would they bring the money here? Not so easy, especially with the FBI watching everything. Besides, to them diamonds are cheap. Having cash here is what is priceless to them. When do we make the purchase?"

"Monday. They have a new address for us. I don't think they stay in any one place too long. Or maybe they are setting us up?"

"They're not setting us up. They need us for now. And don't fret, after we have squeezed every golden egg we can out of this goose we will cut off its head. Our last transaction will be with guns. Someday we'll be heroes to the FBI. But not yet."

Yuri nodded and started to leave, but Petrenko stopped him.

"These store owners," Petrenko said, "let them know their rates are being raised another eighty dollars a month. That they can thank their fellow *zhid* grocery store owner for that."

They pulled up to Joel's house a few minutes before twelve. Dan got out, opened the trunk, took out a trash bag that he had filled earlier and swung it over his back. When Joel answered the door, he met Dan and Gordon with a curt nod, shook hands with Shrini and led them into his living room where his friend Eric Hoffer was reclining on the sofa drinking a Bud. He looked pretty much how Dan remembered him. Small eyes that seemed almost buried in a pig-like face and skin the color of boiled ham. As they were all being introduced, Hoffer grunted and pushed himself forward so he could offer Dan a moist handshake.

"I understand you're the brains of the outfit," he said, forcing a wide grin. He talked slowly, deliberately, as if he'd had a stroke, or maybe had marbles in his mouth. "Thanks for having me along, chief."

Dan freed his hand. "You got your buddy Joel to thank for that."

Hoffer's grin turned somewhat plastic. "Anyway, chief, I'm not gonna disappoint you."

"All right," Joel interrupted. "Enough fucking pleasantries. We have business to go over."

Gordon had talked incessantly during the trip to New Hampshire. Once he stepped inside Joel's house he clammed up. He carried a kitchen chair to a spot near the wall so that he could lean back and sat with his arms folded across his chest. Shrini also seemed more reserved than usual as he sat quietly on the sofa.

Dan went over the details of the robbery. As he talked, Gordon closed his eyes, his head dropping towards his chest as if he were dozing off. Hoffer just kept nodding enthusiastically, his plastic grin firmly in place. Shrini sat quietly, attentive. Joel was beside himself. He kept looking over at Gordon, becoming more and more agitated. Finally, he had enough. He got up and kicked out one of the chair legs, almost sending Gordon and his chair crashing to the floor except that Gordon was able to fling his arms out and grab the wall and somehow maintain his balance. Breathing hard, he positioned his weight forward so that the chair's front legs fell back to the floor.

"*Schmuck*," Joel swore, his face white with anger. "You're going to sleep through this? You think this is some sort of game?"

"What is your problem?" Gordon demanded. "You do something like that again and you'll end up with my shoe up your ass, understand?"

"You fucking clown."

Indignant, Gordon turned to Dan. "I don't have to take this from that weasel. I'm out of here!"

"Weasel, huh?" Joel said. "I didn't like it when you nicknamed me that at Vixox and I don't like it any better now."

Gordon stood up, his large fleshy hands balling into fists. "Then don't act like one!"

"Joel, Gordon, for Chrissakes, both of you sit the fuck down," Dan implored. "I know we're all stressed out here. I mean, shit, whoever thought we'd be talking about a bank robbery. But let's not ruin this over something stupid."

Reluctantly, Gordon lowered himself back into his chair. Joel stood where he was.

Patiently, almost as if talking to a child, Dan asked Gordon to repeat what he had been saying before Joel acted like an asshole.

"You were explaining how after the robbery we're going to sit on the money for several months to make sure it's safe."

Dan turned to Joel. "Joel, take a deep breath. We can do this if we just stay calm, okay?"

"Don't fucking lecture me. I thought he was sleeping."

"He wasn't. He was paying attention, probably much more than you. Why don't you get us some beers, see if we can relax a little."

Joel looked like he was going to say something, but instead he clamped his mouth shut and left the room. Hoffer followed him. When they returned, the two of them handed out beers. Gordon grudgingly took his.

"I won't charge for these," Joel told Dan. "'Cause you're right, I acted like an asshole. Next round, though, you pay for them."

"Okay, Gordon," Dan said, ignoring Joel. "This is as much

of an apology as you're ever going to get out of this guy. Are we all friends again? Or are we going to walk away from this?"

"Hey, don't look at me," Gordon said. "I was just sitting here minding my own business."

"You okay now, Joel?"

"Yeah, I'm just peachy. I got a question. Where are we going to keep the money while we're sitting on it?"

"Two years ago I rented a storage locker to hold some old furniture. I got stuck with a five-year lease so I'm still holding on to it. I'm going to hide the money there."

"Why do that? I have twenty acres up here. There's plenty of places to hide the money. Why take the chance of having the police search your locker?"

"That's not going to happen," Dan said.

"Famous last words. Let's take a vote. Anyone else agree it makes more sense to hide the stuff here?"

Only Hoffer's hand went up. Sneering, Joel gave a slow look around the room. "That's the way it's going to be, eh?" he asked. "You're going to outvote me three to two on everything. Fine, I'll just shut up, then."

"Joel, if you don't trust me, let's end this right now."

"Fuck you, I trust you. Let's just move on, okay?"

"Good enough, we'll move on." Gordon and Shrini both sat stone-faced. Hoffer's grin only grew wider, making him look more like a village idiot. Dan picked up the garbage bag he had carried into the house and dumped its contents on to the floor. Inside were work overalls, gloves and ski masks. He handed them out, asking if they'd try them on.

"I only got four sets of these," Dan said to Hoffer. "I didn't know that you were going to be along for this when I got them."

"No problem there, chief. I have stuff at home I can use."

"Anyone going to be able to recognize it?"

Hoffer shook his head. "Not a chance." He sat on the sofa with his grin intact while the rest of them put on their outfits. With the overalls, ski masks, and gloves, they looked like they could be bank robbers instead of the odd collection of out-of-work software developers that they were. Gordon was studying Shrini. "We're supposed to look like Italian mobsters, right?" he asked. "I'm going to have to put some makeup around Shrini's eyes, lighten up his complexion somewhat. Or maybe he could wear sunglasses."

"I think I'll wear the sunglasses, dude," Shrini answered.

"And what's with the tape over the mouth hole?" Gordon asked.

"I'm hoping it helps muffle our voices."

"What if one of us has a stuffed-up nose? We'd suffocate."

"Come on, Gordon—"

"Well, I could always just talk like this," Gordon said, imitating a Swedish accent.

"For Chrissakes," Joel swore under his breath.

"When we're in that bank it's important that we talk as little as possible," Dan said. "Only when absolutely necessary. And no foreign accents, okay? Just try to talk as low and guttural as possible. All of you practice that. And whatever you do, don't use any of our real names. I did a little research and found some names of Raymond Lombardo's associates. If for whatever reason we need to talk to each other I'll be Ray, Joel, you're Tony, Shrini, you're Vinnie, Eric, you're Sal, and Gordon, you're Charlie."

"Why do I have to be Charlie?" Gordon asked. "Why can't we pick our own names?"

"I fucking give up," Joel spat out. "He's nothing but a goddamned infant."

"Relax, okay?" said Dan. "He's just doing a riff on *Reservoir Dogs*."

Gordon's belly bounced up and down under his overalls as he laughed at his joke. A glint in his eyes showed there were still hard feelings from before and this was partly payback for that. "What's wrong with you, Joel, too much high-octane before we got here? Jeez, lighten up, guy. Take that stick out of your ass."

"Gordon, it's been an absolute pleasure not working with you the last seven years. Too bad we have to break that streak now."

"Same here, Joel."

Joel ignored him and turned to Dan. "Eric and I are going to be using assault rifles to keep control in the bank. Nothing like looking down the barrel of a Kalashnikov to shut you up. You three are going to be carrying Smith & Wesson forty-five caliber pistols. They're good guns and they're made right here in the USA."

"I don't need a gun."

"Sure you do. All three of you do. No fucking way I'm going into that bank otherwise."

"Dan, I have to agree with your friend," Shrini said.

"We're going to be in and out of that bank in ten minutes. There's not going to be any shooting. No one is firing any guns. Shrini and I don't need them."

Joel took his ski mask off. "Let me explain something to you, pal," he said, his black eyes smoldering. "When we walk into that bank, this gets serious. All bets are off. You may not want to shoot anyone, but if a cop ends up wandering into that bank he's sure as hell going to want to shoot you. Or me. I'm only willing to do this if you're prepared to do what it takes.

And that means backing me up and shooting someone if you need to. Obviously, nobody wants that to happen, but we have to be ready for it."

Dan turned to Shrini and Gordon. They had both taken their masks off. "The weasel's right," Gordon said.

"I don't even know how to use a gun," Dan said weakly.

"Typical Massachusetts liberal," Joel sneered. "Expect others to fight your battles for you. Not this time, buddy boy. I have my own private shooting range dug out in the basement. I'm going to teach you how to fire a gun. And I want to see how your two buddies do also. All of you, downstairs now."

Joel led the way down to the basement. When they got there, Joel picked up a Kalashnikov AK-47 rifle and admired it. "Eric and I have to get two of these babies into the bank. How long will it take us to get from the parking lot to the front lobby door?"

"Maybe ten seconds running."

"I could try hiding this in my pant leg, but I don't see much point. Five guys entering a bank in overalls and ski masks will be suspicious whether or not we're carrying these Kalashnikovs."

He put the rifle down and unlocked a cabinet, taking out a handgun and a box of shells. After handing out cheap earplugs, he put a more expensive set of earmuffs on himself. A narrow alley of about forty feet ran the length of the basement. At the end of it was a target attached to a large dirt pile. Gordon held out his hand to Joel.

"You want me to go over how to use this first?" Joel asked.

"Just hand me the gun and some shells."

Joel did as asked. Gordon slid out the magazine, loaded it, then, snapping the magazine back in place, he held out the gun as he weighed it in his hand for a few seconds, and then squeezed off five rounds. Joel squinted as he peered towards the targets. "Three bullseyes, two near bullseyes," he muttered. "Nice shooting."

"A little rusty," Gordon said. "You can't blame me. It's been over thirty years since I fired a gun." He handed the weapon back to Joel.

Joel went over the basics with Shrini and Dan, showing them how to hold the gun and how to use the front and rear sights to line up a target. Shrini learned quickly. By his fourth round he started hitting the target. Dan just couldn't see the damn thing. He was having trouble focusing, the targets blurring into the dirt wall. He went through two magazines and missed wildly.

"What the hell's wrong with you?" Joel asked. "Are you blind?"

"It's too dark down here," Dan said.

"Don't give me your excuses. It's plenty light enough. When we're in that bank you're not going to be able to control how well lit the room is." Joel gave Dan a hard look, his eyes dulling. He nodded to himself as if he understood he was dealing with damaged goods. "Just hand me that gun. I've let you waste enough shells. If we're in that bank and you need to shoot, make sure you're close enough to your target so you don't blow my head off by mistake. Okay?"

The five of them went back upstairs. They finalized their plans and agreed on a time and location for them to meet before the robbery. As they were leaving, Gordon asked for the ski masks, suggesting that he could do something with them to help with their disguises.

Walking back to the car, Dan couldn't shake a sense of uneasiness. It was almost as if when he breathed he could feel the uneasiness deep in his lungs. Kind of like a tingling sensation. Over the years he had gotten together many times with these people in different combinations for beers and to shoot the breeze. While this meeting had the same juvenile feel, they weren't just bitching about pointy-haired managers and screwed-up projects. This was something that was going to change their lives. Something that once done, they wouldn't be able to turn back from. He just prayed that it would work as planned and that there would be enough money to justify him losing a bit of his soul.

None of them seemed to feel like talking. Even Gordon sat quietly in the backseat, a somber expression darkening his face. When Dan let him out at his condo, Gordon told him he was going to spend a few days at the Jersey shore but he would be back by Tuesday night. After they pulled away, Dan asked Shrini what he thought.

"Your friend Joel is very excitable," Shrini said.

"That's one way of putting it. We could be kind and call him passionate. He's not what worries me, though. What did you think of his buddy, Eric?"

"He looked like a small hog walking on two legs. Dude, something's not quite right about him."

Dan nodded, feeling his uneasiness now every time he exhaled. "So what do we do, call this off?"

"I still want to do this," Shrini said. "Our plan makes too much sense not to go through with it. How about you?"

"I don't know, man. I'll have to think about it."

"Just a case of nerves, dude. Don't think too much."

"I'll try not to." Dan laughed. "Damn, I had been feeling pretty good about this. I don't know, something about Joel and his buddy put me off."

"Just nerves, dude. You'll be fine."

When they arrived at Shrini's apartment, Dan joined him inside for a few shots of tequila. After his third shot, his uneasiness faded somewhat.

Dan pulled into his driveway a little before five and was surprised to see Carol's car there. Usually she didn't leave work until five. He found her sitting alone in the kitchen, an open bottle of wine on the table in front of her. Carol was not a big drinker, but it looked like several glasses had already been poured. She looked up at him, her eyes watery, her face pale and drawn. She told him she had been fired.

"They waited until four o'clock to tell me," she said, almost as if in a daze. "They claim I'm being fired for cause. Because I was late for a meeting. All of three minutes late."

"They're firing you for that?"

"That's what they're claiming. The real reason's because I happened to be standing nearby when Nancy told the senior partner to go screw himself. That little egotistical prick probably couldn't stand the idea of having me around after that."

Dan rubbed a hand across his jaw considering what Carol told him. "So fuck them," he said. "You didn't like it there anyway. You'll look for another job, collect unemployment—"

"You don't understand. I was fired, not laid off. They're going to fight any unemployment claim I make."

"Can they do that?"

"That's what they're doing. How can I fight an office full of lawyers?" As she looked at Dan, her blank expression gave way to hopelessness. She appeared utterly, completely lost. "Please tell me again that your interview went well."

He stared at her for a moment before he remembered what

she was referring to. "Yeah," he said. 'It seemed to go well. We'll see next week. The follow-up is scheduled for next Thursday."

"I don't want to put pressure on you, but if you don't get that job I don't know what we're going to do. We have no money coming in now and I don't know how I'm going to be able to find another job. Other firms are going to know I've been fired."

He struggled trying to think of something to say.

"Please," she pleaded. "Whatever you do, don't say everything's going to be okay. Whatever you do, don't say that. I'll go insane if you do. I swear to God I will."

Dan nodded. He fully accepted now that he was going to go through with the bank robbery. He couldn't help feeling somewhat dead inside. "Where are the kids?" he asked, his voice barely above a whisper.

"Brandon's dad is taking Gary to a baseball game. Susie left a note that she's with Julie and will be home by seven." Carol showed a sad smile. "I need you to join me upstairs in the bedroom. Please, for the next hour try to be with me."

He followed her out of the kitchen and up the stairs. When they got to the bedroom, they both took their clothes off, neither of them saying a word. For that one hour he lost himself.

12

Gordon set his alarm for six and was on the road by a quarter past. By eleven-thirty he was pulling into the Asbury Park Beach. A couple of teenagers leaning against a Mustang convertible and playing gangsta rap on a boom box smirked at him as he made his way by. Gordon ignored them, ambled along to an empty spot on the beach, and plopped himself down on the sand. He started to take his shirt off, noticed how white and flabby his stomach looked and slipped his shirt back on.

After feeling the sun on his face for a few minutes, he pushed himself into a sitting position as two girls walked by. Both were around eighteen, thin, long-legged and darkly tanned. Both were wearing string bikinis. One had long black hair that fell past her shoulders, the other had bleached her hair blond.

Gordon called out to them, asking if they were Brazilian. They stopped, their mouths falling open as they stared at him. "What you saying to us?" the bleached-blond demanded. "What you mean by that?"

"Nothing at all." Gordon could feel himself start to sweat.

"I'm about to date a girl from São Paulo and I just wanted to ask if you were from Brazil."

"We look like we're from Brazil?" the dark-haired girl asked angrily.

"I don't know. You're both thin and tall and beautiful. I thought maybe you were."

"We were born here in New Jersey, asshole!"

"I wasn't trying to insult you."

The dark-haired girl turned to her friend. "I think this old fat *pendejo* is trying to pick us up." The bleached-blond snickered and slowly licked her lips as she stared at Gordon. "Is that true?" she asked. "You think we would want anything to do with a *pajero* like you?"

"First of all," Gordon said, jutting out his chin. "I resent being called old. I don't have a single gray hair or wrinkle. For all you know, I could be in my thirties."

The dark-haired girl shook her head. "Can you believe this guy?" she asked. The bleached-blond just kept staring at Gordon, licking her lips in an exaggerated motion. "You didn't answer my question, stud," she said. "You think you have a chance with either of us?"

"Well, I don't know. What if I were rich?"

"He thinks we're whores," the bleached-blond said to her friend. Then to Gordon, "Who you try to fool? You don't have no money, but even if you did I would never let you touch these." She cupped her breasts, staring defiantly at him.

"I could have a lot of money," Gordon said. "More than you could imagine."

"Look," the dark-haired girl said as she pointed at Gordon's crotch. "This old *pajero* has a stiffy. I think he's going to start fingering himself."

"I don't have an erection," Gordon insisted.

"*Creep! Pendejo!*" the bleached-blond yelled as she grabbed her friend and pulled her away. The dark-haired girl spat in the sand. As they walked away, Gordon made a gun with his thumb and forefinger and shot imaginary bullets through their thin beautiful torsos. He was still doing it when they stopped to talk to two muscle-bound guys in their twenties. The guys stared in Gordon's direction and then started moving fast towards him.

"Oh, jeez," Gordon murmured to himself, then got the hell out of there.

13

Petrenko looked dully at his Arab hosts while his jeweler sat at a table in the corner and examined the diamonds. Abbas stared intently back. There was a fourth Arab this time. Three of them made a show of the Glocks they were carrying. The one with the scowl had his right hand bandaged and was holding a gun with his left. The only noise came from the old jeweler grunting occasionally as he shifted positions.

Petrenko had brought both Yuri and Sergei with him. He also had four other men sitting in a car outside. They were listening in on an open line from a cell phone that Petrenko had slipped into his shirt pocket. If they heard a commotion, they'd be in the house in seconds. Petrenko didn't expect any trouble. His gaze shifted to his two men. Both of them were standing like marble statues.

Petrenko, bored, winked at Abbas. "They could stand like that for hours and not move a muscle. Maybe I should make a little extra money and rent them out to guard that palace in England. What do you think?"

Abbas ignored him. Petrenko fell back into his dull stare. It was hot and stuffy in that house and these Arab bastards couldn't even offer him a drink. No business sense whatsoever.

There were a few more grunts from the old jeweler before he pushed himself out of his chair, approached Petrenko and nodded, indicating that the diamonds were of the same quality as the others.

Petrenko considered briefly trying to squeeze a few more dollars from the price, but decided he had pushed these Arabs as far as he could. He handed Abbas the attaché case he had brought with him. Abbas opened the case and counted through the stacks of hundred-dollar bills inside. When he was done counting, he closed the case and indicated to the other Arabs that the money was all there. While they all acknowledged him, none of them bothered to put their Glocks away. Or loosen their grips.

Petrenko stood up and collected the diamonds. Walking back to Abbas, he extended a hand. The Arab looked sourly down at it before reluctantly offering a weak grip in return.

"If you need to sell more diamonds you know how to reach me," Petrenko offered.

Abbas nodded sharply and somewhat angrily.

When they were alone in their Mercedes, Yuri mentioned to Petrenko that he didn't believe the Arabs were happy with their price.

"No, I don't believe so either," Petrenko agreed. "We have had a very good day. First, let us store these stones in a safe place, then we will have a small celebration."

Yuri pulled away from the curb and drove towards the Lynn Capital Bank.

14

Dan spent the four days leading up to the robbery taking his family on day trips. Nothing that cost more than a few bucks; a couple of trips to the beach and once to an amusement park, but everyone seemed to have fun. One night he splurged and took Carol and the kids to a minor league ball game. He was amazed at how fast the time flew by. The past year he had felt a growing estrangement from his wife and daughter, but during those four days it was as if they were a family again. As if all past sins had been forgotten. Susie most of the time seemed happy, letting her guard down and laughing the way she used to. She even sat on Dan's lap a few times with her arms wrapped around his neck – something she hadn't done in ages. Carol surprised Dan even more. He didn't know how she would be after losing her job, but she acted the way she used to – relaxed, affectionate with the kids and playful with him. Gary was Gary. He was always a good-natured kid, and had seemed oblivious to the tension and financial strain that had been pulling the family apart. Now, though, he had picked up on the general good mood of the rest of them and acted more rambunctious and good-natured than ever.

At first Dan was confused about Carol's behavior. He thought maybe she was putting on an act, trying to be positive for the kids, but eventually he realized that she was in denial. Maybe she had convinced herself that he was going to be offered the position that she thought he was interviewing for, or maybe she simply couldn't deal with worrying any more. Whatever the reason for her change, he was grateful for it. A few times he caught her staring off into the distance while a brittle look formed on her face, but she seemed to snap out of it quickly.

When Wednesday morning came he felt the way he always felt whenever he had an unpleasant task to do, like a trip to the dentist or filling out tax forms. Something you just had to suck up and get over with. Mostly, though, he felt okay. Maybe some nervous energy and a little tightness in the stomach, but not too bad. Probably more anxious than anything else.

He squinted at the clock radio and saw it was eight minutes to eleven. At first he refused to believe it was that late, and then with kind of a knee-jerk reaction he reached for Carol and realized that he was alone in bed. He had set the alarm for seven thirty. Somehow he must've slept through it. There was no way he would be able to meet Gordon at eleven as planned. Everything had been timed out to the minute and he couldn't afford to be late, not even ten minutes.

Stumbling out of bed, he dressed quickly. As he headed down the stairs Carol yelled to him from the kitchen.

"You're up finally," she said. "You looked so dead to the world that I thought I'd let you sleep. Why don't you join me in the kitchen. I'll make you a late breakfast."

So she had turned the alarm off. Great. He checked his

watch and felt the tightness in his stomach intensify as he saw it was three minutes to eleven. He went into the kitchen and told Carol he was supposed to meet Shrini in a few minutes. Shrini was a safer choice. He knew he wouldn't be able to explain needing to meet Gordon.

"I was hoping we could spend the day together," she said. "After all, if things go well we might not have another chance to spend time like this during a weekday."

He looked at her dumbly before realizing she was referring to the interview she thought he was going to be having the next day. He told her that he'd like to spend the day with her, but he had promised Shrini that he would meet him. Carol had brewed a fresh pot of coffee and he poured a cup into a travel mug. "We want to talk over some possible business ideas," he continued. "I should keep my options open in case things don't work out tomorrow."

"I thought you said the first interview went well?"

"It did, but you never know with these things."

"Do you think there's a chance you won't get an offer?" The same brittle look that he had caught glimpses of over the last few days had resurfaced. He felt a pull on his heart as he forced a reassuring smile. "I know you hate it when I say this, but I'm sure everything's going to work out fine. I really have to get going. I'll try to be home by five."

He gave her a quick kiss. On his way out the door, she told him that she was going to miss him. "Be careful, please, darling." There was a heartfelt concern in her voice that almost stopped him and made him turn back to her. Instead, he took a deep breath and kept walking.

While he drove to meet Gordon, he couldn't help feeling bad about leading Carol on. He didn't have any choice, though.

She'd be freaking out otherwise. Also, while his plan was to use Shrini's future company in India as a way to funnel his cut of the robbery back to him, that could take six months or longer. He was going to need access to some of the money before then and he was playing around with the idea of using a bogus software contract as a way to explain the money he would be bringing into the house.

He thought about her plea for him to be careful. She had always been very intuitive and must have sensed that something was up. What exactly she thought he should be careful about he had no idea. She probably didn't either.

When Dan arrived at Gordon's complex, he found Gordon waiting for him in the parking lot, pacing furiously. He pulled the car up to him.

"Jeez, Dan," Gordon said, worry lines creasing his forehead. "You're late."

Dan glanced at the cell phone Gordon had in his hand. "You didn't try calling me, did you?" he asked. "We agreed no phone calls."

"No, but I almost did. You're twenty minutes late. I told you I need a full hour."

"I know you did. I'm sorry. Let's go upstairs and get started, okay?"

While they walked to Gordon's apartment, Gordon complained how he needed at least an hour to do the makeup. Dan just murmured along agreeably. He had heard this same type of complaining countless times from Gordon over the years. Gordon was okay with deadlines as long as he could set them and make sure there was enough fat in his schedule to provide a comfort zone, but if you tried pushing him he would go to pieces.

When they got to his apartment, Gordon had Dan sit next to the computer while a set of photos of Raymond Lombardo were displayed on the monitor. His hands shook as he started to apply a compound to Dan's jaw.

"Relax," Dan told him. "Take a deep breath, okay? You have the full hour. I'm not going to rush you."

"What about your schedule?"

"I padded it," Dan lied. "We're fine. Don't worry about the schedule."

Gordon slowly relaxed into his old goofy self. His hands moved faster and steadier as he made a thicker jaw and nose for Dan. As he worked, he talked incessantly about the twenty-eight-year-old dental hygienist from São Paulo that he was thinking about contacting. After finishing the jaw and nose, he attached a wig to Dan's hair using pins and then glued on sideburns and a mustache. He finished the job by adding acne scarring along Dan's cheeks. When he was done, Dan popped in his cosmetic lenses and studied himself with a hand mirror. The resemblance was good. If he looked hard enough he could tell the nose and jaw were fake, but when videotaped from a distance the disguise would work fine.

Gordon handed him a ski mask. "Try taking this off a few times. I want to see if the compound holds."

Dan did as he was asked. The compound held. "Let's get the overalls on," he said.

Gordon helped him into them. With the extra padding, the overalls were somewhat clunky, but he was able to move around in them okay. "What do you think?" Dan asked.

Gordon appraised Dan slowly, nodding. "You look enough like him to fool a security video."

Dan checked his watch. Gordon had finished fourteen

minutes early. They were almost back on schedule. "You're straight on where you're meeting us?" he asked.

"Don't worry, I'll be there." Gordon exhaled, made a face as if he had bitten into a lemon. "By the way, I went to the Jersey Shore for the last time this weekend. I don't know, that place has lost its appeal for me."

"Why don't we talk about this later."

"Sure, I know, I better let you get going." Gordon handed Dan a rolled-up paper bag. "The ski masks and everything you need to remove the makeup are in the bag." He hesitated, rubbing a hand across his jaw. "I need a favor, Dan. This weekend I'm going to fly down to São Paulo. I'm not planning on coming back. I have over four thousand dollars left. That should leave me enough for six months if I'm careful. When the bank money is safe, I'm going to need you to wire me my cut."

Dan nodded. The request didn't surprise him. "I'll take care of it, buddy. You're meeting us at one-thirty sharp, right?"

"Righto."

They shook hands. As Dan left he couldn't help feeling a bit nostalgic. Gordon, Shrini, Joel; he had known them for years and they were all going to be out of his life soon enough. When the robbery was finished, that was it. But there was more to it than that. There were so many more aspects of his life that were going to be shut off forever. He felt a panic start in his chest. He took several deep breaths and tried to block out his thoughts and simply concentrate on the road. He opened both front windows, afraid that he might pass out if he didn't have fresh air blowing hard on his face.

When he arrived at Shrini's, Shrini was wearing his overalls and gloves and waiting where he was supposed to. Dan pulled up alongside him. From the driver's seat of his Honda Civic,

Shrini gave a big shit-eating grin as he looked at Dan. "Hey, Raymond Lombardo, how's it going, dude?"

Dan got out and took the passenger seat in the Civic. He was still shaken from his near panic attack and waited until Shrini pulled out on to the street before answering him. "Great day for a bank robbery," he said, trying to force a bravado but his voice sounded flat and lifeless to him. "You have everything in the trunk?"

"Everything's there, dude." Shrini took a quick sideways glance at Dan. "Believe me," he said. "Gordon is truly an artist. He should be working on Broadway, or better yet, Hollywood."

Shrini handed Dan a piece of paper. Written on it were addresses of cars they had scoped out. All the addresses were in Revere. If none of the cars were available, that was it, the robbery was over. The deal they had was if anything went wrong they would walk away from the robbery if they could.

Dan directed Shrini to the first three addresses on the list before they found what they were looking for. He got out of the car, took a slim jim and a screwdriver from the Civic's trunk, and walked over to a rusted-out older model Chevy Camaro that was parked on the street. Sliding the slim jim between the window and door panel, he had the car unlocked in seconds. He pressed the trunk release. While he pulled out the ignition wires with the screwdriver, Shrini transferred the contents of his trunk to the Chevy's.

A minute later he had the ignition wires clamped together and the car engine running. By using a clamp, he could easily turn on and off the ignition. He put the car in drive and pulled into the street. Shrini trailed behind in his Civic. All the practicing paid off. While he had been unable to figure out the newer cars, older cars like this Camaro he could unlock and start in less than two minutes.

Dan checked his watch as he entered the Revere Mall parking lot. Shrini was still behind him, but he tailed off as they had agreed. He kept driving until he spotted Joel and Hoffer sitting in Joel's car. He pulled up next to them and they quickly left their car and got into the backseat of the Chevy. Both of them were carrying what looked like large gym bags. Joel was wearing his overalls, Hoffer had on an old running suit.

Dan next drove to the area of the mall parking lot where Gordon was supposed to be and spotted him pulling up as they got there. He checked his watch again. They were only a couple of minutes off schedule. Gordon took the front passenger seat and made eye contact with Joel and Hoffer before facing front.

Dan drove to where Shrini was waiting and stopped so that Shrini could squeeze into the backseat next to Hoffer.

"Okay, dudes, let's rock and roll," Shrini said. No one bothered to answer him. Gordon and Joel both seemed deep in thought. Hoffer still had his stupid grin plastered across his face. As they headed towards Lynn, Joel remarked to Gordon how he'd done a fucking fantastic job making up Dan. "Our son of a bitch friend up there actually looks like that Mafioso," Joel said. "I also have to tell you, you impressed the hell out of me the other day with your shooting."

Gordon looked back, nodded soberly. "Thanks, Joel. Believe it or not, that means a lot to me coming from you."

"All right," Dan interrupted, trying to sound both confident and in charge. "Before we all start crying and joining in a group hug, we're five minutes from the bank. As of right now, thanks to some crappy work by an Indian contract house and a little help from yours truly, their alarm system will be disabled for the next twenty-eight minutes. That should give us enough time. We'll go in there and get this over with fast." Pausing, he added, "No shooting, understood?"

"Unless we need to," Joel snapped.

"Unless one of our lives is at stake," Dan corrected him. "But if something goes wrong and we're in a position to surrender peacefully, that's what we do. Agreed?"

Joel sat glaring, his lips pressed into tight lines.

"Joel, you already agreed to this last week. Agree again or I turn around."

"All right, all right. I don't like it but I agree."

Dan drove past the side street that the Lynn Capital Bank was on and instead took the next right. Next he swung into a parking lot for a vacant storefront. Directly behind the parking lot was the bank's lot. Cut through shrubs separating the two lots and you had a ten-second run to the bank lobby. Thanks to its location, the bank had little foot traffic. While they were taking a small chance someone would see them during those ten seconds, Dan thought it unlikely.

Joel handed out forty-five caliber pistols along with extra magazines. "That gives each of you fourteen shots," he told them. Dan stuck his gun in a front pocket and then passed out the ski masks. Gordon had added hair to the edges of the ones that both he and Joel ended up with, making them look like they had long black curly hair. Shrini slipped on a pair of tinted aviator glasses and put his ski mask on over them. They all sat for a moment collecting their thoughts and then Dan whistled to get their attention. He got out of the car and took a duffel bag from the trunk. Shrini followed, also taking a duffel bag. Joel and Hoffer both opened their bags and brought out Kalashnikov rifles.

"Fuck it," Joel said. "Let's get moving!"

He led the way, pushing though the shrubs and running at full speed towards the bank. Dan followed behind. He felt strange, almost as if he were watching himself from outside his body. Dreamlike more than anything else.

The scene didn't seem real to him as they descended on the bank, guns drawn. Customers and bank employees looked on with confused and shocked expressions. An older woman started screaming. Joel smacked her on the back of the head with the rifle barrel. That shut her up as she sat on the floor holding the area where she'd been hit. As Dan looked around he could see the light going on in some of their eyes as they realized what was happening. Two of the tellers had their hands below the counter. He knew they were pressing the alarm signal. One of them showed a thin smile, as if he had some joke over them that they didn't know about. Of course, the alarms were disabled, but they didn't know that. Joel and Hoffer were rounding them up, making them lie on their stomachs while Gordon wrapped their wrists and ankles with duct tape. Dan ran to the bank manager's office. The manager looked up at Dan, scared, and told him the silent alarm had been pressed.

"You might as well leave now while you still can," he said. "Before someone gets hurt."

This was the same manager who had made the decision to farm the software development to India instead of letting Dan build it. Dan signaled with his gun for him to stand up. As he got out of his chair and started for the door, Dan pushed him hard from behind. The manager tripped and fell to his knees before stumbling back to his feet. Joel spotted him, ran over and dragged him to the others.

Dan caught Shrini's eyes. The two of them made a beeline

towards the room where the safety deposit boxes were kept. That was what they were after. The robbery plan had come together once Dan hacked into the bank's customer database and saw that one of the customers owned eight safety deposit boxes. After researching who this customer was and realizing he was a renowned Russian mobster it had all clicked. This man, Viktor Petrenko, wouldn't be able to go to the police about what was stolen, and without that, how could the police catch them? And why would they ever suspect a bunch of geeky software engineers of pulling this off – especially if they had physical evidence linking the robbery to a reputed Mafia member?

There were electric outlets in the hallway. Dan and Shrini both opened their duffel bags and took out extension cords, plugging them into the outlets. The door to the room containing the safety deposit boxes was unlocked. If the alarm had been working, the door would've been bolted shut.

Inside, the two of them took high-performance power drills out of their duffel bags, plugged them into the extension cords and went to work. Dan had bought the same make of safety deposit box over the Internet. They were paid for with money orders and delivered to an address in Revere, a block from Raymond Lombardo's home; he had been able to pick them up without anyone knowing about it. He and Shrini had practiced on those boxes and learned how to open them. There were three bolts that needed to be drilled through and then the boxes slid out easily. It still seemed like a dream as he drilled open the boxes belonging to Petrenko and dumped the contents into his duffel bag. There seemed to be a lot of money in the boxes, mostly packets of hundred-dollar bills held together by elastic bands.

Both of them were finishing up when they heard a gunshot.

It was louder than Dan would've ever imagined and just seemed to echo on forever. They both shut off their drills.

"Is that what I think it is?" Shrini whispered.

Dan held up a palm for him to be quiet as he tried to listen to what was going on. He heard a woman yelling and then another shot.

"Let's get the hell out of here," he told Shrini.

"Wait a second." Shrini turned his drill back on and finished cutting through the last bolt. Dan stood and watched, feeling like his heart was going to explode. After Shrini dumped the contents into his duffel bag and zipped it shut, the two of them grabbed their bags and headed back to the lobby.

What was going on there didn't make any sense to Dan. There were no cops, no reason for any shooting, just Joel and Hoffer standing with their rifles while Gordon stood over two women, his body rigid, his arm fully extended as he pointed his gun at them. A large red puddle was leaking outward from one of the women. She couldn't have been much older than twenty. Her shirt looked like it was drenched in blood. Her eyes were closed. Her skin bloodless. There was no question she was dead. The other woman, maybe in her forties, moaned loudly as she squirmed on the floor. She had been shot in the stomach. Gordon asked her several times if she had anything else she'd like to say to him.

Dan looked over at Gordon and then at Joel, trying to figure out what had happened. Joel shook his head angrily and headed quickly towards the lobby door, Hoffer joining him. Dan followed, his head buzzing, trying to understand how those two women got shot. As he was running, Shrini grabbed him and gestured towards his ski mask. Still in a daze, Dan took his mask off near one of the hidden security cameras. That was a big part of the plan since he knew the location of all the hidden security cameras. He paused for a moment and then kept going. When he got to the Chevy, Joel was waiting for him, livid.

"I told you not to bring him," he spat out through clenched teeth.

"What the hell happened in there?"

"Ask your loon buddy."

Gordon was pushing through the shrubs, breathing hard.

"Gordon, what the hell...?"

"Dan, you should've heard what those two said to me."

"We have to get out of here," Joel said, taking the ski mask from Shrini and collecting his gun. Dan blindly handed Joel both his gun and mask.

"Gordon, do you realize what you did to us?"

"Come on, Dan, I didn't do anything to us. What difference does it make if I shot those two?"

"What difference...?"

Joel interrupted Gordon, slapping him on the arm. "Hey, loony, give me your mask."

Annoyed, Gordon threw his mask at Joel before turning back to Dan. "Anyway, what did you expect?" he asked. "You invited me along and gave me a gun. Jeez, you should've known I'd do something like that."

All Dan could do was stare at him. Joel moved forward, his hand out in front of Gordon's eyes as he snapped his fingers. "Your gun, now!" he barked. Gordon turned to him, his face red. "What is your problem!" he yelled back, shoving the gun, barrel first, into Joel's outstretched hand.

Joel without any hesitation flipped the gun in his hand and shot Gordon in the middle of his forehead. Gordon rocked back and forth on his heels and then fell straight back as if he were a piece of timber that had been cut.

Joel pointed the gun at Dan. From the corner of his eye, Dan could see Hoffer aiming his rifle at Shrini, his plastic grin now a hard sneer. "Take his overalls off," Joel said softly. "Both of you."

"Joel, what are you doing?"

"You got twenty seconds," Joel said, his face white, his eyes glassy. "I'm counting now. Otherwise, I'm leaving you and your Indian buddy here with this loon."

He started counting. Shrini moved first, kneeling by Gordon's dead body and unzipping the overalls. Dan joined him, his hands shaking. He could hear Hoffer standing behind him laughing softly. Somehow they got the overalls off before Joel finished counting. Underneath, Gordon had on a Grateful Dead T-shirt and a pair of shorts. Hoffer balled the overalls up and threw them into the Chevy's trunk, along with the duffel bags.

"Take his car keys," Joel ordered.

Dan went through Gordon's pockets and pulled out both his wallet and keys.

Joel waved his gun at Dan. "We're getting out of here now. Dan, you drive, Gunga Din here can sit in the back with Eric."

They moved quickly into the car. Dan could feel himself trembling as he gripped the wheel, not out of fear but from a white-hot rage. He pulled the car on to the street and headed towards the highway.

"You would've shot me back there," he said.

"If you didn't get those overalls off in time, yeah."

Dan drove another minute stewing in silence. Then he reached into his pocket and pulled out a cell phone.

"What do you think you're doing?"

"I'm calling for an ambulance. That woman in the bank, the one shot in the stomach, needs one."

"Forget it. I'm sure someone heard the gunshots, and I'm sure plenty of ambulances are on their way."

Almost prophetically the sound of sirens could be heard in the distance. Within seconds the noise grew louder until it was almost deafening, and then just as quickly it faded. The police cruisers and ambulances must've traveled past them on a parallel street.

"You fucked us," Dan said to Joel after it became quiet again. "It was bad enough what Gordon did, but what you did fucked us. The police are going to tie him to the robbery. You screwed up the frame we had in place for Lombardo."

Joel squeezed his jaw with one hand while he used the other to hold a gun on Dan. "I made an executive decision," he said. "No way I was going to trust my life with that loon, not after seeing what he did in that bank. Fuck him anyway, he got what he deserved for what he did to those two women."

"You still fucked us."

"I didn't fuck anything. I used the same gun he used. That means ballistics are going to match up and the cops are going to figure that he was shot by the same bank robbers, probably so they could take his car. They'll look at him as simply being in the wrong place at the wrong time."

"That's right, chief," Hoffer snickered from behind. "Nothing at all to worry about."

Joel glanced back at him, giving him a look to shut up.

"What happened in there?"

"Exactly what you should've expected." Joel showed a pained expression, shook his head. "Even worse, exactly what

I should've expected. I never should've agreed to let you bring Gordon."

"He just started shooting them?"

"Pretty much. He started talking to that girl, the one he shot in the chest. I don't know what the fuck he was saying to her, shit about Brazil and the Jersey Shore and God knows what else. She called him a couple of pretty rough names and he flipped her over and shot her in the chest. Then that other woman started mouthing off, and he flipped her over and shot her also."

"You couldn't stop him?"

"How?" Joel asked. "What could I have done?" He shook his head angrily. "No, pal, this is your fault. You insisted that he be part of this. You promised me you could control him for ten lousy minutes." His voice choked off as he stared at Dan, his features hardening, making him look like an old man. Then, softly, "I didn't sign up for a felony murder rap. Sorry, Dan, but this changes everything. You're going to drive to your buddy's car, the two of you are going to get out and you're going to forget about any share of the money."

"This isn't right, Joel."

"The price you have to pay, Dan."

"What about me?" Shrini asked from behind.

"Sorry, Gunga, but that's your price also. As far as I'm concerned Gordon was as much your mistake as Dan's. My advice, go back to India and forget this ever happened."

Dan turned into the mall parking lot where they had left their cars. He pulled up to Shrini's Civic.

"This is not a good idea, Joel."

"Why not? You're going to tell the police on me?" Joel made a face. "I don't think so." His eyes glazed over as he trained the gun on Dan's chest. "If either of you do anything other than quietly get into that car, I'm going to cut the two of you down right here and take my chances. Have a nice life, okay, pal."

"Nice seeing you again, chief," Hoffer added.

Dan sat frozen until he felt the barrel of Joel's forty-five push into his ribs. He turned to say something, but the look in Joel's eyes convinced him that it would be useless. He got out of the car. Shrini stared helplessly at Dan before joining him. They stood and watched as Joel slid over into the Chevy's driver's seat and Hoffer moved up front. As they drove off, Hoffer rolled down his window and saluted them with his middle finger.

15

Alex Resnick noted the location of the surveillance cameras as he entered the bank. Two other detectives, Tom Stillwall and Phil Hollings, were already inside talking to a witness. Resnick nodded to them and then glanced at the dead woman. Over the years he had grown mostly numb to the sight of dead bodies, but seeing this girl weakened him in the knees. She was just too damn young to have something like that happen to her. He heard a low groan, and saw his partner staring in her direction.

"Damn, there's a lot of blood," Maguire said.

Stillwall approached the two of them, both hands pushed deep in his pockets, his face frozen in a constipated frown. He was a big man, messy, his hair uncombed, a thick six o'clock shadow already showing. His suit, which was several sizes too big, looked as if it had been slept in.

"Hey, boyos," he greeted them, his constipated look growing more pained, "what a mess, huh? We're going to be here all goddamn night. And just my luck, I've got Sox tickets for this evening."

"Two people were shot?" Resnick asked.

"Yeah, we had two of them all right." Stillwall consulted a notepad. "One Mary O'Donnell, forty-two, lives right here in Lynn." He closed his notepad. "She was in pretty rough shape when they took her out, shot point blank in the stomach with a forty-five. Whoever did that wanted to inflict much pain, my friend.

"Now this poor girl," Stillwall went on, waving a hand in the direction of the dead woman. "Margaret Williams. Only barely twenty-three. Always hard to imagine when they're dead, but she must've been something to look at when she was among the living. This was a pure execution. And like the other shooting, a forty-five was used. Two shots, two casings. We got them both."

"Why's she still here?"

"FBI's sending over one of their CSI experts, although I don't see the point of it. I mean for crying out loud, we know what happened, and even if we didn't we'll be watching videotape of it later. But what are you going to do, rules are rules." Stillwall moved closer to Resnick. "Let me give you a quick rundown," he said, lowering his voice. "Six or seven guys stormed in here, all wearing masks, all with guns drawn. Several of them had assault rifles, maybe AK-47s. They laid everyone out on their stomachs and taped their wrists and ankles behind them."

Stillwall stopped in his tracks, his frown deepening as he held his stomach. "Damn acid reflux," he said after a while. "I had a sausage sub for lunch and I've been paying the price ever since."

"So everyone's on the floor…" Resnick said patiently, trying to get Stillwall back on track.

"Okay, so after everyone's on the floor, they go for the safety deposit boxes. They didn't try for the vault or bother with any of the money from the cashier drawers."

"What about the shootings?"

"I'm still not clear on what happened. That guy over there with Phil, the pencil-necked individual who looks like he's about to pass out, is one Craig Brown, the manager of this fine banking establishment. According to Brown and several other witnesses, there was something going on between the two victims and one of the gunmen." Stillwall edged closer, his voice dropping to a low growl. "Now something I find interesting; this bank has a new state-of-the-art security system. We tried it five minutes ago and the system worked like a champ, yet during the robbery the damn thing's a bust. You got to ask yourself why."

"You think there was someone on the inside?" Resnick asked.

"I don't know how else to explain it. The system is locked away in a cabinet. Brown unlocked it for us and showed us that everything was up and running. I have to think the system was turned off before the robbery. And according to Brown, he's the only one who has the key to the cabinet. Figure that one out, boyo."

Stillwall raised an eyebrow, waiting for a reaction from Resnick. When he didn't get one, he turned to Maguire. "Your partner's a hard man to please. Just about talk your ear off if you let him, but you must know that by now." He waited a few seconds and then sighed after still getting no reaction from either of them. "No sense of humor, the both of you."

Stillwall led the way to the back of the bank where the safety deposit boxes were kept. Two extension cords plugged into outlets in the hallway snaked through an open door. Resnick walked into the room. Both cords were attached to drills that lay on the floor. He counted the number of safety deposit boxes that had been dumped on the floor. Eight of them, each with three holes drilled into them. Examining one of the boxes, he saw that the holes had cut through bolts that would've kept the boxes from being able to be opened.

"Seems they knew what they were doing," Resnick said.

"That it does," Stillwall agreed.

Maguire stood squinting at the rows of safety deposit boxes. "I wonder how they happened to pick the ones they did," he said.

"Do we know who owns them?" Resnick asked Stillwall.

Stillwall showed a thin smile. "So far Brown's not being very cooperative. He's making noise about the privacy of his customers, crap like that, but he doesn't have a leg to stand on. We could get a court order by tonight if we had to, but I think if we lean on him a little he'll cave fast enough. What do you say, Alex?"

"Sure, just give me a minute." Resnick stepped back and took several shots of the damaged safety deposit boxes before sliding the digital camera back into his jacket pocket.

They got to the lobby as two FBI agents were entering the bank. Resnick knew immediately they were FBI from their dress and body language. One was a tall, thin man in his late forties with a long dour face; the other an athletic dark brunette around thirty who would've been very attractive if her face hadn't been set in a humorless, rigid expression. Phil Hollings joined them and there was a quick round of introductions. The woman, Kathleen Liciano, was the crime scene investigator, and she quickly left them to go and examine the dead body. The other agent was Donald Spitzer. Stillwall gave him a quick rundown, more tersely than he had with Resnick and Maguire.

"The government is going to be seeking the death penalty for the people behind this," Agent Spitzer announced glumly. "We've been looking for a case like this in Massachusetts ever since the federal death penalty was expanded."

"I hope we'll be able to oblige you," Stillwall said. "The perps who did this deserve at least that much. We were about to talk to Mr. Craig Brown and try to find out, among other things, why the bank's security system magically stopped working before the robbery. Would you care to join us?"

Spitzer indicated that he would. Brown, who was standing across the lobby, turned a bit green as four detectives and an FBI agent approached him. Stillwall did the introductions. The bank manager had put out his hand to the FBI agent, but pulled it back after Spitzer ignored it.

"We'd like to talk to you someplace quiet," Resnick said.

"All of you?"

"You don't have a problem with that, do you?" Spitzer asked

"No, of course not." Brown's eyes jerked from Resnick to Spitzer. He took a handkerchief from his suit pocket and wiped the back of his neck. "My office should be fine."

After they got situated in the bank manager's office, Resnick asked Brown about the shootings.

"They had us all lying face down. I don't think any of us saw the shootings. When that first shot happened I thought it was a bomb. I never heard anything so loud." Brown's voice wavered, probably as he replayed the moment in his head. As his attention focused back on Resnick, his skin looked paler, almost waxy. "I still can't believe this happened," he muttered. "I feel like I'm going to have a heart attack or something."

"Do you require medical attention?" Maguire asked.

Brown shook his head. "Maybe a glass of water." He

picked up a coffee mug from his desk and started to get up, but Maguire took the mug from him. "I'll get you the water," he told him.

"Why do you think those two women were shot?" Resnick asked.

"One of the robbers was talking to Peggy. I don't know exactly what he was saying, some strange things, like about a Brazilian bikini wax. I think he was trying to pick her up. Peggy just let him have it, told him what she thought of him. Then he shot her."

"Peggy – you mean Margaret Williams. You knew her?"

"I've known her since she was seventeen. I know her parents also. Peggy was a beautiful girl. Also very feisty – someone who wouldn't take guff from anyone."

"Did you have a relationship with her?" Hollings asked.

"What? No, of course not."

"Why do you think your security system didn't work?" Spitzer asked. There was a hard edge to his voice and the bank manager flinched at the sound of it, almost as if he had been punched.

"I have absolutely no idea," he said. Maguire had brought back his coffee mug. Brown's hands shook as he drank from it, some of the water spilling on to his suit jacket. "Right after I was freed, I checked the cabinet and found that the system was still on. I tested it later with two of the detectives here and the system worked the way it was supposed to. I have no idea what happened."

"Who was with you?" Spitzer demanded.

"What do you mean?"

"When you checked the cabinet, who was with you?"

"I was alone…" Brown's mouth closed slowly as he realized

what Spitzer was getting at. As he stared at the FBI agent, a shadow fell over his eyes. "I don't like what you're implying," he said. "Maybe I should consult a lawyer."

"That's your right," Resnick said. "And if you're involved in this, it would probably be a good idea."

"If you do want to lawyer up, we'll be more than happy to bring you down to the station for official questioning and make sure the media knows all about it," Stillwall added.

Brown's complexion turned a sickly white as he looked from Spitzer to Stillwall. "This is ridiculous," he said. "I had absolutely nothing to do with this."

"You can understand why we would be suspicious," Resnick said.

"No, I don't understand that."

"Anyone else have a key to that cabinet?"

Craig Brown shook his head.

"There you go," Hollings offered.

"Add to that your unwillingness to cooperate with us," Resnick said.

"Unwillingness to cooperate?" Brown sputtered. "How am I not cooperating?"

"A woman is shot to death, another critically wounded, and you can't tell us why your alarm system didn't work," Stillwall said.

"I've been telling you, I don't know."

"You won't even tell us who owns the safety deposit boxes that were broken into," Resnick said.

"Which is just plain silly," Stillwall explained. "If we go to a judge, we'll have a court order within the hour forcing you to provide us with that information."

"You would make things easier for me if you got a court

order," Brown said. "The person who owns them wouldn't be happy if I gave you the information voluntarily."

"One person owns all of the boxes that were broken into?" Maguire asked.

Brown nodded. Then, very softly, "Viktor Petrenko."

Resnick's voice cracked as he asked Brown to repeat the name. Brown repeated that Viktor Petrenko owned all of the boxes that were robbed.

Resnick could feel his heart beating a mile a minute. "Did he own any others?" he asked.

Brown shook his head. "Only the ones that were broken into."

There was a knock on the door and a patrolman stuck his head in. "We found another dead body out back," he said.

"What do you mean out back?"

"In a lot behind the bank's. A male Caucasian, around sixty, shot once in the head."

Resnick exchanged glances with his partner and then Stillwall, who lowered his head into his hand and squeezed his eyes. "I might as well throw my Sox tickets away," he moaned.

Resnick and Maguire left with the patrolman, the others staying behind to continue questioning Brown. Resnick had to get out of that office anyway. Hearing that Petrenko owned those safety deposit boxes had sent a burst of adrenaline pumping through his system and he had to get moving. Petrenko must have had more than just money in those boxes. Probably also weapons and other incriminating evidence. If Resnick could get his hands on what was taken from those boxes, he had no doubt that he would be able to put Petrenko away for a long, long time.

As they walked towards the lobby, Resnick was so caught up in his thoughts that he only half heard his partner ask the patrolman whether the media had picked up on the robbery yet.

"It's a zoo out there," the patrolman was saying. "Reporters from all the local stations and newspapers are parked out front."

"Any of them know about the dead body out back?" Resnick asked.

"Not that I know of. We're trying to keep them away."

When they got to the lobby, Resnick noticed that Margaret Williams' body had been removed. A large puddle of blood remained where she had died. When they left the front lobby door, a burst of voices yelled out to them. Resnick looked up and saw a mob of reporters and cameramen being restrained by a line of uniformed cops. He ignored them and moved quickly towards the parking lot in back. The patrolman led the way, pushing through a thick row of shrubs about three feet high. Maguire cursed as his pant leg caught on a branch and the fabric ripped.

On the other side of the shrubs, Kathleen Liciano was kneeling by the dead body. She looked up as Resnick approached her.

"He was shot once in the forehead with a forty-five caliber," she told him.

Resnick scanned the empty lot. "Could he have been shot in the bank's parking lot and dragged here?"

"No. I found the bullet casing here. Also, there would be plant debris on his clothing if he had been dragged through those bushes."

Resnick looked down at his own suit and brushed away some

small leaves that had attached themselves to it. Maguire walked over to him, still cursing over his torn pants.

"I just bought this suit," he complained. He looked down at the dead body and shook his head. "I don't know what's wrong with these old guys having to walk around as if they're still at Woodstock. He should've been shot dead just for dressing like that. Do we know who he is?"

Liciano shook her head. "He had no identification on him."

"Car keys?" Resnick asked.

"No. His pockets were empty."

Resnick stared at the dead body. There was a small entry wound in the middle of his forehead. Without looking, Resnick knew there would be a large hole blasted out of the back of his skull. The dead man's body looked bloated, his skin grayish. There was a smallness to his face, though. Almost as if it had shrunk in death. Resnick looked past the body and could see small pieces of brain and bone fragments littering the pavement.

"I wonder what he was doing here?" he asked no one in particular. "This store has been vacant for years."

"Probably lousy luck more than anything else," Maguire offered. "Maybe he was going to cut through to the bank, ran into the perps, and got shot either because he saw something, or maybe for his car."

"But why would he park here?" Resnick asked. "Why not in the bank's lot?"

"Who knows?"

Kathleen Liciano stood up, stretching. She removed her latex gloves. "I'm done here," she said. She handed Resnick a card. "Call me in a day and I'll let you know if the autopsies reveal anything." An ambulance had pulled up next to them.

She turned to talk with the EMT workers about the removal of the body.

Resnick took one last look at the dead body and then faced Maguire. "Let Tom and Phil handle the witnesses," he said. "Get the surveillance tapes and I'll meet you back at the station."

"What about you?"

Resnick gave a thin smile, one of the few Maguire had seen from his partner during the three months they had worked together. "I have an errand I need to run," he said.

16

Shrini drove while Dan lay slumped over in the backseat. Both of them had taken their overalls off. Dan had also taken off his wig and had been able to remove the mustache and sideburns using the solution Gordon had left him, but he didn't want to risk anyone else seeing him until he had the rest of the makeup off.

Shrini was fuming, too furious to talk. Every few minutes he'd punch at the wheel and let loose with a string of curse words, both in English and Hindi. That seemed to go on for about forty minutes. Then, after some quiet, he told Dan in a tight angry voice, "If your friend thinks I am going to go quietly back to India, he's in for a very big surprise, believe me."

"Joel just needs to cool off. When he does, he'll give us our share," Dan said, his own voice sounding brittle and odd to him. He still had this strange sensation that he was only a spectator to what was going on around him, almost as if he were watching everything from outside his body.

"No, I don't think so. I believe this is what your friend intended from the beginning."

"Come on, Shrini. He went over the top because of what happened with Gordon. He'll cool off."

"Come on yourself, dude! Why do you think he demanded his pig-friend be included?" Shrini's voice choked off. Dan could see from the reflection in the rearview mirror that Shrini's dark eyes were simmering with fury. "Believe me," Shrini continued when he could. "I am going to receive my share from that little peacock friend of yours, and after I do I am going to kick his ass all over the place."

Dan lowered his head back on to the seat and closed his eyes. As enraged as Shrini was, he himself felt nothing but a gnawing anxiety in his gut. He couldn't blame Joel for what he'd done; after all, he was the one who had promised that Gordon would behave himself during the bank robbery. Joel was right, he had a price to pay for what happened, although he still couldn't comprehend Gordon shooting those two women. It just made no sense to him.

"What was it with that Gunga Din talk?" Shrini demanded. "Was that supposed to be some sort of racist insult?"

"He was just trying to get under your skin. Try to calm down, okay? If we give Joel a couple of days to cool off, he'll come to his senses."

"I don't want to give your friend any days. I say we buy two rifles and wait outside his house and welcome him the same as he did to us. Then we take the money and split it between us."

"What are you saying? You want us to ambush him? Kill him?"

"Sounds good to me."

"Shrini, please, man, calm down. We're not killers."

"I hate to break it to you, dude, but we are. Once Gordon killed that girl we became killers."

"How could we have expected Gordon to do that?"

"It doesn't matter; if we get caught we will all be treated as killers. That's the law."

"We're not going to get caught," Dan stated stubbornly, but he wasn't so sure whether he believed it himself. Joel shooting Gordon changed everything. He hadn't been able to think it through enough to understand the ramifications of what Joel had done. Every time he tried, his mind just seemed to shut down on him.

"I still say we buy two rifles," Shrini insisted, his tone now more petulant than angry.

"If we did, we'd probably be the ones getting our heads blown off. Joel is one paranoid son of a bitch. He'd probably smell that we were out there. Let's just give him some time and things will work out."

Shrini started to argue, but instead punched the steering wheel one last time. They were only a mile from Gordon's condominium complex. When Joel had ordered Dan to take Gordon's car keys, Dan realized then that he had better take Gordon's wallet also. Now that the police were going to find Gordon's body, he had to make sure that there was nothing in Gordon's apartment linking him to the robbery. He just had to hope that there was no other identification on Gordon, at least nothing that would lead the police to his apartment within the next hour or so.

Shrini pulled into the complex and parked in one of the visitor spots. The two of them looked at each other, and Dan took a deep breath as he nodded. There was a risk someone would see them going into Gordon's apartment, but they had no other choice. They moved quickly, Shrini keeping about thirty yards behind Dan as they walked across a courtyard to a side door. Dan looked up briefly and didn't spot anyone. When he got to the side door, he fumbled with the keys for what seemed like an eternity before opening it. He kept the door open long enough so that Shrini would be able to follow him, then went straight to Gordon's apartment, this time opening the door almost without breaking stride. Once he got inside he leaned against the hallway wall, his heart pounding in his chest. Shrini followed seconds later.

"You think anyone saw us?" Dan asked, breathless.

"Relax, dude. It's three twenty-five. No one's around."

Dan held his stomach as he caught his breath. "Okay," he said, "I need to get this makeup off. While I'm doing that, check Gordon's computer and get rid of any pictures of Lombardo. Also, get rid of his anonymous email account."

"Any other orders you wish to give me?"

"Come on, man, we don't have time to get pissed at each other right now."

Shrini pointed his finger at Dan, his mouth poised to spit out something, but instead he swallowed back whatever he was planning on saying. Shaking his head, he sat over by the computer and turned it on. Dan watched for a moment, immobilized by a deep sense of dread. It seemed to take every bit of strength he had to force himself to walk towards the bathroom. When he got there and saw his reflection in the mirror, he broke out laughing. With the wig and facial hair removed, he looked like some sort of weird hybrid of himself and Raymond Lombardo.

Getting the rubber compound off was harder than he would've thought. The damn stuff just didn't want to come off. He kept scrubbing with the solution Gordon had given him, but it didn't seem to do any good. He ended up having to chip the stuff off with a nail file. When he was finally done, he saw that the compound had left a dark reddish discoloration around his jawbone, chin and nose.

Goddamn it, Dan thought, *what else you got for me? Frogs, locusts, boils? Bring it on, asshole.*

He stood staring at himself in the mirror and then, resigned to the situation, joined Shrini in the other room. Shrini's head cocked to one side as he noticed Dan.

"You got a bad rash on your face."

"Yeah, I know."

"It looks like it's where the makeup was. I don't think this is good."

"I agree. Any suggestions?"

"This is not working out." Shrini sat staring at Dan for a long moment as he shook his head. "I could try buying medication from a pharmacy," he said. "Maybe if you spend the night on my sofa your rash will be gone by tomorrow."

"I don't think I could do that, but we can talk about this later. Right now I better search the apartment and make sure there's nothing here that can connect Gordon to the robbery. How are you doing with his computer?"

Shrini shrugged. "I'm doing Gordon a favor and also getting rid of all the porn. Believe me, there's a lot of it. I'm almost done."

"Okay, I'll probably need ten minutes."

Dan found a garbage bag in the kitchen and made a quick search of the apartment. Aside from the rubber compound and pieces of a wig that Gordon had used to make up the facial hair, the only other incriminating evidence Dan found were some printed photos of Lombardo. He also found a roll of hundred-dollar bills hidden in a dresser drawer. He counted four thousand two hundred dollars. He hesitated on what to do with the money, then slipped it into his pocket. When he joined Shrini, he showed him the roll of bills.

"You can have half of it, buddy," he told Shrini.

Shrini considered it, then shook his head. "I don't think so. It would make me feel too much like a grave robber. I will just be satisfied with my share of the robbery. And trust me, I am going to get it."

Dan nodded, understanding Shrini's feelings. "Are you ready to leave?"

"I've been ready for five minutes."

Dan wiped off the keyboard and mouse and then rolled the garbage bag up under his arm. He opened the door, made sure that the hallway was empty, and signaled for Shrini to leave. Then, stepping out himself, he locked the door behind him and tried to appear calm as he walked out of the building. By the time he got to Shrini's Civic, he was sweating like crazy and could hear the blood pounding in his head. He just about collapsed into the passenger seat.

"Breathe, okay?" Shrini said. "The last thing I need now is for you to drop dead in my car."

"Thanks for your concern."

They drove in silence after that. Dan tried to think through what had happened during and after the robbery, but just felt too exhausted. He had to close his eyes. As his consciousness started drifting away, Shrini's voice woke him.

"I am going to get my money from your friend," he stated.

"We both will."

"I want us to see him tomorrow."

"Shrini, trust me on this, we're better off giving him a few days."

"I will give him two days at the most. That's all." His face darkened with anger as he thought over the events. "Believe me, I will not forget the two of them pointing guns at us."

Dan nodded. He tried to keep his eyes open, but his lids were just too damn heavy. Again, Shrini's voice woke him.

"I wasn't going to abandon you," he said.

"Yeah, I know," Dan muttered, not quite sure what Shrini was talking about.

"I mean it. When I asked your friend for my share, I was planning to split with you whatever he gave me."

Dan just stared straight ahead. After another couple of minutes of silence, Shrini asked Dan what he was going to do about his rash. "I think it looks worse now," he said.

"I don't know. I guess as long as the police believe Lombardo's involved, this rash doesn't much matter."

Shrini pulled into his apartment complex. After parking, he asked if Dan wanted to come up and help him finish off the rest of the tequila. "We should have a drink in Gordon's memory," he said.

Dan thought about it and shook his head. "Carol's waiting for me."

"I'll have to finish the bottle off myself then." Shrini's face grew somber as he seemed to lose himself in his thoughts. Snapping out of it, he looked at Dan. "I'll see you in two days," he said.

Dan nodded and left the car.

"Money, it's a gas. Grab all you can and smoke some hash."

"Will you shut the fuck up!"

Hoffer, a big grin plastered across his face, asked, "What's your problem? You don't like my singing?"

Joel grimaced, slowly rubbing both his temples, holding the steering wheel in place with his elbows. "You're fucking tone deaf, that's my problem."

"Money, it's a hit. Just don't light up any of that bad shit."

"I told you to shut up." Joel took a sideways glance at Hoffer. "I'm not going to tell you again."

Hoffer could barely contain himself as he rocked back and forth in his seat. "You're just jealous, man."

"Fuck you. Not only is your croaking giving me a headache but you're screwing up the lyrics, you asshole. You're fucking ruining Pink Floyd for me."

Hoffer smacked his fist several times into an open palm. "I am so jacked right now," he said. "Fuck, I wish I had some good weed on me."

"Yeah, that would be just brilliant. Why don't I flag down the first cop I see and beg him to search my car? Asshole."

"Shit, you worry too much. Let's do something, man. We got guns and ski masks. First gas station we see, man. We can grab some more cash and watch some asshole shit bricks staring down a couple of AK-47s."

Joel gave him a slow cold stare, his upper lip twisting into a sneer.

"Why don't you go back to butchering Pink Floyd," he said. "It would be better than listening to these brilliant ideas of yours."

Hoffer flipped him the bird and held it steady until Joel took a swipe at his outstretched finger.

"I don't understand you, Joel. We did it, man. We robbed

that bank. We got away with it and we have all the money. Why are you sitting there sulking?"

"In case you didn't notice I killed someone," Joel muttered half under his breath.

"I couldn't hear you, man. What did you say?"

"I said I fucking killed someone! You say another word, make another sound, and I'm putting you out of the car. I mean it!"

Hoffer was about to start drumming on the car's dashboard, but the look Joel gave him made him pull his hands back. After only a few minutes of quiet, Joel screwed up his face, looking like he'd been punched in the gut. "Why would he have to shoot those two women?"

"Because he was a wacko."

"Do you know what he was even saying to that girl?"

"Not a clue."

"She should've known better." Joel shook his head, his upper lip separating from his teeth as he grimaced. "You don't give someone lip who's holding a gun on you. I don't care what the loon might be saying to you."

"Maybe she was pissed."

"And why would that be?"

"I dunno. Maybe she thought he was the one who grabbed her ass."

Joel's color paled as he looked at Hoffer. "What the fuck do you mean?"

Hoffer's wide stupid grin came back. "She had a sweet ass, man. Like two big juicy peaches wrapped tight together."

"Yeah, so?"

"So I couldn't help myself. I took two big handfuls when I had my chance."

"You really are an idiot."

"Hey, how was I supposed to know that wack job was going to start hitting on her? Boy, though, she really let him have it. And shit, he really let her have it."

Joel sat straight in his seat, his eyelids falling while he studied Hoffer. "Tell me again how you ended up getting arrested."

"What for? I told you about that years ago."

"I want to hear it again."

Hoffer's tongue wetted his lips while he thought about it. "There's nothing really to say. I had too much to drink and was taking a leak in an alley when some high-strung little princess saw me and started yelling rape. That's all it was, man."

"That's not what you told me before."

"No?"

"No. What you told me was that you had a hooker in your car and she yelled rape when a cruiser pulled up."

Hoffer's eyes turned dull as he nodded. "Yeah, that's the way it could've been."

"You son of a bitch. You've been lying to me all these years. So you did try to rape some girl."

"What difference does that make now? We got two bags of money in the trunk, one for you and one for me. That's all that matters now."

"What do you mean one for you and one for me?"

"We're splitting the money. That's what I mean."

"Fuck you we're splitting the money. You're getting twenty percent."

"I don't think so."

"You don't think so? That was the deal, asshole."

"The deal changed when you killed that wack job and cut out the Chief and his little Indian."

"Says who?"

"Fair is fair." Hoffer crossed his arms, his small pale eyes as hard as stone. "One way or another I'm getting half that money."

As Joel looked at Hoffer, his car drifted over the center line and he had to swerve to avoid a head-on collision with a pickup truck. The driver of the pickup, red-faced and eyes bulging, blasted his horn and yelled bloody murder. Joel gave the driver a cold stare before turning straight ahead, his knuckles white as he gripped the steering wheel.

"You want to rip me off and go back on our deal, fine," he forced out, his voice barely a whisper. "We'll split the money, asshole."

"You're giving me your word then? Fifty–fifty?"

"Isn't that what I just did?"

"Man, just say it."

"Fine. You have my word. We split the money. Anything else you want to extort out of me?"

Hoffer pumped a fist in the air. "Man, it's only right that we do this. So we'll divide it up when we get to your place."

"Fuck you we will. Neither of us are touching that money until it's been cooled off."

"What do you mean?"

"I can be connected to Gordon. Which means there's a chance the cops will come to me looking for that money."

"So we'll stash it at my place."

"You really are an idiot, aren't you? If the cops can connect me to Gordon, they can connect you to me. I got twenty acres. We'll bury the money on my property."

Hoffer's wide face seemed to shrink as he thought over what Joel was suggesting. "I have a better idea. You hide one bag, I'll find a safe place for the other."

"Sorry, pal, this is too important. I'm not betting my life on you not doing something stupid."

"I don't see what the big deal is—"

"I already told you, and besides, I gave you my word. That's not good enough for you?"

Grudgingly, Hoffer accepted that it was.

"You've known me, what, fifteen years? Have you ever known me to go back on my word?"

"Okay, already, it's good enough for me."

Joel gave Hoffer a hard stare before facing straight ahead. When they arrived at his house, he had Hoffer take the duffel bags while he went to get two shovels. When he returned, Hoffer had one of the bags open.

"What the fuck are you doing?"

"I need some money, man. I'm just taking a thousand bucks."

"Show me what you got."

Hoffer held up ten hundred-dollar bills. Joel made a face, but nodded. "Fine," he said. "Put that money away and grab those bags."

Hoffer shoved the bills into his pockets. They walked behind Joel's house to a small clearing of grass. Beyond that were acres of woods. As they made their way through the woods, Hoffer spotted a forty-five caliber pistol sticking out of Joel's waistband.

"Why are you bringing that?" he asked.

"For Chrissakes, use your brains. This is the gun I shot Gordon with. Why do you think I'm bringing it?"

Hoffer's tongue licked his lips as he stared at the gun. "I dunno," he said.

"'Cause I need to bury this also, you putz."

"That's all?" Hoffer asked, his eyes jerking nervously from the gun to Joel's face.

"Yeah, what the hell else do you think I'm going to do with it?"

"You gave me your word before."

"I know I did. What's your point?"

Hoffer shook his head as he thought about it. "Never mind," he said.

They walked another ten minutes before Joel decided that they had gone far enough. "We'll bury the bags near that boulder," he said.

There was an empty clearing about twenty feet from the boulder Joel had pointed out. The two of them went to work. When the hole got to three feet deep, Hoffer, sweating like a pig, dropped his shovel.

"That should be deep enough," he said.

"I don't think so. If we get a heavy rain it will seep into these bags. We need to make this deeper."

"You make it deeper then, I'm done."

Hoffer started to climb out of the hole. He had one leg out when Joel grabbed him from behind and swung him down so he landed hard on his side. The fall knocked the wind out of him. When he opened his eyes he saw that Joel was pointing the forty-five at him. Backing up, Joel scrambled out of the hole.

"You gave me your word," Hoffer said, his voice trembling.

"And I'm going to keep it," Joel said. "But I told you we need that hole deeper."

Hoffer slowly got to his feet.

"You better start digging."

Hoffer picked up the shovel and started digging. As he dug, his knees buckled on him. At one point he fell to one knee.

"Just keep digging."

"Joel, forget the split. All I need is twenty percent."

"I said keep digging."

"I said I'll take twenty percent."

"And I said keep digging."

Looking up, Hoffer burst into tears. "You gave me your word!" he cried.

"And I plan to keep my word. You should know me well enough to know that."

"You're going to kill me!"

"I told you, I'm going to keep my word."

Bleary-eyed and sobbing, Hoffer forced himself back to his feet. His arms shook as he lifted and dumped out each shovel full of dirt. When the hole got past four feet deep, Joel told him that was enough.

"Put down the shovel," Joel said as he aimed the gun at Hoffer's chest.

"You gave me your word!" Hoffer screamed.

"And if you were still alive when we split the money, you'd get half," Joel told him in a flat tone. He shot Hoffer in the chest, the impact knocking Hoffer off his feet and on to his back.

Hoffer, dazed, touched his chest and then watched the blood drip from his fingers. He looked up at Joel. "We've known each other for fifteen years," he implored.

"I knew Gordon longer than that," Joel said as he fired three more shots into Hoffer's body. At first Hoffer lay still, then he started moving feebly as he tried to push himself into a sitting position. Cursing that he didn't bring another magazine with him, Joel tossed the empty gun into the hole. He grabbed a shovel and started to fill the hole up. Even after he had Hoffer's body covered with a foot of dirt, the guy was still trying to push himself up. It was almost as if a wave was rolling through the loose dirt. Hoffer's body didn't seem to come to rest until the hole was completely filled and the ground packed hard.

Joel stood and watched for a long ten count, waiting to see if anything would upset the stillness. His plan was to later plant raspberry bushes over Hoffer's grave. After wiping his brow, he grabbed the two duffel bags and headed back to his house.

Alex Resnick tracked Petrenko to a small Russian restaurant on Essex Street. Petrenko was sitting at a table with three other men, in front of him a bottle of Cristall vodka in an ice bucket and a platter of caviar. All four men were drinking. Petrenko looked amused as Resnick approached his table.

"Detective, I would offer for you to join us, but our table is too crowded as it is."

"I didn't come here to drink with you."

"No? A pity. This vodka is quite nice. Of course, it is also chilled to the right temperature, something you Americans always fail to do. Add a few of these lingonberries and you have something close to extraordinary."

The three other men at the table were all smiling, amused. Resnick said, "Yeah, well, I prefer bourbon anyway."

Petrenko made a comment in Russian, eliciting some laughs from his companions. Turning back to Resnick, he smiled thinly. "You should learn to broaden your horizons. Here, at least try some of this. Beluga Malossol, the finest caviar you will ever find."

Petrenko had spooned a small amount of caviar on to a

cracker and held it out to Resnick. The detective looked down at it and shook his head.

"Fish eggs – I don't think so. I need to talk to you privately. Maybe your friends can leave."

Petrenko shook his head sadly at the detective as he placed the cracker into his own mouth and chewed it slowly. "You don't know what you're missing," he said. "And I doubt on your salary you will have many more opportunities to sample something as exquisite as Beluga. That is your problem, though. What do you wish to talk to me about?"

"Police business."

"I gathered as much. My friends will stay. So what happened, Detective, did another old man fall and bump his head?"

"There was a bank robbery. One woman was killed, another critically wounded."

"And what time did this bank robbery occur?"

"Around two."

Petrenko made another comment in Russian, drawing more laughs from the others sitting at the table. Matter-of-factly, he told Resnick, "You're wasting your time. I've been here with my friends since noon. Maybe, though, I should talk to my lawyer about this harassment."

"You misunderstand me. I'm not here to accuse you of anything."

"Then what?"

"Your safety deposit boxes at the Lynn Capital Bank were robbed. I need to get a statement from you."

The amusement in Petrenko's eyes dried up, leaving behind something hard and cold. "These games you're playing, Detective—"

"Sorry, I'm not playing any games." Resnick took a notebook from his inside jacket pocket and read Petrenko the numbers of the safety deposit boxes that were robbed. "I also took digital photos if you'd care to see them."

Petrenko moved his head in a slight nod. The color had bled out of his face, leaving behind a dead whiteness. He accepted the camera from Resnick and scrolled through the pictures, studying each one in the camera's LCD display. When he handed the camera back to Resnick, Petrenko's facial features had been transformed into something not quite human, almost reptilian.

"Funny thing was, your boxes were the only ones broken into."

"No other safety deposit boxes were robbed?"

"Nope, it looks like you were targeted. Any idea who might have been out to get you?"

Petrenko sat still, no perceptible movement, his eyes dead as he stared straight ahead. Resnick watched for a moment, having to bite down on his tongue to keep from smirking.

"I need to know what you had in those boxes," he asked, in as businesslike tone as as he could manage.

Petrenko looked at Resnick, confused, as if he couldn't understand why this man was still standing there. When Resnick's words finally registered, he shook his head angrily. "That is personal, Detective. Now if you will excuse me—"

"Sorry, a felony crime has been committed. You do have to answer me, or if not me, I'm sure I can arrange for you to testify in front of a grand jury. In the meantime, I'd be more than happy to arrest you for obstructing a criminal investigation."

Petrenko sat expressionless, his dead eyes holding steady on Resnick's. After several minutes passed, he looked away and poured himself a glass of vodka. "I had nothing in those safety deposit boxes," he said.

"You've been paying for eight empty safety deposit boxes?"

"I've been meaning to close my account at that bank."

"Who else knew your box numbers?"

Petrenko shrugged. "No one that I can think of. Detective, this vodka has made me very sleepy. Please, I doubt I can be of any further assistance to you."

"That's quite all right. And don't worry about a thing. I'm sure there must've been items in those boxes that you've forgotten about. Maybe papers, maybe other things. I want you to rest assured that I am going to dedicate myself to finding who did this and recovering what was in those boxes. I'll be working on this twenty-four-seven if I have to. You can count on it. And when I find what was stolen, you'll be the first to know."

The two men stared at each other. There was no misunderstanding what Resnick was promising. After Resnick left, Petrenko sat staring blankly as his hands slowly clenched into fists.

"That fucking *zhid*," he swore. "He came here just to rub it in. Someday soon, I will make it my pleasure to take care of him personally." He then turned to Yuri Tolkov, who had been sitting to his right. "Find out if these Arabs were stupid enough to have kept that briefcase."

Yuri nodded, pushed his chair back and got up from the table. The other two men followed him, leaving Petrenko alone, clenching and unclenching his fists.

17

Carol gave her husband a concerned look when she saw him. "What happened to your face?" she asked.

Dan ran a hand lightly across his jaw. "Shrini made lentils with green curry for lunch. I got some sort of allergic reaction from it."

Thin lines creased Carol's brow as she moved closer to him. "That's funny," she said, her eyes narrowing, studying the pattern that the rash made. "You've had Indian food before without having any reaction. And this rash seems so isolated, mostly on your nose and jaw."

"I guess it's just one of those things." He waved a hand in the air as if that would wave the issue away. "I am so damn beat right now. I'm going upstairs to take a nap."

She was still frowning as she nodded to him. "Dinner will be ready soon. I'll let you know when the food's on the table. Oh, I almost forgot, Gordon called."

For a second Dan felt as if his heart had turned to slush. Barely under control, he asked Carol what time that was.

"Right after you left this morning."

"Did he say anything?"

"Only that he wanted to talk to you."

"I'll call him back after I take a nap," he said.

As he walked up the stairs, he really did feel exhausted. All he wanted to do was lie down on the bed and close his eyes. Just hide someplace dark. When he got to the bedroom, he pulled the window shades down, then collapsed on to the bed. Lying there, he thought about all the lies he'd been telling Carol. Before this robbery business he had never lied to her. Not once. Now he was telling her one lie after another. At first, he had felt guilty about it, maybe even remorseful. Now he felt almost nothing. It was amazing to him how easy the lying was becoming.

He was drifting off when the lights turned on. He saw Carol moving towards him, her face flushed with excitement.

"You won't believe what's on the news," she said, breathless.

Dan pushed himself up and sat helplessly as Carol turned on the television set. The top story was about the bank robbery. When they showed a high-school graduation picture of Margaret Williams, all Dan wanted to do was slink off into some dark corner and die. According to the report, the other woman, the one shot in the stomach, was in intensive care and the doctors weren't sure yet whether she was going to make it. "We'll know more in the next forty-eight hours," one of the doctors was saying. The story seemed to go on forever. Dan sat there dreading what was going to come next, praying that they wouldn't show a photo of Gordon. When they came to report on the dead man found outside the bank, they described him as being in his early sixties, wearing a Grateful Dead T-shirt and shorts. Police were working on the assumption that the robbers killed him either for his car or because he might've seen something. Instead of showing a photo of Gordon's corpse, the news aired a police drawing of what the dead man would've looked like if he were alive. They asked for anyone with information about him to contact the Lynn Police. Carol gasped when she saw the drawing.

"Do you know who that looks like?" she asked.

Dan could feel himself shaking his head.

"I swear that could be Gordon. And that Grateful Dead T-shirt—"

"Come on," Dan half heard himself saying, "a lot of guys wear those types of T-shirts. And that doesn't look at all like Gordon. Jesus Christ, that's a drawing of an old man."

"It looks a lot like Gordon to me," she said. "Go ahead, call him, see if he's home."

"I'll call him later."

"I'm telling you, that's him. If you don't try calling him, I'm going to."

Dan picked up the phone and dialed a movie phone line. He waited until he got the recorded message as to what was now playing, pretended to leave a message for Gordon, and hung up. All the while, Carol watched, anxiously pulling at her fingers.

"He's not home right now," Dan said. "But that doesn't mean anything. He's always out. Who knows, he could be on his way to the Jersey Shore right now."

"I'm going to call the police," Carol said. "I'm sure that's him."

Dan stopped her as she reached for the phone. "Come on, you know how Gordon is. If you send the police to his apartment, the guy will get weird on me and probably never want to talk to me again."

"You're saying that as if it's a bad thing," Carol said, only half-joking.

"Gordon's not that bad."

"He's very strange. Most of the time when he's talking to me, I don't know what he's saying." Carol shook her head. "I wonder what he was doing at that bank."

"How can you be so sure that's him? From that one police drawing?"

"I really think it's him," she said, but some doubt had edged into her voice. She hesitated for a moment, her mouth opening slightly. "When I was watching the news downstairs, they mentioned something about the bank's security system not working. Isn't that what you built for them?"

"I architected the system, I didn't build it. If they had let me code it instead of farming the coding out, I bet you it would have worked today."

"You don't think the system not working was because of a mistake you might have made?"

"No, I don't. What's wrong – you're worried no one's going to want to hire me after this?"

Carol tried to smile, but it faded fast. "I guess I'm worried about everything these days. It just doesn't sound like a very good endorsement having a bank security system you built—"

"Architected," Dan corrected.

"Okay – architected – being broken into. Maybe you should remove that last contract from your resumé?"

"Probably not a bad idea," Dan agreed.

"Do you think they could try suing you?" Carol asked, her face now racked with worry.

"I'm sure my design was sound. If there are any problems with that system, it must be in the implementation. But that's what you get when all you care about is price and you have the software developed by the lowest bidder. Don't worry about this, okay?"

"I'll try not to. This whole thing is just so freaky. Especially that drawing looking so much like Gordon."

Dan tried to make an innocuous comment. Standing up, he felt as if all his strength had bled out of him leaving him sluggish, like he had a bad flu. On their way downstairs, Carol knocked on both kids' doors, telling them to come down for dinner. While they sat at the table together, Dan couldn't look at his children and couldn't stand the thought of them looking at him. He could barely lift his head enough to look past his plate. After the robbery, he had been mostly in shock. Now, the full magnitude of the events was hitting him.

Two people dead, another critically wounded, and it was his fault. Gordon, that young girl, both lying in a morgue now because of him. Because of him…

What did I do? he thought. *Jesus Christ, what the fuck did I do?*

Carol was telling the kids about the bank robbery, about how it was the same bank Dan had worked at only a month earlier. As she talked, he involuntarily shrunk inwards, as if her words were blows that he needed to protect himself against.

"Wow," Gary said, "Dad, what would you have done if you were there today and a bunch of guys came in with guns?"

He could feel Gary's eyes boring into him. Sitting there he felt dirty, diseased, as if he were contaminating his wife and children. He couldn't stand it.

What the fuck did I do to myself? To them? What in the world did I do to them?

"I don't know," he said, his words catching in his throat.

Susie was now asking about the robbery. How could he just

sit there and listen to them talk about it? How in the world could he possibly do that?

He pushed his chair away from the table.

"I'm not feeling well," he told Carol. "I'm going upstairs to lie down."

His wife's brow furrowed the way it did whenever she was surprised. "Do you want me to bring you up the rest of your dinner?" she asked after a short hesitation.

"No, that's okay, I really don't have any appetite."

He caught a glimpse of their faces as he turned from them. Carol showed mostly a mix of worry and confusion, maybe even a bit of the brittleness he had seen flashes of before. Susie was staring straight ahead, her features now pinched and angry. Even Gary seemed taken aback.

Jesus Christ, even without trying he was hurting them...

Moving slowly, he left the room and headed towards the staircase. His legs cold, dead, almost as if they were disconnected from his body. Looking up the stairs, he didn't know how he was going to make it, but he had no choice. He needed to lie down and figure out a way to convince himself that things were going to be okay.

Captain Kenneth Hadley's pale blue eyes did not look happy as Resnick entered the station. In fact, his soft round face seemed to be sagging under the stress of the day's events. He indicated with a short wave for Resnick to join him in his office.

After Resnick took a seat across from him, Hadley asked his detective where he had been, his voice showing a touch of exasperation.

"I was getting a statement from Viktor Petrenko."

"Walt's been back over two hours."

"Petrenko can be a tough man to track down."

"In case you've forgotten we have had a bank robbery with two fatalities and another victim lying in intensive care with her stomach mostly gone. I need you working this case. I can't have you running around on a personal vendetta."

Resnick shrugged. "We needed to get a statement from Petrenko."

"That could've waited." He paused. "You didn't do anything to get yourself or the department in trouble, did you?"

"Me? Of course not. I was very sensitive about his loss, letting him know that we would do everything possible to recover his stolen items."

Hadley let out a lungful of air, the noise escaping from him in a slow hiss. "What did he have to say?" he asked

"Among other things, his safety deposit boxes were empty at the time of the robbery."

"So he doesn't want to tell us what was in them."

"Probably for a damn good reason." Resnick edged forward in his seat. "This shook Petrenko up. He's desperate right now. God knows how much he lost, but probably worse for him, he can't afford to let us find what was in those boxes. Let's put him and his people under surveillance for a few days and see where it leads us."

Hadley blinked several times while he stared dumbfounded at his detective. "Not a chance. We're short-handed as it is. Every man I can free up is going to be working this bank robbery until it's solved."

"You've got no imagination, Ken."

"Maybe not, but what I do have is everyone on my ass until we've cleaned up this mess."

Resnick nodded blankly, realizing the futility of trying to argue. "We should put someone on the bank manager. Unless you want to end up with another dead body on your hands."

"You think he's involved?"

"I think Petrenko's going to think so."

"What about you?"

"I don't know. The guys who did this found out Petrenko's box numbers either from Petrenko himself or from someone inside the bank. I can't imagine Petrenko letting anyone close enough to get that information from him. And you've also got someone in the bank shutting down their security system before the robbery and turning it back on afterwards."

"You still haven't answered my question. Is this bank manager involved?"

"Logically, he seems like he'd be the guy, but I don't know. I couldn't get a good feel one way or the other. Tom and Phil were still working on him when I left. Have you talked to them yet?"

"They're still at the bank." Hadley shook his head slowly, a pained expression washing over his face. "Maguire's looking at the security videos. Why don't you go join him? And tomorrow take another crack at this bank manager. I need to know if he's involved. I need this mess wrapped up before I develop any more ulcers."

"What about having someone watch over Brown?"

"I'll take it under advisement."

Resnick started to get up, stopped. "The body we found outside the bank – do we know who he is yet?"

"Not yet."

Resnick nodded and left Hadley looking miserable, his pale blue eyes staring off into the distance. He found his partner alone in the video room – a windowless eight by ten foot room with a single VCR and monitor, all that the department could afford. A stack of videotapes lay in front of Maguire, who looked up briefly at Resnick with a sour smile before turning back to the monitor.

"Back from your personal errand, huh? Must be nice."

"Not quite personal. I tracked down Petrenko for a statement."

"No kidding? How'd that son of a bitch take the news?"

"Not good."

"Damn, I wish you had brought me. It would've been worth the price of admission seeing his reaction. And I bet you had a hell of a lot more fun than what I've been going through."

Resnick looked away, knowing what his partner was going to tell him.

"Margaret Williams' parents came down to the station. Hadley, the fucking coward, had me break the news to them. I guess I can be thankful I didn't have to escort them to the morgue."

The one part of the job Resnick couldn't deal with was breaking the news of a child's death to the parents. At some subconscious level that was a good part of the reason he took off to find Petrenko, and probably also why it took him as long as it did to find Petrenko at that restaurant. Resnick knew if he had been back at the station Hadley would've roped him into notifying the dead girl's parents.

"Must've been rough," Resnick said.

"Yeah, it was, but I guess it's part of the job, huh? Anyway, while you were off having your fun, I've had my nose to the grindstone. And guess what? There's a surveillance camera covering the cabinet that alarm system is locked away in. I've gone through the tapes. No one opened the cabinet from midnight last night until after the bank robbery."

"The security system could've been turned off days ago."

"Maybe, but watch this."

Maguire ejected the tape that was in the machine and plugged in one that he had separated from the others. Checking his notebook, he fast-forwarded to a tape position that he had written down, and then hit the play button. The tape showed the bank manager, Craig Brown, running to the cabinet, duct tape still attached to his wrists. He looked out of breath as he stood fumbling with his keys, a thin sheen of sweat covering his neck and forehead. After he opened the cabinet, he froze for a long ten count as he stared into it, a look of puzzlement breaking out on his face.

"Did you see that?" Maguire asked. "At no point does he touch anything in that cabinet. He didn't turn on the security system because it was already on. Which means it was on during the robbery."

"Why didn't it work then?"

"Maybe nobody pushed any of the alarm buttons."

"Brown claims he did," Resnick said.

"I called Tom. Supposedly three other tellers swore they did also. Maybe they're all lying."

"Four people on the inside involved?" A dull throbbing had started in the front of Resnick's skull. He squeezed his eyes shut trying to block out the pain. "That's too many people. It wouldn't work. One of them would screw up their story. The alarm system was probably hacked into. Ah shit, this is going to get complicated."

"We'll see. I called Tom and asked if he could have all the alarm buttons dusted for prints."

Resnick didn't see the point in that, especially since tellers were probably always touching the buttons, if for no other reason than to make sure they knew where they were. He didn't bother to mention that to Maguire; he was just glad to see his partner taking more of an initiative.

The throbbing in his head had become more of a dull pounding. He always carried a bottle of aspirin with him, and he popped a couple of tablets into his mouth and chewed them slowly. He wished it had been as simple as the alarm system being turned off. The thought of having to worry about how the system had been hacked into made the pain in his head worse.

"Have you watched the robbery yet?" Resnick asked.

"Yeah, let me show it to you."

Maguire plugged in a second tape that he had separated from the stack and positioned the tape to where the robbers were about to appear. The surveillance camera was angled to capture most of the bank lobby, but not the lobby door. Resnick watched as men poured into the bank lobby, two of them carrying assault rifles, another brandishing a handgun. He reached over and paused the tape.

"I count five men," Resnick said.

"That's all I counted also."

"Do you think any others could've slipped by without the camera picking them up?"

"I dunno. Maybe."

Of the five men, four of them were dressed in red overalls and ski masks. A fifth man was wearing a yellow running suit. He also had on a ski mask, but it didn't match the others.

"They must've planned the robbery for four guys and added a fifth at the last minute," Resnick said.

"Look at the firepower those guys had," Maguire said. "Two assault rifles and that big guy with the long hair is waving a forty-five. If you ask me, that's overkill for a bank robbery. You're going to make a lot of noise firing off those weapons."

"You're going to make a lot of noise firing off any gun. They probably wanted to scare the hell out of whoever was in there and get control fast."

Maguire thought about it. "Maybe," he conceded. "By the way, that big guy waving the gun is the one who ends up shooting those two women. He's probably also going to turn out to be the one who shot the Grateful Dead guy in the parking lot."

Maguire hit the play button and watched as the tape showed three of the robbers rounding up the bank employees and customers, forcing them on to their stomachs, then taping their wrists and ankles. The two other robbers had duffel bags slung over their shoulders. Maguire pointed them out as they started sprinting towards the hallway leading to the safety deposit boxes.

"Unfortunately, there's no camera where the safety deposit boxes are kept," Maguire said. "According to Brown, they would be violating the privacy of their box owners if they videotaped what was being put in them."

Resnick nodded, realizing the bank manager was right.

"Nothing much happens until the shootings," Maguire continued. "Let me fast-forward until we get there."

As the tape sped along, Resnick thought he saw something. He stopped the tape, rewound it and played it back. At one point, the guy in the running suit kneeled by Margaret Williams to check the duct tape wrapped around her wrists. Resnick paused the tape at that point and played it at slow speed. The guy in the running suit had his back to the camera, and while that mostly obscured what happened, you could see for a second him slipping both hands under the young woman's skirt.

"That little fat fuck," Maguire swore. "He's molesting her."

After that Resnick played the tape at regular speed. At one point the guy who had been waving the forty-five around wandered over to Margaret Williams.

"This is where it happens," Maguire said.

The man started saying something to Williams. His attitude looked casual, relaxed. After several minutes of that she turned her head, straining to look back at him. Her face was livid, veins streaking her neck as she yelled something to him. At first the robber started glancing from side to side, looking like he just wanted to run away. Then, almost as if a switch had been flipped, his body stiffened and he grabbed her with both hands and flipped her on to her back. Within a blink of an eye, he had his gun arm extended, then a flame exploded from the gun barrel. Margaret Williams' body bounced on impact. When it settled down her head rested to one side.

Hard lines tightened along Resnick's jaw as he watched the shooting. He stopped the tape and rewound it. Maguire groaned. "I don't think I can watch that again," he said.

"I want to show you something," Resnick said. "The guy in the running suit – take a look at the way he's acting while she's yelling at the shooter. His shoulders are bouncing up and down. He's laughing, he's enjoying what's happening. Now look at the third guy. He's clearly agitated. As the shooter extends his gun, this guy starts to lift his rifle as if he's going to shoot him instead. There's definitely chaos going on at that point."

Resnick replayed the tape, pointing out his observations to Maguire.

"Okay," Maguire said. "So we've got a couple of psychos involved. How's that going to help us?"

Resnick stopped the tape. The hard lines along his jaws stretched tighter while he stared at the monitor. "In some ways this seems like a professional job – the way they shut down the alarm system, the precision in drilling open the safety deposit boxes – but I can't believe those three guys are anything but amateurs."

"They could just be wack jobs," Maguire offered. "Are you ready to see the other shooting?"

Resnick nodded grimly. The tape was started again. Mary O'Donnell had been lying next to Williams. After Williams was shot, O'Donnell started screaming. She turned her head back, trying to face the shooter. For a long moment the man stood frozen, then he started yelling back at her. He pushed her on to her back with his foot and without hesitation shot her in the stomach. While she lay writhing on the floor, he seemed to be talking to her. Resnick noticed that the guy in the running suit had stopped laughing. The third guy's body language indicated that he had given up trying to control the situation.

Resnick watched the rest of the tape, watched as the two other men ran back into the bank lobby, both carrying duffel bags. He watched as four of the men fled the bank. The shooter stayed behind. Almost as if he were in a trance, he stood over O'Donnell, his gun arm fully extended. Then, realizing he was alone, he lumbered out of the bank.

Maguire let out a tired sigh. "Watching this crap is wiping me out. I need to take a break and get something to eat. You want anything?"

Resnick shook his head. "Which of these haven't you looked at yet?"

Maguire went through the stack and pulled out six tapes. "These are all from outdoor surveillance cameras." He got out of the chair, stretched and pushed a hand against the side of his head, cracking his neck. "I'll be back in a half hour."

Resnick took his place and fast-forwarded through four of the tapes without seeing anything useful. The fifth tape showed the five men running towards the bank, all with their ski masks and overalls already on. He fast-forwarded to the point where they were fleeing the bank. One of them stopped, took off his mask and looked back before running out of the view of the camera. Resnick rewound the tape and froze the picture at the place where the man's profile could be seen clearly. For a long moment all Resnick could do was stare at the screen, his heart beating a mile a minute. Then he just let out a long whistle.

Joel had dumped out the contents of the duffel bags on to the floor and was now counting the money for a second time. The first time he had counted four hundred and three packets of bills, each packet held together by two rubber bands. They all seemed to be of the same thickness. Picking a dozen of them at random, he counted fifty hundred-dollar bills in each. Thumbing through them he saw nothing but hundreds. That meant he had over two million dollars. He finished his second count and came up with the same number.

Outside of the money they had also taken photographs, documents, videotapes and computer disks from Petrenko. He separated those items out and packed them away in a box. At first he thought about sending the box anonymously to the police. While he liked the idea of fucking that commie asshole one more time, he decided it would be safer to just destroy the items. For all he knew the FBI would be able to trace that package back to him no matter how careful he was in sending it. Better not to be a schmuck. Just keep the money and be satisfied. Anyway, it was no skin off his nose whether or not Petrenko ended up in prison.

The robbery also netted six silk pouches and he had their contents spread out on the kitchen table. Diamonds. Ninety of them. He picked one of them up. The diamond felt substantial, heavy, and it sparkled like crazy as he held it to the light. Squinting at the stone, it looked flawless to him, but what the hell did he know? He had an uncle who worked in the diamond district in New York. In a few days he'd visit him, find out what they were worth.

One day he's down to his last few thousand bucks, the next he's sitting on over two million large. When Dan had first told him about the robbery, he thought he'd be lucky to clear fifty grand from the job. He had to hand it to the guy, Dan knew what he was talking about. Outside of Gordon going nutso in that bank, things worked out exactly as planned. He felt a tinge of regret about the way he had cut Dan off, but he had warned him about bringing Gordon along, told him a number of times he'd hold him responsible if that nutjob acted up and, if nothing else, Joel considered himself a man of his word. Being cut off was the price Dan had to pay, and besides, he'd had plenty of warnings.

As far as Gordon went, Joel had no regrets whatsoever – except that he hadn't taken care of that nutjob before they ever entered the bank. Thinking how Gordon shot those two women while they were both bound and defenseless made his blood boil. May he rot in hell! Given the opportunity, he'd shoot him again, and be glad to do it.

He had no regrets about Eric either. The prick was going to have the audacity to go back on the deal they had and try to hold him up for fifty percent of the take? When he was brought in, it was for a twenty percent cut, and he damn well knew it! Just because things might've changed with the others didn't affect what Eric was entitled to. Besides, molesting that girl inside the bank probably triggered the episode with Gordon. He deserved what he got as much as Gordon did. And realizing how Eric had lied to him over the years about how he had ended up in jail gave Joel the creeps. They might've known each other for fifteen years, but so what? What did they really have in common? Politics, guns, drinking beer? Eh, good riddance.

Joel gathered the diamonds back into the silk pouches and stacked the money into one of the duffel bags. The diamonds had to be worth at least half a million. With two and a half million dollars, he was going to be able to do whatever he wanted. While there were certain things about his house he would miss – the privacy, twenty acres of woods, having a shooting range in his basement – maybe it was time to move. Maybe he should just go to Florida and get the hell out of where he was. He didn't have to rush into a decision, though. He'd have some time to think about it. For now, he'd spend a little money, fortify the house a bit, do some of the improvements he'd been wanting to do for years.

A grin broke over his face as he thought about how his fortune had changed. His eyes rolled up towards the ceiling, his grin stretching wider. "You're finally letting me roll sevens. About fucking time."

18

Stillwall and Hollings showed up at the station minutes after Resnick had played the surveillance tape showing Raymond Lombardo.

"You lose our FBI friend?" Resnick asked.

"At five o'clock on the dot he was gone," Stillwall said, scratching his chin. "Joys of being a federal employee."

"That's a shame. I've got a few things I'd like to show him."

Resnick showed them instead, first playing the tape of the robbery and then the one of Lombardo taking his ski mask off. Stillwall's large face dropped into a hangdog expression when the tape froze on Raymond Lombardo's profile. "You got to be kidding me," he complained. "We waste all this time questioning witnesses when we had this tape all along?"

"Them's the breaks," Hollings said, shaking his head in awe. "This is huge, my friends."

Resnick knew he should've felt better than he did, but there was something about the tape that bugged him, something he couldn't quite put his finger on. He was replaying it frame by frame when Maguire walked in.

"Fucking unbelievable," Maguire said.

"We're going to be here all goddamn night," Stillwall moaned. "Not even a chance now of catching the last few innings."

Hadley was brought in. After a flurry of phone calls with the district attorney, FBI, and Lombardo's lawyer, an arrangement was made for Lombardo to surrender at ten the next morning. No one seemed happy at that.

"A double murder and another woman in intensive care, and we're going to let him waltz in here at his convenience?" Stillwall asked.

Hadley's soft face looked worn out. "It's out of my hands. There's more to this, Tom. We've got to work with the organized crime task force, an ongoing federal prosecution—"

"This still sucks. Ah well, tomorrow morning then."

"Not here, though. Raymond Lombardo will be surrendering at the FBI building, downtown Boston."

"They better not make a deal with that murdering son of a bitch." Stillwall's voice trailed off, anger flushing his face. "You should see how those two women were shot," he said when he could. "Alex, maybe you should play the captain that tape."

"I don't need to see the tape."

"Any leads yet on the dead guy?" Hollings asked.

Hadley's round face deflated. He shook his head. "Nothing yet," he said, a weariness edging into his voice.

Resnick hung around for another few hours, ran out of things to do, and headed out after waiting to see if the eleven o'clock news would draw any leads on the dead man. It didn't. On his way home he stopped off for some Chinese takeout.

He got back to his apartment a little before twelve and stuck the food in the microwave oven to reheat it. After the oven's buzzer went off, he dumped the food on to a plate and brought it over to a small dark wooden table that used to belong to his parents. When Brian was alive he couldn't wait to get home each day so he could have dinner with Carrie and his boy. Now this was the part of the day he dreaded most.

He tried to eat quickly before memories of the past could seep in, but his mind drifted. Before he could help it, he started thinking of Carrie and how happy she used to be. She had the most beautiful smile when she was happy; she could almost stop his heart with it.

It had been over ten years since he had seen that smile. With a start, he realized it had been almost five years since he had last heard from her. She called once to check on how he was doing and then swore she would never do that again. So far she had kept her word.

Thinking of that call made him uncomfortable. The last thing she told him was she couldn't deal with '*his constant running from Brian's death*'. Absent-mindedly, he moved his thumb along the edge of the table until he felt a small groove in the wood. Brian had made that when he was four. Resnick remembered the mischievous look Brian gave him after he carved out the groove with his fork. His boy was so proud of himself as he waited for some sort of reaction from his dad. As much as Resnick tried to give Brian his stern look, he couldn't do it, not with the way his boy was looking back at him. He ended up breaking out laughing which made Brian giggle like crazy.

Resnick jumped out of his chair and started pacing the

apartment. He had to move. He had to keep moving. As he paced the studio apartment, there was nothing but blank walls for him to look at. He had no photographs or personal effects anywhere in his apartment. There was nothing, outside of a few books, that could identify him as living there.

The tightness in his chest eased up. He could breathe again. The urge to go out for a few drinks overwhelmed him, but he fought it. He'd drink occasionally after work, but he knew if he went out for drinks every time he felt this way, he'd be out every night. And he also knew there was a real risk of him developing into an alcoholic. He couldn't afford to let that happen. Working as a detective kept him busy. Almost every week he'd work the full seven days, usually staying on the job until he was exhausted. Then he'd be able to go home and fall asleep without having to think.

Without having to worry about absent-mindedly thinking of Brian...

Petrenko had been hitting the heavy bag for over three hours, trying to release the restless energy pent up inside him. It didn't help. But what else was he going to do? Sit still and wait? So even though his arms felt heavier than cement, he repeated the same combinations over and over again. *Jab, jab, hook. Jab, jab, uppercut.* He tried to empty his mind and focus solely on his foot work and body movement, but flashes of rage kept breaking up his concentration. The eleven o'clock news had reported that witnesses inside the bank thought men of Middle Eastern descent were involved in the robbery. Hearing that was like adding gasoline to the fire. What was he, stupid? Nothing but an idiot *mudack*? When Resnick told him about the robbery, he knew instantly that those Arabs were behind it. It was no accident that they had come to him. Sell him diamonds one day and rob him the next. And have a long hard laugh at his expense.

He had to get his hands on those Arabs. But for that to happen, he had to hope they were dumb enough to keep the briefcase he had given them and not realize there was a tracking device planted in it. While he had other holdings outside of what was in those safety deposit boxes, he had nothing that was liquid, nothing that he could quickly convert to cash. More important, he had documents in those boxes that he couldn't afford to let fall into the hands of the FBI. If they did, he would be going away to prison for a long time – if he wasn't taken care of first. He knew the only reason he was alive was because certain powerful people couldn't afford to let those documents go public. If he didn't quickly recover what was stolen from him he would have to disappear, maybe slip back into Eastern Europe, and he'd have to do it without the funds needed to sustain the lifestyle that he had grown accustomed to.

The bank manager also needed to pay. Someone gave those Arabs his box numbers and that little nothing of a man was as good a bet as any. Petrenko hit the bag harder as he thought about conversations he had with the bank manager, how Brown told him straight-faced that their new security system was foolproof and would make the bank safer than Fort Knox. And Petrenko, the idiot that he was, believed him and bought six more boxes, consolidating his cash and private documents at that bank. He never would've thought it possible that Brown would dare try something like this, but then again, even the most gutless hyena can be emboldened to snap at a lion if it believes the beast is helpless.

A knock on the door interrupted Petrenko's thoughts. He lowered his arms and barked out in Russian for the person to enter. When Yuri walked into the room carrying a briefcase, Petrenko felt a wave of relief wash over him. Moving stiffly, he took the leather wraps off his hands and noticed with indifference how bloody and raw his knuckles were.

"These were very stupid men," Yuri said.

"All of the money still there?"

"Almost. Ninety-six thousand dollars."

"And the Arabs?"

"We found two of them – the ones that were in charge. They were surprised to see us. Right now we have them waiting at the warehouse."

Petrenko picked up a gold Rolex and saw that it was two-forty in the morning. While he was anxious to take care of the matter, he knew it made more sense to go into it rested and with a clear head. A few hours wouldn't make any difference.

"They can wait for us," Petrenko said. "All of us should get some sleep. They'll keep." He hesitated as he rubbed his knuckles. "Did you find anything?"

"Not yet."

Petrenko tried to appear unperturbed by that bit of news. He picked up a towel and wiped off his arms and neck, and then walked over to a table where he kept a bottle of vodka chilling. Pouring a glass, he drank it slowly, waiting until he was sure he could hide his disappointment before telling Yuri to meet him at the warehouse at noon.

"We will have a long day ahead of us," he added. "Everything is ready, correct?"

"Yes. The plastic coverings have been put down. Everything that you will need is there."

"Our Arab guests are not too uncomfortable?"

Yuri smiled broadly, showing yellowish, crooked teeth that were badly in need of dental work. "Sorry, but they were left very uncomfortable."

Petrenko nodded, violence darkening his pale face. "That's fine, then," he said.

19

Dan had a mostly restless night. As much as he tried to fight it, his mind kept racing, jumping back and forth to different images from the previous day. The dead girl, her chest caved in, an ever-growing pool of blood leaking from her; the other one, the middle-aged woman moaning on the floor in agony, her intestines clearly showing; the back of Gordon's skull blowing out; Joel pointing a gun at him, the look in his eyes while he tried to decide whether or not to pull the trigger...

It was as if those images were looped together to play endlessly in his head. Even when he opened his eyes he would see them. They would linger like ghosts in the dark before fading away.

At some point, exhaustion took over. Then there was nothing, just a drifting along. He felt almost at peace then. After a short time he could hear a voice calling him. It sounded familiar. He tried to ignore it, but it was persistent.

"Jeez, Dan, turn around already."

Sighing, he turned around. Gordon was waiting for him,

but he didn't look quite the same to Dan – smaller, older, a harshness to him, with none of the goofiness that Dan had come to associate with him.

"I always told you Joel was a weasel," Gordon said.

"Joel's not that bad—"

"Not that bad? That weasel blew my brains out!"

"I'm sorry about that."

"What the fuck, what's done is done."

"I'm still sorry."

"Yeah, I know, but I'm past that. What about you?"

"What do you mean?"

"Jeez, Dan, you know what I mean. How are you going to get your cut from that weasel?"

"He'll give it to me. He just needs a few days to cool off."

"Not a chance. He'll never give you a dime. You know that."

"Maybe, I don't know… Jesus, Gordon, what the hell happened in that bank?"

"Dan, that wasn't my fault."

"But you shot them."

"You should've heard what they were saying to me. I mean, come on, Dan, you would've done the same thing if you had some snotty little bitch calling you a filthy disgusting pervert. Telling you that she'd rather be fucked by a pig than by you. What did you want me to do, just walk away?"

"Gordon, she was tied up, helpless. Yes, you should've just walked away."

"Look, I've been walking away from cunts like that my whole life. I wasn't going to do it this time – not while I'm holding a gun. Fuck her, fuck both of them. Anyway, I couldn't walk away, not when Joel's fat little friend's standing there laughing at me."

"What about the other woman?"

"Same thing. She had the fucking nerve to tell me that she hoped I'd rot in hell for all eternity. I decided to give her something else to think about instead."

Dan felt off-kilter. The person in front of him was Gordon, but it also wasn't. There was a coldness to him, an emptiness. He seemed only a shell, a soulless version of the man Dan used to know. Nothing left in his eyes but bitterness and rage.

"Why'd you have to start talking to her?" Dan asked, a rush of anger choking his words. "You promised me. Jesus, Gordon, why'd you have to do that?"

"I was just goofing around, that's all. Killing time, trying to be friendly. I didn't see what the big deal was."

"You didn't see what the big deal was? We had so much at stake! What could you possibly have had to say that you thought she'd want to hear?"

"I was just telling her about Jersey and some interesting facts about Brazil, that's all."

"I got news for you, Gordon. Nobody cares about your interesting little factoids!"

"You don't think I know that?"

"Then why, Gordon? Why did you have to jeopardize all of us over some mindless small talk?"

"Why?" His mouth closed while he thought it over. Then shrugging, he said, "I don't know. What else was I going to talk to her about?"

"But why say anything?"

"Oh, come on, how many chances am I going to have to talk to a cute girl with a nice little ass like she had? And, Jeez, Dan, I'm holding a gun, I'm being polite, she should've just laid there and listened to me. Let me at least pretend that I had a chance of fucking the shit out of her – what's wrong?"

"Nothing, it's just until now I've never heard you swear before."

"Yeah, well, I figure I'm dead, so what the fuck?"

"I don't know, it doesn't seem like you."

"Well, it is, Dan, and… why do you keep looking away? Do you have someplace else you'd rather be?"

"I guess I'm tired."

"How can you be tired? You're asleep after all."

"I know, but I'm beat. Why don't we call it a night."

"You're kidding, right? I mean, Dan, I'm dead. This might be the last chance we ever have to talk and you're going to blow me off?"

"Gordon, I'm sorry, man, but I'm really beat."

"Forget it. Fine. If that's the way you want to be. But at least answer my question. The one you keep avoiding. How are you going to get your cut from that weasel? Because you're royally fucked if you don't."

"I'll figure something out."

"No you won't. And you really are fucked, Dan. You realize the police will be calling you soon. They're going to want to know why the bank's security system didn't work."

"I know."

"Are you prepared for it?"

"I think so."

"Are you prepared for what's going to happen when they realize I was one of the robbers?"

"That's not going to happen."

"I'm not so sure."

"Right now the police believe you were an innocent victim. There's no reason for that to change."

"There are plenty of reasons, Dan, as you well know. If you had your cut, you could make a run for it. But as things stand, you're nothing but a sitting duck. If they connect me to the robbery, you'll be next. And then you're sunk. You'll lose everything – Carol, your kids, your life. And for nothing. Because Joel won't even give you a dime."

"Gordon, I've had enough."

"What do you mean you've had enough? Come on, just one more thing and then you'll never have to hear from me again—"

"No, I'm serious, I'm done."

Gordon's mouth slowly closed. He stood staring at Dan, his eyes vacant, distant. Then his lips puckered up in an exaggerated display of self pity. His voice bitter, he swore, "Fuck you, anyway. I'm out of here!"

With that Gordon was gone.

Dan felt relieved, but also an emptiness. At some level, he knew he was only dreaming, but at the same time there was something odd about it. Almost as if there was an order and logic to it, not the chaotic and out-of-control feeling that his dreams usually had. Maybe that really was Gordon – the pure essence of him, anyway. An overflowing of self-loathing, bitterness, and rage.

Whether or not the police ever connected him to the robbery, he knew he had already lost everything. He had lost Carol, lost his children, and lost his future. At least at some level. What happened in that bank was his fault. Even if nobody ever found out about it, how could things ever be the same?

He had risked everything of value in his life for nothing.

Realizing that, the emptiness inside him expanded until he felt completely hollow inside. As if his chest could be crumpled like tinfoil.

Carol woke him. His chest ached, his face felt sticky and wet. He realized he had been sobbing.

"What's wrong?" she asked.

"Nothing," he said, choking back one last sob. "Nothing but a bad dream."

20

Resnick had gotten to the station at six the next morning. There were still no leads on the dead man they had found. He went through the witness reports Stillwall and Hollings had made and then played both videotapes; the one showing the robbery and the other one of Raymond Lombardo taking his ski mask off. There was something about both tapes that bothered him. He figured out what it was about the Lombardo tape. It was an eye movement that Lombardo made, almost as if he were locating the surveillance camera before he stopped to take off his mask. Resnick played the tape back several times. He wasn't a hundred percent sure about the eye movement, but that's what it seemed like. Anyway, it made no sense. Why take the mask off there? There was something also about the robbery tape that bugged him, but he couldn't quite figure it out. Kind of like a name on the tip of your tongue that you just can't quite pull from your memory.

Shortly after eight o'clock, Hadley wandered in, spotted Resnick and chewed the fat with him for a few minutes, remarking several times how glad he was they'd been able to wrap up that nasty business from the other day so quickly. Resnick was no longer so sure of that, but he held his tongue. Hadley seemed, for him anyway, buoyant, almost a sparkle in his dull eyes, and Resnick didn't see any reason to ruin that over a hunch. But his gut kept telling him that this was something other than what it looked like.

He was surprised there were still no leads concerning the dead man. That meant the guy was either from out of state or a loner with no family or friends. He checked the Lynn police logs, saw that there were no reports of abandoned vehicles and then got on the phone to neighboring police stations, asking the desk sergeants to call him back if they found any vehicles that had been abandoned recently. With some luck they'd track down the dead man's car. If he had a car.

Maguire came in a little after nine carrying a bag of donuts and two cups of coffee, one of which he handed to Resnick when they headed out together for the FBI building in Boston.

"I didn't sleep well last night," Maguire confided. "I dunno. I wish I hadn't seen that videotape."

He didn't look like he had slept much, his complexion grayish, the skin under his eyes swollen. Resnick didn't bother saying anything. After all, what was there to say? That you get used to seeing young girls shot to death? It wasn't true. Maybe you get hardened to it, maybe you get to the point where you don't lose sleep over it, but how can you ever get used to something like that?

When they arrived at the FBI building, Resnick found Kathleen Liciano in her office. Her handshake had a cool, dry quality to it. She looked more relaxed than the other day, more professional and matter-of-fact than rigid. Resnick told her they still hadn't identified the dead man they had found behind the bank. He gave her a copy of the surveillance tape showing the robbery.

"I was hoping you could help us build a profile of the men involved," Resnick said. "Heights, weights, other physical characteristics you might be able to detect."

"We have computer modeling software I can use. I'll start working on this today." She took a folder from her desk and handed it to him. "This copy's yours," she said. "Ballistics showed that the same gun was used on all three victims. Death was instantaneous for both Williams and the unidentified man—"

"You mean the Grateful Dead man," Maguire interjected, smirking.

"...found in the back lot," Liciano continued, ignoring Maguire's miserable pun as her eyes held steady on Resnick. "Concerning the dead man, height is six foot one, weight two hundred and twenty-three pounds. Age sixty to sixty-five. He had a scar along his left thigh where I found a fragment of shrapnel consistent with mortar that was used during Vietnam."

"So he was a Vietnam vet, probably decorated with a purple heart," Resnick said.

Liciano nodded. "Hopefully that will help in identifying him," she said. "No other distinguishing scars or marks. No calluses or cuts on his hands. He was probably a white-collar professional."

Maguire inspected his own hands. "Could also be a cop," he said.

Liciano continued to ignore him. She said to Resnick, "If I can help you in any other way or you'd like to talk about this report, call me any time."

"Thanks, I appreciate your help." They shook hands again, her grip still cool and dry like before, but there was also a firmness to it that Resnick liked. Maguire, still sulking, didn't bother to offer his hand and Liciano didn't seem to notice or mind.

While they were leaving her office, Maguire muttered to Resnick, "Damn, that's one uptight lady. Someone should take that stick out of her ass."

Resnick ignored him.

"So how do you suppose she'd like to help you?" Maguire asked, and then answered his own question by making an obscene gesture using his thumb and forefinger on one hand and his middle finger on his other.

"That's not very nice," Resnick told him. At first Maguire thought his partner was joking, but the look on his face made Maguire realize quickly that he wasn't.

"I'm sorry," Maguire said. "I told you before I didn't sleep well. I spent the whole night thinking about that girl, how she was shot down like a dog... I don't know, I guess it put me in a lousy mood. Besides, I thought my Grateful Dead man joke was funny."

"Forget it."

"But it's still pretty obvious she's interested in you, partner."

"Just shut up, okay?"

"Man, your first wife must've really fucked you over."

Resnick stopped in his tracks. "How do you know I had a wife?" he asked coldly.

"Stillwall told me—"

Resnick raised a finger and pointed it at his partner as hard lines showed along his jaw. "Here's the deal, Walt. You don't talk about my personal life, ever, and I don't demand that Ken assign me a new partner. Deal?"

Maguire was taken aback by Resnick's tone. "Excuse me for taking an interest," he said. "Fine, whatever. Be a miserable fucking hermit for all I care."

"Thanks for your permission."

It was a quarter to ten when they got back to the front security desk. Resnick called Agent Spitzer on his cell phone. The security desk was then called back and an arrangement was made for them to be escorted to one of the interrogation rooms. Stillwall and Hollings were already there, Stillwall with his eyes closed, hands clasped behind his neck and feet up on the desk, giving the impression that he was napping. Hollings wore a thin, sarcastic smile and greeted his two fellow detectives with a wink. Also sitting at the table was a big linebacker type with a square jaw and wearing a suit stretched too tight across his chest and shoulders. He was introduced as Jim Taylor, an investigator out of the FBI's organized crime unit. He acknowledged them with a short nod. Spitzer's long dour face looked almost cheerful as he shook hands with Resnick and then Maguire.

"This could end up being very big," Spitzer said. "We've been trying to loosen up Raymond Lombardo for over a year now. I think we've finally got him."

"Let me guess, you're going to let him walk on this," Maguire said. "It doesn't matter that two people are dead, another critically wounded."

Spitzer gave him a stern look, any previous signs of cheerfulness fading fast from his long face. "Sometimes you have to look at the big picture."

"This could help us shut down mob operations from Boston to Providence," Taylor stated.

"What if he's not involved?" Resnick asked.

"What?"

"Something's not quite right about that tape."

Stillwall had opened an eye. "Tell me more, boyo."

"Before he takes his ski mask off, you can catch an eye movement as if he's trying to spot where the surveillance camera is."

Spitzer's thin lips disappeared into two pale lines while he considered Resnick. "Sometimes if you look too hard you can see things that don't exist," Spitzer said, his voice thin, tight. "There's no question the man on that surveillance tape is Raymond Lombardo."

"Why would he take off his ski mask?" Resnick asked.

A slight twitch showed near Spitzer's right eye. "Maybe he got hot," Spitzer said. "Maybe he was pissed off about what happened inside the bank. Who knows, and you want to know something, who the fuck cares?"

"Maybe there's some computer analysis you could do—"

"Can you believe this guy?" Taylor interrupted. He was staring at Resnick as if his head were a football that needed to be separated from his body. "It's bad enough what we have to deal with now with defense lawyers who pull every underhanded trick imaginable and juries who won't convict unless we can play them back the crime on videotape, but now that we actually have a videotape, this joker's trying to claim that's not even good enough."

Spitzer held up a hand to stop Taylor, then faced Resnick, his expression grim. "We don't need to do any computer analysis." He waved a thumb in the general direction of a door on the opposite side of the room. "I think it would be better if you and your partner watched from the observation room. I'm afraid we might overwhelm Lombardo with too many people."

Maguire started to argue, but stopped when Resnick

shrugged and headed towards the door, Taylor glaring at him as he left. Stillwall now had both eyes open and was looking on with amusement. Maguire reluctantly followed Resnick out of the room.

"The nerve of that guy," Maguire said. "This is our investigation and he's going to push us aside? Asshole."

"It doesn't matter," Resnick said. "We'll have just as good a view from in here."

He turned on the monitor in front of them and settled back in his chair. Maguire took a donut from his bag and offered Resnick one, who declined.

"You really think there's a chance that wasn't Lombardo?" Maguire asked.

"I don't know. It bothers me that he stopped the way he did to take off his mask. Almost as if he were posing for the camera."

"I think you're reading too much into it. Sometimes you have to look for the most obvious explanation."

"And what would that be?"

Maguire considered that as he chewed his donut. "Lombardo screwed up. He's not too bright. He was too pissed off to think straight. Take your pick."

"You could be right, Walt," Resnick conceded, shrugging in a way that indicated he didn't think there was much chance of that.

At twenty past ten Raymond Lombardo was escorted into the interrogation room. He was a big man, heavy, with rolls of fat around his middle. Instead of long stringy black hair, sideburns and a thick mustache, he was clean-shaven and had a short buzz cut, his hair now dyed yellow with orange highlights. Accompanying him was a square red-faced man who charged into the room like a bull. He introduced himself as Russ Korkin, Lombardo's attorney.

"This is outrageous!" Korkin exclaimed, his eyes nearly bulging. "I hear that some Girl Scout had her cookie money taken away from her. You going to charge my client with that also?"

"If we have a videotape of him doing it, sure," Taylor said.

Korkin's eyes narrowed suspiciously. "What do you mean by that?"

Spitzer tried to smile, but it came off more as if he had gas. "A picture's worth a thousand words," he said. Using a remote control, he turned on a monitor that was positioned in the opposite corner of the room. When the videotape got to Lombardo taking his ski mask off, he froze the picture.

Lombardo had been showing a big smart-alecky grin, but as he watched the tape his grin faded. "That ain't me," he told his attorney.

"You don't have to say a word," Korkin said, his manner now more subdued.

"I'm telling you that ain't me," Lombardo repeated. "This is a frame-up. They manufactured that tape."

"We didn't manufacture anything," Stillwall said. "We retrieved the tape from one of the bank's outdoor surveillance cameras."

"That's bullshit!" Lombardo forced himself to take a deep breath. Shaking his head, he showed a wide grin that didn't come close to reaching his eyes. "You guys screwed up," he said. "I mean, look at my hair in that bullshit tape."

"I've been noticing that," Taylor said. "You cleaned yourself up, huh, Raymond? What happened, after the bank job you decided to change your appearance?"

"This bank got hit yesterday, right?" Lombardo asked.

"You think we're stupid?" Taylor asked. "You know damn well when that bank was hit."

"Yeah, well, this is where you screwed up your frame. I had my haircut and shave at my barber's last Saturday."

Taylor blinked several times. "You're a lying sack of shit, Raymond."

Hollings spoke up. "Now why would you happen to have gotten your hair cut this past Saturday?" he asked.

Lombardo showed a self-conscious smile. "I didn't like the way I was looking in the papers," he said. "I thought my hair and mustache made me look heavier and older than I am." He turned to face Taylor, a wide toothy grin showing. "What do you think, asshole, I look better now?"

"You'll look better after a lethal injection," Taylor said. "Don't think for one second I buy this bullshit of yours. What went down in that bank is felony murder, fits right under the new federal guidelines for the death penalty. I promise you, Raymond, I'll be front and center when they inject potassium chloride into your fat lard body."

Korkin had recovered some of his bluster. "This is so goddamn outrageous," he exclaimed, his round face again turning a bright red. "You have the audacity to pass this fraudulently manufactured tape off as evidence? I'm going to see all of you brought up on charges for this!"

"Calm down," Stillwall said. "The tape is genuine. As far as I'm concerned your client wore a wig and fake facial hair to the robbery."

"That is asinine."

"Maybe, maybe not. But if your client cooperates with us,

tells us where he was from two to three yesterday, we'll try to clear this up."

"There's nothing to clear up," Korkin stated emphatically. "As far as I'm concerned this charade is over. Unless you're charging my client, in which case I'll be more than happy to—"

"Russ, this isn't worth wasting time over. I played golf yesterday. Eighteen holes at the Swampscott Greens." Lombardo rubbed his jaw, his expression thoughtful. "If that tape's for real, then the guys behind this did a first-rate job planning that robbery," he said. "Their execution may have sucked, but whoever thought this out, fucking first-rate all the way. If you catch the guy and can't build a strong enough case to convict, tell him he's got a job with me anytime he wants. No hard feelings on my part."

"Awfully generous of you, Raymond. How about the names of your golf buddies?"

Lombardo rattled off the names of his foursome.

"We done here?" Korkin asked as he pushed himself out of his chair.

"I don't think so," Spitzer said. "I still like the idea of your client disguising himself under a ski mask, assuming he did get his hair cut on Saturday like he claims."

"What do you mean like I claim? You think I'm lying about something so fucking easy to check up on? Or about playing golf yesterday?" Lombardo demanded.

Spitzer ignored him. "We're going to be holding your client for the next twenty-four hours while we decide whether or not to press charges," he added.

Korkin shook his head, exasperation showing in his bulging eyes. "I'm heading straight to Federal Court to file an injunction," he warned. Then to Lombardo, "Ray, don't say another word to these people."

"You don't have to worry about that," Lombardo said. "They're nothing but a bunch of fucking clowns."

Resnick was pouring himself a cup of coffee when Agent Spitzer approached him.

"There's no doubt in my mind that that's Lombardo on the videotape," Spitzer said.

"What if you end up with a dozen witnesses claiming he was playing golf yesterday?"

"Then he paid those people off." Spitzer paused, then added, "You were right all along about him intentionally posing for the surveillance camera. That was a good pick-up."

"You think this is all some elaborate scheme on Lombardo's part?" Resnick asked, struggling to keep his incredulity in check.

"Why not? You know how juries are. This allows him to claim we're framing him, but we screwed up not realizing he had cut and dyed his hair."

"Sounds too complicated to me," Resnick said. "Why bother with something like that?"

"Because he thinks he's smarter than we are."

"I don't know. Exposing himself so he can later claim he's being framed doesn't make sense to me."

"Then what's your explanation?"

"Either we've got some very clever bank robbers who knew where the surveillance cameras were hidden or someone very stupid in the FBI trying to sneak that tape in to frame Lombardo."

"No one in the FBI manufactured that tape!"

Resnick took a sip of his coffee. "In that case we've got some very clever bank robbers."

Dan had tried to ignore the phone ringing, but Carol shook him until he opened his eyes.

"Craig Brown from the Lynn Capital Bank is on the phone," Carol told him. Dan wanted his wife to just go away, but he knew that wasn't going to happen. He pushed himself up into a sitting position, the sunlight hurting his eyes and forcing them shut again. Shielding them, he squinted at his wife. "What time is it?" he asked, his voice barely above a croak. It was funny how he felt like he had a bad hangover. Not even as much as a beer the previous day.

"It's already eleven thirty," she said, her expression both brittle and alarmed. As lousy as he was feeling, the look on her face made him feel worse. He took the phone from her, grunted okay a few times and hung up.

"What did he want?" Carol asked.

"He wants to hire me to find out why their security system didn't work. I'm meeting him at the bank at one thirty."

"When's that other man supposed to call?"

"This evening," he said, remembering he was supposed to have a second interview that day. "After seven o'clock."

As he pushed himself out of bed, a wave of nausea rolled through him. He had to steady himself against the bedpost until it passed. God, he felt sick, like he had suffered food poisoning. Slowly he trudged off to the bathroom.

When he looked in the mirror, he saw that his rash was gone. All at once it struck him how goddamn pathetic his situation was. He started laughing and, as he did, his stomach hurt like hell. But he couldn't stop himself. At least he could be thankful for something, even if it was something as insignificant as his rash disappearing. The thought of that just made him laugh harder.

21

The two men were chained to a bar so that their arms were stretched over their heads and the tips of their toes barely able to touch the floor. The room they were in was soundproof, so there was no real reason for the gags in their mouths other than for the psychological effect and also to keep their screaming from giving Petrenko a headache. They were both animated now, both trying to make noise. Petrenko ignored them as he slipped on a butcher's apron and then a set of goggles. He picked up a pair of latex gloves and pulled them over his hands, then stood clenching and unclenching his fists, making sure his fingers would have the flexibility to do what they'd need to. When he felt ready, he gave Yuri a nod.

Yuri and two other men unchained the heavyset Arab and carried him to a table that was wrapped in plastic. Plastic sheeting was also laid out under the table covering a good area of the floor. After a night chained in the position he had been, the man would have no strength in his arms, no ability to fight back. Yuri and the two other Russians dumped the Arab on the table like he was a sack of flour and then handcuffed his wrists and ankles to metal rings at both ends of the table. Petrenko picked up a scalpel and held it to the light.

The other man, the one named Abbas, tried to scream through his gag when he caught sight of the scalpel, his body contorting wildly. Petrenko shook his head sadly at the man and addressed him as if he were addressing a child.

"There's no point in acting this way," Petrenko told him. "You are going to die later today. Nothing you do will change that. Whether you die easily or not will be up to how long it takes you to tell me where my money is. And you will tell me. Believe me, you will be begging to tell me."

Abbas was nearly epileptic as he tried to make a noise through his gag.

"You don't understand," Petrenko said. "I don't care what you might have to say now. After you watch what happens to your friend, then I will care."

He turned away from Abbas and walked over to the heavyset Arab handcuffed to the table. The man's eyes grew wide as he saw the scalpel. He tried frantically to talk through his gag. In his panic he started choking on it. Petrenko couldn't afford to let him die so quickly. He had no choice but to remove the gag.

"Please," the man was saying as he gasped for air, tears streaming down his face. "I will tell you anything you want to know, anything..."

Petrenko in Russian asked Yuri to get him some cotton. He waited patiently for Yuri, all the while listening to the heavyset man blabber on and on about how he would tell Petrenko anything he needed to know. When Yuri returned with a bag of cotton, Petrenko tore off two pieces and stuffed them in each ear. Otherwise, he knew, this man would give him a headache.

The heavyset man's voice was now barely a hoarse whisper; still though trying repeatedly to convince Petrenko that he would tell him anything he wanted to know.

Petrenko stopped him. "Unfortunately for you," he said, "you have nothing to say that I care to hear." Then pushing the edge of the scalpel against the man's bare chest, he went to work.

Joel had been on the road for five hours before he arrived in Manhattan. The first thing he did was stop off for an onion bagel with cream cheese. Closing his eyes, he savored every bite of it. Back in New England the bagels were *dreck*, nothing but glorified rolls. After he finished it, he bought another one. He'd have no problem eating a dozen of them in one sitting, but he would have to limit himself to two. His waistline couldn't afford more than that. As it was, he was going to have to pay later by doing several hundred sit-ups when he got home.

After his lunch, he headed over to Forty-Seventh Street and found the jewelry store his uncle Hyman worked at. Entering the store, he spotted his uncle, sitting on the same stool he had sat on for over fifty years. Eighty-two years old, half a foot shorter than Joel, with only a few white wisps of hair left on his mostly bald head. Along with his big ears and large veined nose, he looked like some gnarled figure that could've been carved out of wood instead of flesh. The old man did a double-take when he saw Joel. Sliding off his stool, he moved with a surprising quickness to meet his nephew.

"What are you doing here?" he asked. He took hold of one of Joel's hands with both of his, his own hands thick and swollen. "I haven't heard from you in three years and you just pop in here, just like that. What's wrong with you, you can't call first?"

"I'm sorry, Uncle Hymie, but I decided kind of spur of the moment to drive down here. I've got something I'd like to show you."

"Eh, that can wait. You have lunch yet?"

"Yeah, I had a couple of bagels."

"Bagels? You call that lunch? Let me take you to a deli, get you a nice brisket sandwich. Maybe some matzoh ball soup?"

"I don't have time for that now, but I plan on stopping off at the Carnegie and taking a few pounds of pastrami and corned beef home with me. Also a bag of potato knishes. Can I show you what I got?"

"Always in a rush." The old man shook his head, making a tsking noise. "You haven't seen me in three years and you can't even spend time to have lunch with me."

"All right, if you're going to make a federal case out of it—"

"Never mind, you're in too big a hurry. What do you have that's so important for me to look at?"

"Can we go to the back room?" Joel lowered his voice to a whisper. "I'd like a little privacy."

The old man eyed his nephew suspiciously. "Did you do something to get yourself in trouble?" he asked.

"No, of course not," Joel muttered, indignant, his voice still barely above a whisper. "I'd just like a little privacy, that's all, I don't need everyone in this store gawking at what I want to show you."

There were only half a dozen other people in the store, none of them paying Joel or his uncle any attention. The old man shrugged and led Joel to the back of the store and into a small room that was only slightly bigger than a closet.

"So what do you have?" his uncle asked, now showing a little curiosity.

Joel took a silk pouch from his pocket and emptied a diamond into his hand. His uncle took the diamond from him, studied it and then looked back at his nephew.

"What are you doing with an uncut diamond?" he asked.

"Let's just say I found it."

"Tell me the truth. Did you steal this?"

Joel made a face. "Of course not," he said. "Come on, Uncle Hymie, just tell me what it's worth, okay?"

The old man stuck a magnifying glass in his eye and studied the diamond. "This is very good quality." He popped the glass out of his eye and held the diamond in his open palm. "Two and one quarter carats." He gave his nephew a long, careful look. "Retail, this would go for twenty-two thousand, wholesale, fourteen thousand. If you were someone off the street, I could probably get you nine for it. You, if I forgo my commission, twelve. Do you want to sell?"

Joel rubbed a hand along his jaw as he did the math in his head and realized that he had over a million dollars in diamonds. "Not right now," he said. "Maybe in a little while. What if I'm able to get my hands on more diamonds like this?"

"How many more?"

"Fifty, a hundred, I don't know yet. How many would you be able to buy?"

"Joel, what did you do?"

"Nothing. This is all above board. So tell me, Uncle Hymie, how many diamonds like these would you be able to take off my hands?"

"Everything is so above board that you had to show me this diamond in private, eh?" The old man sighed heavily. "But, I guess if not me, you'll get yourself in trouble with someone else."

"Look, Uncle Hymie, I'm not in the mood for a lecture. How many diamonds like these can you buy?"

"*Gott im Himmel,*" the old man muttered to himself, then to Joel as he smiled wistfully, "Uncut, this quality, as many as you have."

When Dan was brought into Craig Brown's office, the bank manager introduced him to Alex Resnick, telling him that Resnick was a Lynn police detective investigating the bank robbery. Dan shook hands with the man and sat down.

"I hope you don't mind," Brown was saying, "but the detective is also trying to find out why our security system didn't work. You won't mind answering a few of his questions?"

"Of course not," Dan said. As he smiled at Brown, he thought, *You sneaky underhanded little prick, trying to waylay me like this. Goddamn sneaky underhanded bastard.*

"Any idea what happened?" Resnick asked.

"Off the top of my head, maybe a couple of ideas." Dan then turned to Brown. "Have you tested the system since the robbery?"

"Of course. We tested each alarm button. They all worked."

"How about the system status?"

"What does that tell you?" Resnick asked.

Dan gave the detective a thin smile. "How long the system has been up and running. If the system was turned off before the robbery, we'll be able to tell that."

Brown made a show of looking through a stack of papers. "I don't think I've gotten around to checking that yet," he said.

"We're wasting our time until we do," Dan said, trying to keep his tone pleasant, all the while his mind spinning while he tried to figure out how he was going to handle this. He had known he was going to have to talk to the cops at some point, but he hadn't expected it this quickly.

That little prick, he thought as he followed Brown out of the office. *Goddamn underhanded little prick!*

For a moment Dan daydreamed that he had pistol-whipped the bank manager when he'd had the opportunity. It had taken quite a bit of self-control on his part to only shove Brown the other day. He didn't like the man – and this was even before Brown made the decision to farm out the software to India – and he resented the condescending comments Brown made to him afterwards.

"You don't need this type of work," Brown had told him. *"After all, haven't you made millions already in high tech? From what I've read, anyone who's any good has."*

And…

"I don't understand why you would want this – isn't this only menial work? Anyway, I can't justify paying you fifty dollars an hour when I can hire four Indian programmers for the same price."

There were other jabs, many others. All made with a smug little smile.

When they got to the security system, Dan moved Brown aside so he could type in a command at the system's console. He showed Resnick the response which indicated that the system had been up and running continuously for over thirty-four days.

"Too bad," Dan told the detective. "This would have made things easy if someone had simply turned the system off before the robbery."

"Could someone have hacked into it?" Resnick asked.

"Not if the system was built the way I designed it."

"It was built exactly to your design," Brown interjected, his tone defensive.

"If that's true, then the system will only allow outgoing calls. No one can connect into it."

"I'm not sure I understood something you said. What do you mean *if the system was built the way you designed it*?" Resnick asked.

"I had nothing to do with the implementation, only the design." Dan grimaced as he straightened up. "I'm getting too old to crouch like this," he said. "My knees can't take it. What do you say we head back to Craig's office?"

Resnick was frowning. "Anything you can tell by looking at it?"

"No. If it wasn't turned off, then there are only two possibilities I can think of. Number one, no one pushed the alarm buttons during the robbery—"

"That's ridiculous," Brown interrupted. He was trying to appear indignant, but his act fell flat. He knew the FBI agent had suspected that and the accusation weighed heavily on him. As hard as he tried, he couldn't muster up any genuine indignation.

"Well then, the only other explanation I can think of is that a backdoor was put into the software."

"What do you mean by a backdoor?" Resnick asked.

"One or more of the programmers built in a way to make the system fail—"

"That's preposterous!"

Dan turned to Brown, his affable grin hardening. "No, it isn't. What's preposterous is you having some firm halfway around the world building critical security software for you because they're the cheapest ones you could find."

"There was nothing wrong with what we did," Brown insisted. He cleared his throat. "Would you be able to examine the software and figure out why it failed?"

"Sure, I could do that. Two hundred dollars an hour, one hundred and sixty hours guaranteed. Paid in advance."

Brown's head jerked as if he'd been sucker punched. "That's r-ridiculous," he sputtered. "We only paid you fifty dollars an hour to design the system!"

"If you don't like my price I'm sure you could always offer it to the lowest bidder. Maybe that same firm in India who you had build the code. I'm sure for two hundred dollars an hour, they'd be able to get twenty people."

Dan stared evenly at the bank manager. Brown blinked several times before looking away. "I think we'll need to talk to other firms," he said gruffly.

"That's your choice, although I'd have to think you'd want to resolve this as quickly as possible. I'd also think you'd want the guy who designed the system to be the one looking at the code. But if you don't care about the public relations aspect of this, that's your business." Then to Resnick, "Any more questions, Detective, before I leave?"

"Not right now. I'll need a number where you can be reached."

Dan handed Resnick a business card. "This has my home and cell numbers." As he turned to leave, Brown stopped him.

"I'll get you a check." Brown met Dan's eyes briefly and then lowered his gaze. "How quickly can you start on this?" he asked.

"Right away. I'll need the full amount up front."

Brown nodded. "Give me a minute," he said. After he locked up the security system, he started towards his office. Dan was going to follow him, but Resnick stopped him. "If you don't mind, I'd like to talk to you alone," he said.

"Sure." Dan maintained his pleasant smile. He was amazed at how calm he was able to appear. In reality it was more of a numbness. Almost as if he were on autopilot, reacting without any thought or plan. But still, no perspiration, no heart palpitations, nothing but a flat evenness.

Brown wavered as if he wanted to eavesdrop on the conversation. Reluctantly, he kept walking. After he was out of sight, Resnick asked Dan what he thought. "Could Brown be involved in this?"

"I don't think so. I don't think he'd have the balls to try something like this. It's a nice thought, though."

"You don't like him much, do you?"

"No, not much. I warned him about the dangers of sending out this type of code to a place where there would be no oversight and he ignored me. I even offered to do the work at a discount." Dan paused, his amiable smile fading. "I don't want to appear insensitive," he added. "I know people were killed during this robbery, but this thing really fucked me over too. I make my living designing security systems. Who's going to want to hire me after this? All because some incompetent bank manager wouldn't take my advice."

"Are people going to know you worked on this security system?"

"Yeah, it's a small industry, word gets around. Plus I've got dozens of resumés circulating now that mention this last contract."

Dan stopped and let his smile drop completely. "What you asked before about Brown being involved – there is something that seemed odd to me. In my original proposal I had a backup line that would've been tied directly to the alarm buttons and would bypass the security system. This way if the system was down for any reason, the police would still be called if any of the buttons were activated. Brown got rid of it. The damn thing would've only cost about three hundred dollars a month. I just assumed he made his decision out of shortsightedness, but who knows?"

Dan spotted the bank manager walking towards them. As Brown handed him a check, he made a lame joke about how the bank was being robbed for the second time in two days. Dan noticed that Resnick was looking at Brown differently now, more intensely, and Brown seemed to notice it also, his smug little smile quickly growing strained. Dan told the bank manager that he'd be calling him as soon as he found something and then shook hands with Resnick, who thanked him for his time.

As Dan walked through the bank lobby, sights from the other day rushed through his mind. *The dead girl, the other one squirming along the floor, all that blood leaking out of them*. He squeezed his eyes shut, trying to rid his mind of those images. Stepping outside, the numbness he'd been feeling was gone. A tight fist squeezed his heart. His knees buckled.

Damn, it would be something if I passed out right here. What the hell would that cop think?

Somehow he stayed on his feet. Staggering, he made it back to his car, amazed that he had been able to pull off talking to that cop. But as he'd been noticing with Carol, lying just keeps on getting easier.

Petrenko pulled the latex gloves from his hands and dropped

them into a garbage bag. Grimacing, he grabbed his fingers and rubbed them vigorously. It had been a grueling four hours.

"He didn't know anything," Petrenko said.

"No, I don't believe so," Yuri agreed.

"We have lost a lot so far," Petrenko noted bitterly. "Not only what was stolen yesterday, but all the potential millions we could've gained in future diamond purchases." He stopped for a moment to rub his eyes. "We'll find them. Sooner or later I'll get my hands on them and they'll suffer worse than these Arabs did."

Petrenko gazed off into the distance, his expression turning somber. Slowly, he looked back at Yuri. "We'll offer a reward," he said at last. "If any diamond dealers have come across uncut diamonds, we'll find out about it. Take care of it."

Yuri nodded and left the room.

Petrenko glared at the two other Russian men working for him. "Why are you two standing there?" he demanded. He waved a hand in the general direction of where the remains of the dead Arabs lay. "Take care of this mess!"

22

After Dan Wilson had left, Resnick stuck around to try and gauge whether Brown could've been involved in the robbery. Somebody inside the bank had to have been. Somebody had given the robbers Petrenko's box numbers, and it made sense that somebody had arranged with the offshore programmers to put a *backdoor* into the software. Brown seemed as good a bet as anybody. What bothered Resnick, though, was remembering the look on Brown's face when he had discovered the system was still on after the robbery. To Resnick, it looked as if Brown had fully expected the system to have been turned off. Of course, it could've been an act – the bank manager knew where the surveillance cameras were so he would know he was being videotaped – but still it would've been a damned good act, close to Academy Award caliber.

When Resnick tried asking Brown why he chose not to have a backup line for the alarm system, the bank manager first got flustered and then indignant. He claimed it was his fiduciary responsibility to avoid unnecessary expenses and that there was enough redundancy built into the system as it was. Resnick tried shaking him on that, but couldn't get anywhere. After that, he had Brown go over the payments that were made to the Indian contract firm, hoping he could catch an extra payment or some other irregularity. If Brown had used bank funds to pay something extra to one of the offshore programmers, he did a good job hiding it. Resnick decided he was going to have to ask for an audit and he was sure Hadley wouldn't be happy about that.

When he got back to the station, he was surprised to find Maguire wasn't there waiting for him. They had separated so that Maguire could stick around the FBI offices and see how the Lombardo investigation progressed, but he should've been back to the station by now.

Resnick checked his phone messages. A desk sergeant working out of the Revere station had called about an abandoned car found at the Revere Mall. Resnick couldn't help smiling when he brought up the owner's driver's license from the Registry of Motor Vehicles database. Printing out a copy, he brought it into Hadley's office.

"You're back," Hadley said stiffly. "I've been wanting to talk to you."

"Take a look at this first."

Resnick showed him a copy of Gordon Carmichael's driver's license. Hadley stared blankly at it for a moment before he recognized who it was.

"How'd you find this?" he asked.

"I was checking around for any abandoned vehicles. This guy's car had been dumped at the Revere Mall."

"Raymond Lombardo's neighborhood," Hadley observed.

"Yeah, it's almost as if someone's trying hard to connect the dots to Lombardo," Resnick said. "I'm going to head over to the Revere Mall, see if they have any surveillance cameras covering their parking lot—"

"Stop."

Resnick gave Hadley a puzzled look. "What's up, Ken?" he asked.

"I've had a long talk with Agent Spitzer and we've both come to the conclusion that Raymond Lombardo is responsible for the bank robbery." Hadley took a deep breath. As he exhaled, his round face deflated like a punctured tire. He added, "As far I'm concerned, this case is closed."

"Has anyone tried to verify Lombardo's story?"

"And what would that prove? I'm sure his barber is going to say whatever Lombardo tells him to. Same with his golf buddies."

"We have so many leads we haven't checked out yet," Resnick said, shaking his head angrily. "Someone inside that bank has to be involved. If we shut this down now, we're never going to get to the bottom of what happened."

"We know what happened. It's over, Alex. We have the man who did this on videotape. That's more than enough for me and it should be for you too. Let the FBI finish this up."

"Ken, this stinks. We're going to just let the FBI force Lombardo into a deal and watch this case quietly disappear?"

"Sometimes it works out that way."

"And it doesn't matter how many people were hurt?"

"Of course it matters." Hadley sighed heavily, his eyes empty as he stared at his detective. "But unfortunately, not this time."

For a long moment all Resnick could do was stare back. His voice low and catching in his throat, he said, "What if Lombardo brings a dozen witnesses forward claiming he was playing golf at the time of the robbery? This could blow up in your face, Ken."

"I don't believe that's going to happen. Anyway, as I said, it's over. A press conference is going to be given at six tonight. As far as you're concerned, I don't want you spending any more time on this. In fact, I'm giving you what you asked for earlier. Until further notice, you're on Viktor Petrenko. Watch him twenty-four hours a day if you can."

"And what about Walt?"

"He's to watch that bank manager, Craig Brown, which I believe is something else you suggested."

"So that's it, huh? How long are you going to keep us on these assignments? Until the FBI finalizes their deal with Lombardo?"

Hadley tried to smile, but it didn't come close to reaching his eyes. They remained as pale and lifeless as glass. "That's as good a guess as any," he said.

23

Later that afternoon Dan was still amazed that he had been able to pull off what he did with that cop. It was like dodging a bullet during wartime. While it's happening, your adrenaline's pumping too much to realize how much danger you're in, how close you are to being turned to shit. Only afterwards does it register. Forget dodging a bullet, he dodged a whole clip from a machine gun. His hands were still shaking when he deposited the check Brown had given him. Thirty-two grand. He still had over four thousand dollars that he had taken from Gordon. All that money should've made him feel better. Instead he felt unsettled.

It was four thirty. He didn't feel up to heading home and facing Carol or his kids. Would he ever feel up to facing them again? Maybe. Given time the robbery could become an empty memory. Something that might or might not have ever happened. He had other empty memories. People he might've once known, but was no longer sure of. Even the first girl he ever had sex with. They were both sixteen at the time and had snuck out on to a golf course one night with a blanket. At some level of his consciousness he knew it had happened, but it also didn't seem possible. He could barely remember it. He could barely remember the girl. Of course, this was different. But maybe over time this could become like all those other distant, vague memories of his past. Maybe years from now he wouldn't be able to believe this had ever happened either.

Now, though, he couldn't stop thinking of that dead girl. Or the other woman. When he was driving to meet Brown, the news over the radio reported the other woman's status as touch and go. He hoped she wouldn't die. But how would her life be now, after having a bullet rip through her stomach? Would something like that ever really heal?

Thinking about it made him start perspiring again. Jesus, he was shaky. If anyone saw him they'd probably think he had some sort of neurological problem. He needed something to calm his nerves. A drink would help.

He stopped at the first bar he came across. The bartender gave him a funny look when he tried ordering a Guinness and a shot of Jameson's.

"Are you okay, buddy?" the bartender asked.

"I'll be better after you bring me my beer and a shot."

"You know, I'm not allowed to serve alcohol to someone already intoxicated."

"I haven't had a drop yet. Honest. What do you want me to do, recite the alphabet backwards?" Dan proceeded to do just that. The bartender lifted up his hands in a show of surrender. "Okay, okay," he said. "I believe you." But as he poured the draft, he raised an eyebrow and gave Dan a doubtful look.

God, he wished he could forget the robbery ever happened.

Let Joel keep the money. At this point he didn't care. He just wanted to distance himself as far from that memory as he could. But he knew that wasn't possible. Shrini wasn't going to let that happen. Tomorrow the two of them were going to drive to Joel's, and he knew Shrini wasn't going to give up on this until he got his cut. Deep down he also knew Joel wasn't going to give in. The damn thing had the potential for spiraling even further out of control. Fucking Joel. If he would be reasonable, they could move past this. The robbery could some day become one of those empty memories.

The bartender brought over his drinks. Dan took the shot and then sipped the Guinness, trying not to drink it too fast. The thirty-two grand would buy him some time, maybe enough so he could find a job and end up with long-term disability insurance. The beer was in one of those promotional glasses that breweries give out. He held the glass at arm's length. In bright light he was still able to make out details, even read text on a computer screen, but here in the dimness of the bar the lettering on the glass was fuzzy and he couldn't make out what it spelled. He wondered how much time he had before he would be unable to function. A year, maybe less.

Next week sometime he would get back in touch with Brown and report why the software malfunctioned. There was no reason to hide anything. Let them think he was being completely honest and above board. The conclusion would have to be that one of the Indian programmers intentionally put a backdoor into the software. Let them prove otherwise. Dan laughed sourly, thinking about how the papers would pick up on the story. Maybe it would end up scaring the shit out of other financial companies that had farmed out critical software. Maybe even drum up some business for him.

That was an interesting thought. He could do more than just scare the shit out of these companies. With a little bit of luck he could create a panic. First thing, write some articles about what happened to Lynn Capital Bank. Fuck, maybe even propose a book about it, detailing the risks to financial institutions and highlighting the case of this bank.

For the first time in a long while Dan felt excited, his mind racing with ideas. All those banks and brokerage firms were going to go crazy when they heard about what happened to Lynn Capital Bank. They'd all be forced to check any software built offshore for possible hidden backdoors. And Dan could do that checking. He could start a software firm tomorrow focusing on that and drum up business with articles and a book. As the ideas swirled in his head, he felt a dryness in his mouth. He looked up and saw the bartender studying him.

"I got to admit," the bartender said. "The drinks did you a world of good. When you came in you looked like shit. You've got your color back. Buddy, you look like a new man."

"Amazing the recuperative properties of a Guinness," Dan said with a wink, his good humor back. "How about another round, both the beer and the shot, see if I can get a bit healthier."

"No problem."

Dan watched him pour the draft. Then his gaze drifted towards the television set and to the Red Sox highlights. The Sox had been playing well of late, winning their last seven games. While he was watching the highlights, they were interrupted by a news flash. The sound was off, but he knew right away what the story was about. Up on the screen as bright as day was Gordon's driver's license photo. Dan felt a sinking feeling in his stomach when he saw that. He had known Gordon would be identified eventually, but realizing it had already happened brought back his uneasiness.

The bartender brought over his drinks. Dan didn't even taste them. He could just as well have been drinking water, or mud for that matter. They had no effect on him. All he felt was an almost unbearable uneasiness and the urge to get moving. He stood up and tossed twenty dollars on to the bar.

He knew the quicker he faced Carol the better. If he waited too long he wouldn't be able to do it. On his way home he decided to play it as straight as possible. Sure enough Carol met him at the door, her face both anxious and excited.

"That was Gordon who was killed," she told him, her words coming out in a breathless rush. "I knew it was him!"

Dan forced himself to meet her eyes. "I know. I was in a bar and saw it on the news."

"This is so unbelievable." Her eyes were wide as they searched his. Dan knew what she was looking for. Some sort of sign that this was a surprise to him too. As strong as the temptation was to look away, he forced himself to maintain eye contact.

"Why would he go to that bank?" she asked.

"I don't know. He was probably looking for work."

Her eyes were still searching his, almost desperately. "They weren't hiring, were they?"

Dan felt himself shaking his head.

"Then why would he go there?"

"God knows. He knew I finished a contract with them. For whatever reason maybe he thought it was worth talking to them. That must've been why he called the other day." He shook his head as he looked away from her. "I have some great news," he said. "This kind of spoils it, though. The bank hired me to examine the software they got from those Indian contractors.

They want me to try to figure out why it didn't work. Guess how much they're paying me?"

Carol shook her head.

"Thirty-two thousand dollars. I had them pay me up front. The money is already in our account."

Dan moved past her. "I know this is kind of weird after what happened to Gordon," he said. "But we should do something to celebrate, maybe go out to dinner."

"Thirty-two thousand dollars," she repeated softly to herself. "Thank God. I was sure we were going to lose the house. But we can't go out. You have your phone interview at seven."

Dan made a face as if he had forgotten about it. "Yeah, well, why don't I blow that off? I've already got a contract."

"It can't hurt to have another one lined up."

She was still studying him, still trying to read something in his expression.

"Yeah, I guess you're right," he admitted. "Well, let's at least have a drink."

The only alcohol left in the liquor cabinet was a bottle of Kahlua that they had brought back from Mexico years ago. Dan opened it, filled two glasses halfway, then added some ice and milk. As Carol sipped hers, the increasingly familiar tense expression returned to her face.

"You don't think Gordon could've been involved in the bank robbery?" she asked.

Dan almost coughed up his drink. Damn, she was intuitive! He knew she wanted to ask more than that.

"You're kidding, right?" he said. "This is Gordon we're talking about. How in the world would he get himself involved in a bank robbery? Come on, let's be serious here."

Her soft blue eyes were holding steady on his, still searching, still trying to uncover something. Finally she looked away. "I don't know," she said. "I guess it was a crazy thought."

"Yeah, it was." Dan finished his drink. Without looking at Carol, he told her he had better go prepare for his interview. He could feel her eyes on him as he left the room. As he sat in his study, he felt shakier than ever. If she was suspecting Gordon of being involved in the robbery, then what else was she suspecting? He already knew the answer to that. He had been able to see it in her eyes. A cold chill went through him. He could imagine what she must be thinking – about his phone calls, his meetings with Joel and Shrini, the rash he had had the other day – and how she must be trying to make sense of all of it. Trying to understand how it could be related to Gordon being killed and that bank being robbed.

He felt both drained and anxious. Like he couldn't move a muscle, but at the same time couldn't sit still. He tried playing back the phone conversations he'd been having, trying to figure out if she could've overheard anything incriminating. He was still doing that when Carol opened the door, her face flushed with relief.

"They caught the person behind the bank robbery," she said. "They just had the story on the news."

"Who was it?" Dan asked. He could feel his heart racing wildly in his chest.

"I can't remember his name," Carol said, a big smile breaking over her face. "Someone connected to the mafia. I think from Revere."

As Dan looked at his wife, he could see all doubt was gone. At that moment her smile looked brighter than any Christmas tree.

Thank God, he thought, *thank fucking God*.

*

Petrenko had sent three of his men to snatch Craig Brown and was pacing impatiently while waiting for them to return. One way or another he was going to get to the bottom of what happened. If it meant skinning another man alive, so be it.

The television set was on in the background. Petrenko was only half paying attention to the news when the story broke about Lombardo's arrest. Slowly, he made the connection between what the reporter was saying and what it meant to him. For a good twenty minutes he stood completely still, the wheels spinning in his head, his eyes as dull and lifeless as sand. In his mind he played out the possible steps he could take next, from kidnapping members of Lombardo's family to having an all-out war with the Boston Mafia. He couldn't see any of them working. The money and diamonds were lost. Dispassionately he accepted that. The best he could do to salvage the situation was to make a deal for the documents that he had lost.

There was a knock on the door. He looked over to see Yuri Tolkov enter the room.

"Did you get him?" Petrenko asked.

Yuri shook his head, his expression blank. In Russian, he said, "A cop was watching him."

"Which one, the *zhid*?"

"No, the other one, his partner, the dumb-looking one. The only way to grab the bank manager is to take care of this cop first. What do you want me to do?"

Petrenko thought about it, frowning heavily. "We'll do it another time. Right now we have more important matters to deal with."

Yuri nodded matter-of-factly. "I heard the news on the radio."

"We'll have to make a deal with the Italians," Petrenko said.

"Are you sure? There are other ways we could handle this."

"None would do us any good."

"I don't know, we could try to—"

"There is no point," Petrenko interrupted, his voice low but edged with violence. "We will do what we need to for now, but later we will pay them back. Don't worry about that."

Dan waited until seven thirty to tell Carol that the hiring manager must be blowing him off.

"He probably found someone cheaper. Son of a bitch couldn't even show me the courtesy of calling me back," he complained.

"These things happen," Carol said.

She seemed a little disappointed, but not too much, probably happy enough that he had gotten his other contract. He knew she was also relieved to think that her suspicions about the bank robbery had been unfounded.

The kids had been home for over an hour. Carol had made a tuna casserole for dinner which none of them really cared for. Still, the mood was better than it had been for the past couple of days, even with the occasional comments Carol made about Gordon. Susie couldn't help smiling a few times at Dan's bland, innocuous jokes and Gary was buzzing about the Sox winning streak. Halfway through dinner Dan had found he was able to look at his kids without being overwhelmed by guilt.

It was now thirty minutes since they'd finished dinner, and the kids were upstairs, Susie plugged into her music and

Gary watching the Sox game. Dan sat on the living room sofa scribbling notes for his book proposal. Carol was next to him, leaning against him while she read the paper. He checked his watch again and saw that it was now seven thirty-three. "The guy's not going to call," he repeated. "Why don't we splurge and take the kids out for some ice cream?"

Carol twisted herself around. Turning his face with her hand, she kissed him hard on the mouth. "That's a wonderful idea," she said. "If we can talk the kids into it."

Susie gave her typical *whatever* response, but her sullen act was half-hearted at best and she joined them without too much of an argument. Gary groused a bit about being torn away from the Sox game, but agreed as long as he could listen to the game in the car. It was the first time they had gone out for ice cream that summer. Since Dan had lost his job they had stopped doing little things like that.

Dan could tell the kids enjoyed the outing. Susie stood close by him, her body at times bumping into his. Gary was his typical good-natured self, happier than usual since it looked like the Sox were on their way to winning an eighth straight game. While they stood eating their ice cream, Carol moved close to Dan and held his hand.

When they returned home there were two messages waiting for him. One from Shrini, another from Peyton Hanes.

"Why don't you call them back tomorrow?" Carol asked.

Dan dreaded calling either of them. "They probably want to talk about Gordon," he said. "I'll call them quickly and get it over with."

"If you have to. Don't spend too long."

Dan nodded. When he got to his study, he stared at the phone for several minutes before calling Peyton. One of Peyton's kids answered and left Dan waiting. After a while, Peyton picked up.

"Hey, hey, Dan," Peyton said. "Man, it's been a while. Can you believe what happened to Gordon?"

"Hard to believe," Dan said.

"Shit, yeah. I saw that drawing on the news last night and it didn't even register that it could be him. Damn, I still can't believe it."

"It's a shock," Dan said.

"Yeah, man, it sure is. Any idea what he was doing in Lynn?"

"With Gordon, who knows?"

"The whole thing is just so fucking bizarre. Listen, I talked to Gordon's parents. The funeral's going to be this Saturday. You'll be there, right?"

"I'd like to, I just don't know if I can make it—"

"Shit, Dan, you've got to come. Gordon's parents are in their eighties. It's got to be tough enough for them to bury their son, but I'm beginning to think no one else is going to show up. Tell me you'll be there, okay?"

"We'll see."

"Man, I expect to see you there."

Peyton gave him directions to the cemetery and hung up. Dan was still staring blindly at the phone when it rang again. From the caller ID he could see it was Shrini. Reluctantly, he picked up the handset.

"Hey, dude," Shrini said angrily. "I've been waiting for you to call back."

"Sorry, Shrini, I just got home."

"You heard the news, right?"

"Yeah."

"Okay, dude, we're on for tomorrow as agreed, right?"

"I think we should wait a few days—"

"Fuck that! You gave me your word before. And believe me, with or without you I'm seeing that little peacock—"

"Okay, okay," Dan interrupted, afraid Carol or one of his kids might pick up the phone and hear Shrini ranting. "I'll stop over tomorrow morning at nine."

"You better, dude."

After Shrini hung up, Dan thought about how he was going to explain this to his wife. At some point the lies were going to have to stop. How many could you keep piling up, one on top of another?

After he had settled on a story, he waited until he could muster the strength to get up, then joined Carol so he could add still more lies to all the rest.

24

At seven the next morning Resnick pulled up in front of Petrenko's address. Settling in, he poured black coffee from a thermos and drank it as he skimmed the stories on the front page of the paper about Lombardo and Gordon Carmichael. After that he found Carmichael's obituary.

As he had guessed, Carmichael was a loner with no wife or kids. The only family mentioned were parents living in Greenwich, Connecticut. The obituary had more about Carmichael's father, a retired industrialist, than it did about the dead man – mentioning only that Carmichael had served in Vietnam, was awarded two Purple Hearts, and after his service earned a degree from Yale before working as an engineer at a number of companies, none of which Resnick had ever heard of.

Shortly after ten, a silver Mercedes pulled into Petrenko's driveway. A man with a thick build, about five foot eight, got out. He was in his late thirties, had blond hair cut close to his scalp and a nose that had been pushed sideways across his face. Resnick recognized him, having seen him with Petrenko several times before, including at the Russian restaurant. The man stared indifferently in Resnick's direction before heading to the front door. It was already eighty degrees in the shade and he was wearing a leather jacket, which told Resnick that the Russian was probably carrying a piece. He considered whether to try picking him up on a weapons charge, but decided to sit still and see where this led.

Ten minutes later Petrenko left the house, escorted by the same man. Petrenko gave Resnick an indifferent look before turning his gaze away. The Mercedes pulled on to the street and Resnick made no attempt to hide the fact that he was following it.

The Mercedes headed into Boston. At Government Center, the car turned towards the North End. When it got to Hanover Street, the car stopped. Petrenko stepped out and walked briskly in the opposite direction, nodding at Resnick as he went past.

Resnick was stuck. The street was too narrow for him to pull over without blocking traffic. He could gamble, drive down Hanover Street, and hope that Petrenko would double back. That seemed like a bad bet. Instead he stayed on the Mercedes. He knew the driver was Petrenko's muscle, and he doubted Petrenko would do any business without him.

At the next street the Mercedes stopped abruptly, forcing Resnick to hit his brakes to keep from rear-ending it. The driver's-side door opened and, in a coordinated move, the driver got out while another man stepped from the sidewalk and took his place behind the wheel. There was still no room for Resnick to pull over. The thick-bodied Russian leered at him as he jogged past. With no other choice Resnick continued following the Mercedes, knowing the best he could do now was pick up Petrenko later. Grudgingly, he had to admire the maneuver Petrenko used to lose him. He made a mental note not to underestimate Petrenko again.

Joel was surprised when he answered the phone and heard his uncle Hymie demanding to know what type of trouble he had gotten himself into.

"Calm down, Uncle Hymie."

"Don't tell me to calm down!" There was a silence, then the old man continued in a low whisper. "A reward is being offered for information about uncut diamonds. Do you want to know who's offering this reward?"

Joel didn't bother answering. He waited for his uncle to tell him it was Viktor Petrenko.

"I've asked about this person," his uncle went on. "He's a thug, a dangerous man. In Russia, he was an interrogator for the KGB. Do you know what that means, Joel? Do you have any idea what type of person you stole from?"

"I don't know what you're talking about. I didn't steal anything."

"You're going to lie to me? You think I'm some *fercockt meshuggina* to believe your nonsense? What's wrong with you to think you could do something like this, getting yourself mixed up with an animal like Petrenko? Do you have brains in your head?"

"Don't you lecture me. I never let Pop talk to me like that and I'm sure as hell not going to let you!"

Joel looked out his window and spotted Dan and his Indian buddy walking up his driveway. *These two fucking momsers have to bother me now?* he thought as he watched them approach.

"You little *pisher*," his uncle was saying. "You're going to talk to your uncle like that?" Then, "Hello, hello? Joel, you still there?"

"Yeah, I'm still here," Joel said. He walked over to his desk, unlocked the bottom drawer and took out a twenty-two caliber semi-automatic handgun. He checked to make sure it was loaded. While he would've liked more firepower, this would have to do. There was a knock on his front door. Peering out a window, he could see the two of them waiting for him. "Uncle, look, I'm sorry about what I said. I lost my temper. But I didn't steal any diamonds." Lowering his voice, "Don't mention any of this to anyone, okay?"

"You really think I'm *fercockt*?" There was a pause, then his uncle added, "Joel, get rid of those diamonds. Throw them away if you have to. Don't be stupid. The next funeral I go to I want to be my own, understand?"

"Uncle Hymie, I appreciate what you're saying. And don't worry about anything."

"I'm not the one who should be worrying. Don't ever talk to me about those diamonds again," his uncle said before hanging up.

Joel stood glowering at the phone handset before throwing it hard across the room. The handset splintered when it hit the wall, scattering pieces across the floor.

That KGB son of a bitch!

He could screw Petrenko several times over if he sent those computer disks and videotapes to the FBI. If they got their hands on that stuff, they'd send that Ruskie to prison for a long fucking time. Joel had looked at enough of it to know what he had. Records of money laundering and payoffs, and if that wasn't enough for that blackmailing KGB son of a bitch, videotapes of sordid sex acts. Well, now the shoe was on the other foot. Joel knew he wouldn't be able to unload those diamonds while Petrenko was on the streets, but if he could figure out a way to send a package to the FBI without having to worry about it being traced back to him...

There was another knock on the door. Joel remembered Dan and his friend standing out there. Holding the gun waist-high, he swung the door open.

"Are you two fucking morons?" Joel asked, his mouth frozen in a hard sneer. "I told you what would happen if I saw either of you again."

Dan took a step back on seeing the gun. His friend inched forward, his muscles tensing.

"Take a step back now, Gunga, or you're dead."

Shrini's eyes moved from the gun to Joel's face. Reluctantly, he followed Joel's order.

"This isn't going to work," Dan said. "You're going to have to give us our cut."

"As far as I'm concerned, it's working just fine. The frame for that Mafioso worked as planned and I'm sitting with all the money. I don't see any reason why I should give you shit."

"Joel, you know this isn't fair—"

"Fuck you. I warned you what would happen if your nutso pal screwed things up for us." Joel grimaced as he absent-mindedly rubbed his jaw. "Because of Gordon I have to live with that dead girl on my conscience the rest of my life."

"We all have to."

"But I shouldn't." Joel shook his head, trying to force out the thought that Eric, and by extension himself, had contributed to what happened. "Sorry, Dan," he said. "You're not getting a dime."

"Joel, we saw how much money we took from those boxes. There's enough for all of us."

"Forget it. You're the one who promised Gordon would behave himself. This is your fault, not mine."

"Okay, let's say it's my fault. At least give Shrini his cut."

"I'm not doing that." Joel shifted his gaze to Shrini. "Take my advice, Gunga, just be grateful you're still alive."

Shrini had been fuming. This was too much for him. "Can you believe this peacock?" he exclaimed. "We plan the robbery, invite him along and he's going to strut about believing he and his pig friend deserve all the money!"

"Peacock, huh?" Joel's mouth dropped into a humorless grin. "Eh, I've been called worse. And guess what? It doesn't matter whether I think I deserve all the money. What matters is I got all the money."

"What do you mean you've got all the money?" Dan asked. He took another small step backwards. "What about your buddy?"

"Eric's not around any more."

"You're kidding, right?"

Joel didn't bother to answer him.

"Dammit, Joel! You're trying to send the police after all of us?"

"Don't get hysterical. Nobody's going to miss him."

As the three of them stood staring at each other, the anger brewing inside of Shrini boiled over.

"You're a coward," Shrini said to Joel. "A peacock with a big yellow tail. Believe me, if you weren't holding a gun I'd kick you and your tail feathers all over the place."

"I'm getting sick of this," Joel said, his grin completely gone, his eyes turning glassy. He faced Dan. "Give me one good reason why I don't get rid of both of you right now?"

"Carol knows I'm seeing you," Dan started to say. His voice cracked. He had to swallow before he could continue. "If I don't come home later, she'll send the police here."

"So? What do you think they'd find? I know plenty of places in New Hampshire where I can bury two bodies." He aimed the gun towards Shrini's chest, then remembered Eric. The cops would probably bring corpse-sniffing dogs to search his property. Those dogs would find him. Even without the dogs, the cops would be able to spot his grave easily enough. If he were to kill these two, he'd have to dig up Eric and move his corpse as well. He'd also have to explain to the cops why it looked like he had a freshly dug grave on his property. The thought of doing all that tired him out. Lowering his gun, he told the two of them to beat it. "If I see either of you again, you're dead," he said.

"I'm not leaving without my money," Shrini insisted.

Giving him one last weary look, Joel shot Shrini in the foot.

"Ow, ow, ow!" Shrini howled, hopping up and down. Dismayed, he turned to Dan. "This peacock shot me," he said, still not quite believing it himself.

"Next one will be through the heart," Joel warned. "Get out of here, both of you."

"Joel, what the fuck's wrong with you?" Dan demanded. He waved a hand towards Shrini's wounded foot. "How are we going to explain this?"

"You're a smart guy. You'll think of something."

"You goddamned asshole—"

Joel stopped him with a look. "I meant what I said before. We're through, Dan. I like Carol, but if I see you again she's a widow. Now you've got ten seconds to get the hell out of here! Ten... nine... eight..."

"Joel, think about what you're doing!"

"Seven... six..."

"For Chrissakes, we've known each other twenty years!"

"Four... Three..."

Dan could tell from the way Joel's eyes had glazed over that none of that mattered. There was nothing he could say. No way to get through to him.

Putting his arm around Shrini's shoulder, Dan helped him down the driveway. He knew if he as much as looked back, Joel would shoot him.

Petrenko sat in the back room of a small Italian restaurant on Prince Street. Yuri stood to his right. Across from him sat "Uncle Pete" Stellini. Stellini, close to three hundred pounds and almost as wide as he was tall, was in his sixties with gray hair that had been dyed black and a face as round as the moon. Petrenko had dug around enough to find out that Stellini's nickname "Uncle" didn't come from his friendly fatherly appearance, but from when he was younger and doing collections. The story was that when he got his hands on a deadbeat, he'd twist the guy's arm behind his back and make the guy say "uncle" before he broke it. Three of Stellini's men now stood behind him, all of them smirking as they stared at Petrenko. They were all out of shape, all carrying at least an extra fifty pounds. Even though Yuri's gun had been taken before they were brought back to meet Stellini, Petrenko had no doubt that he and Yuri could dispatch all of these Italians if they had to.

"What can I get you?" Stellini offered, a warm smile stretched across his face. "Cappuccino, espresso? I can't have you sitting there with nothing."

"Espresso. A double."

Stellini ordered one of his men to get Petrenko his drink. "And bring a plate of biscotti," Stellini said with a wink towards his guest.

"Now, I gotta tell you, I appreciate you coming to talk to us like this," Stellini said. "You could've gone off and done something stupid instead, and Viktor, that wouldn't have been good for anyone. Now here's the thing. Forget about what you've been seeing on the news. Ray had nothin' to do with that bank job."

This was pretty much what Petrenko had expected him to say. "Is that so?" he asked.

"Yeah, it is."

Stellini maintained a casual, friendly appearance as he looked at Petrenko. Absent-mindedly, he popped a couple of pieces of candy into his mouth. Realizing it, he held a paper bag out to Petrenko. "Chocolate malt balls," he said. "You want one?"

Petrenko shook his head.

"I dunno, I'm addicted to these things," Stellini said. "Of all the things I could be eating, it's gotta be this shit. What are ya gonna do, you know?"

One of the wise guys returned with the espresso and biscotti. Petrenko sipped the espresso slowly, his eyes colder than any rattlesnake's as he stared at Stellini.

"Now, as I was saying," Stellini continued, his manner no different than if he had been talking to a long-time acquaintance. "Ray had nothin' to do with that bank. Those pictures, they're fake. This is nothin' but a frame."

"They look authentic," Petrenko said.

"You gotta give the FBI credit. They've been trying to squeeze Ray for over a year now, trying to get him to turn rat. Ain't gonna happen. So this bank job goes down and they must've got the brilliant idea to manufacture that videotape. They did a fuckin' nice job with it too. If I didn't know better, I'd swear that was Ray myself."

"So would I."

Stellini showed a hurt look on his expansive face. "You think I'm lying to you about this?"

Petrenko took a last sip of his espresso before placing the cup on the table. When he looked back up at Stellini there was nothing at all human left in his eyes. "I know the money stolen from me is lost," he said. "But I need the other items returned."

"The *coglionis* on this asshole," one of the wise guys said. "He's going to come here and call you a liar."

Stellini raised a hand to shut the man up. "I don't think he's saying that. The guy's upset, and you know, who can blame him?" Then to Petrenko, "I can't promise anything, but if you want I can ask around, see if I find anything. How's that sound?"

Stony-faced, Petrenko asked what this would cost him.

"Twenty grand," Stellini said. "I'm gonna have to spread some money around, and I'll be lucky to make a nickel out of this, if you understand what I'm saying. But I wanta do this 'cause I'm happy you came to me first, especially under the circumstances. As I said, I can't make any promises. Right now I don't got a fuckin' clue who did this."

Petrenko shrugged. "Twenty thousand, okay."

"Now, as I'm saying, I can't promise nothin'. But I'll do the best I can."

Petrenko leaned back in his chair, his eyes unblinking while he stared at Stellini. "I need those items," he said.

"Yeah, I know. I heard you. Just don't expect any miracles."

"If I don't get them this way, I will have to try another."

"I hope that's not a threat," Stellini said. He frowned,

popped a couple more chocolate malt balls into his mouth. "So far we've left you alone, and I gotta tell you, I got friends who ain't too happy about that. We know you got a nice thing going, but as far as I'm concerned, the world's big enough for all of us, right? So we've been nice and kept out of your business. And now I'm going out of my way to help you out. So a little respect, *capisce*?"

Petrenko told him curtly that he appreciated his help.

"That's all I wanted to hear. I'll try my best to find out who knocked over that bank. When I find out, you'll find out. And forget about Ray. The FBI, they're not as smart as they think. Their frame's not going to hold. A few days, tops, Ray's gonna be exonerated."

Petrenko hoped he was right. At that moment he'd give anything to have Raymond Lombardo out of custody and in his hands.

Dan had to drive around the backwoods of New Hampshire for twenty minutes before he found a drug store. After buying aspirin, antiseptic, gauze and bandage tape, he returned to the car to find Shrini with his sneaker off and in the process of removing a blood-filled sock. His friend looked pale and was sweating badly. Resting for a moment, Shrini swallowed a handful of aspirin. Then, moving gingerly, he finished taking off the sock.

The good news: the bullet had gone through his foot and was found rolling around in his sneaker. The bad news: his foot was a mess.

"Ow, ow," Shrini cried while Dan tried to clean the wound with antiseptic. The bullet had hit Shrini under his ankle and the wound was still bleeding. Since Dan didn't know what else to do, he pushed some gauze against the wound and wrapped it tight with tape. As he applied pressure, Shrini clenched his teeth hard enough that Dan could hear them grind.

"I am going to kill your friend," Shrini forced out, tears streaming down his face.

"Come on, don't talk like that."

"You are joking, right?"

"We're not killers."

"After what he did to me, I will gladly kill him."

Shrini squeezed his eyes shut. "Ow, ow," he cried. "I think that bullet broke bones in my foot."

Dan stared at him, frozen, with no idea what to do. Finally, he started the car. "We've got to get out of here," he said.

For the next half hour the only sound as they drove was Shrini moaning every few minutes.

"I can't drive you to a hospital," Dan said at last. "I'm already connected to the bank because of the security system. If I get connected to this, everything could blow up on us. Do you think you can wait until we get back and drive yourself?"

Shrini nodded, his teeth clenched tight.

"How are you going to explain this?"

Showing a bitter smile, he said, "I am going to tell the police that your friend shot me."

"What?"

"I won't give them his name. But I will describe him and give them his license plate number. I will tell them he shot me after a traffic dispute."

"You can't do that."

"Why not? The police will arrest him. Then we can break

into his house and take back our money." Shrini stopped for a moment, his breathing labored. When he could, he added, "We will teach your peacock friend a lesson he'll never forget."

"Shrini, that paranoid son of a bitch probably has the money so well hidden we'd never find it."

"I am willing to take that chance."

Dan thought about the idea, shook his head. "He'd take us down with him."

"You're the one being paranoid now."

"I don't think so. I know Joel. He'd drag us all to death row just to make a point."

"I don't believe that."

"You can't send the police after him," Dan said. As he thought about the consequences of Shrini doing that his lower back went into spasm, the pain sucking his breath away. For a long moment he couldn't breathe in air. When the spasm subsided, he saw his knuckles were bone-white as he gripped the wheel.

"Dude," Shrini said, laughing weakly, "you're sweating worse than me."

Dan pulled over. He took several aspirin and chewed them slowly. When he trusted himself to drive again, he pulled the car back on to the road.

"We never should have robbed that bank," Dan said.

"Believe me, our mistake wasn't robbing that bank. It was inviting Gordon and that peacock along."

Dan was shaking his head. "We shouldn't have done it, Shrini. We fucked up. The best thing we can do now is forget about the bank and move forward the best we can. I told you my business idea. Let's just do it and make some money together."

Hesitating, he added, "I'll give you half of the thirty-two grand I was paid."

"No way, dude. We robbed that bank and I'm getting my share." Shrini grimaced as a jolt of pain shot through him. His voice tight, he added, "I am not letting your peacock friend get away with this."

"Jesus Christ, Shrini, can't you see how fucking pointless this is? Two people are already dead—"

"Three people. You forgot he killed his pig-friend also."

"Goddamn it, you were shot through the foot. Isn't that enough? When's this going to be over?"

"Ask your friend."

"Come on, man, if we try my business idea, we might end up making more money than we took in the robbery."

"That is not the money I want. Believe me, I am going to get my cut, with or without your help."

Dan turned and saw the determination and anger set in Shrini's face. There was no point trying to talk sense into him, at least not now.

When they were a few miles from Shrini's apartment complex, Dan asked Shrini to give him a week. "Don't send the cops after Joel, okay? Just give me that time to figure something out."

Shrini was shaking his head.

"Please, just one week. That's all I'm asking. Afterwards do whatever you want."

Reluctantly, Shrini agreed. "One week," he said. "After that I'm taking care of matters my own way."

Dan swung into the apartment complex, pulled up alongside Shrini's Civic and helped Shrini into it. After Shrini drove off,

Dan noticed blood stains on the passenger floor mat and seat. The leather interior had been treated so he should be able to clean the blood off the seat, but he was going to have to buy a new floor mat and hope Carol wouldn't notice. If she did, there would be the inevitable questions and yet more lies. That was the least of his problems though.

Even given a week, or a year for that matter, he couldn't see how he was going to figure out anything as far as Joel and Shrini went.

Stopping at a strip mall, he bought some supplies and cleaned up as best he could. There were red smudges ingrained in the leather that he couldn't get out. No amount of scrubbing seemed to help. After a while he gave up trying and tossed the floor mat and the leftover supplies into a dumpster. He'd wait until the next day to buy a new floor mat and to get the interior cleaned. He felt too tired at that moment to do much of anything but head home.

When Carol saw him, she asked what was wrong.

"Nothing. I'm just beat. Why?"

"You have blood on your shirt."

He looked down and saw she was right. "I had a nosebleed. Nothing too serious."

"I can't remember you ever having one before."

"What can I tell you. I had one. It happens, okay?"

"Okay," she said, hurt. "You don't have to bite my head off."

"Sorry, I'm just tired. And having a nosebleed kind of threw me. I'm going upstairs to lie down for a few minutes." As he walked past her, she told him Peyton called. "He's going to pick us up tomorrow at twelve."

Puzzled, Dan asked what for.

Her eyes narrowed as she looked at him. "Gordon's funeral. He said he already talked to you about it. You were planning on us going, weren't you?"

From the way she was studying him, he knew he had no choice in the matter. Not unless he wanted to bring back her suspicions from the other day. "I guess I'd forgotten about it," he said.

25

"You sleeping in there? We've got laws in this city against public loitering."

Maguire opened his eyes but didn't bother looking out his driver's-side window. It was one of those hot, muggy summer days. Not even ten o'clock yet and over ninety degrees. Maguire looked uncomfortable, his shirt collar soaked through, perspiration beading his neck and face. He said, "I saw you when you pulled up behind Petrenko."

Resnick stood next to Maguire's Ford Mustang, holding a cup of Dunkin' Donuts coffee. "I take it Brown's inside."

Maguire nodded. "He's been in there since the bank opened." Rolling his eyes, he added, "I never got a chance to thank you for recommending me for this assignment. Nothing I enjoy more during the summer than sitting for hours in a hot, stuffy car. It's been a thrill a minute."

Resnick took a sip of his coffee and burned the inside of his mouth. "Not my fault. I recommended someone watch Brown. Putting you on him was Hadley's idea. He's trying to keep us busy until the FBI wraps up their deal with Lombardo."

"He's got you on Petrenko?"

"Yeah." Resnick blew on the coffee before taking another sip. "Viktor had some business in the North End yesterday, probably meeting with one of Lombardo's bosses."

"Probably?"

"I lost him for an hour."

"Tough luck. It would've been nice to know who he met with."

"How about you, anything going on with Brown?"

"Sort of." Maguire wiped a hand across his forehead, the sweat spiking up his hair. "Thursday night a van slowed down in front of his house and then drove off. The windows were tinted, so I couldn't see inside, but my gut was they drove off only because they spotted me."

"Did you get a license plate?"

"Yep. Van's owned by a dry-cleaner on Forrest Street. The Russian owner looked scared when I talked to him. He claimed the van was stolen."

Resnick shook his head. "They were going to try to snatch Brown."

"Probably, but nothing we can prove." Maguire raised an eyebrow. "Petrenko's been in there over ten minutes. Do you think one of us should go in and check up on him?"

"Petrenko's not going to do anything. He knows we're both out here." Resnick gave a thoughtful look as he took another sip of his coffee. "Unless he loses his temper."

Maguire started to look nervous. He wiped his hand across his forehead again and up over his scalp, the sweat now matting down his hair. "I'm going to take a lot of shit if something happens to Brown. I better go in there."

"Relax. Petrenko's a bank customer, he's got every right to be in there. And who knows, maybe we'll get lucky and be able to bring assault charges against him. Let's give him another ten minutes."

Maguire settled back in his seat. "Whatever you say. You're the senior detective here."

Resnick finished his coffee, crumpled the Styrofoam cup and slipped it into his pants pocket. "Any idea how long a drive it is to Greenwich, Connecticut?" he asked.

"Over three hours. Why?"

"I'm thinking of going to a funeral."

Shrini's foot hurt like hell. He took another codeine tablet – his fourth since he'd woken up, although with the drugs he'd been given he wasn't so much sleeping as passing out.

As he had suspected, the bullet had broken his ankle and three bones in his foot. The story he gave at the emergency room was that he accidentally shot himself while hunting up in New Hampshire. The doctor seemed skeptical, but didn't push him or get the police involved. Didn't even question him as to why he drove back to Massachusetts before seeking medical attention. After cleaning out the wound and setting a cast from his shin to his toe, he was released. The doctor gave Shrini the name of a specialist for him to contact. If the bones weren't setting right he would need surgery. Also, there was a chance he'd develop arthritis and end up with a limp.

He felt thirsty and wanted a Coke, but that meant he'd have to hobble over to the refrigerator. He had his leg propped up on the sofa, and while he sat staring at the fiberglass cast covering his foot, he thought up ways of getting even with that strutting peacock. One idea in particular struck him. As miserable as he felt, as much as the dull ache from his foot seemed to throb throughout his body, he couldn't keep from smiling when he thought over that particular idea.

Craig Brown crossed one leg over the other, his face set in a smug frown as he talked in circles about why the bank wasn't responsible for Petrenko's losses. Petrenko had already heard one mealy-mouthed excuse after the next about why the security system had failed to work properly, and now this. When he first entered the bank manager's office there was a small amount of fear in the man's eyes. But as Brown mistook Petrenko's seemingly patient, almost passive behavior for acquiescence, the fear dissolved, replaced by an air of superiority. The more he talked the more emboldened he became, thinking that Petrenko was here to play by the rules. This worm of a man actually believed he had the upper hand.

"It's stated in the contract you signed that we can't be held responsible for any items lost from a safety deposit box," Brown explained. He stopped to search through a stack of papers before finding a copy of the contract. He held the paper out to Petrenko, who ignored it.

"The contract states clearly that it is your responsibility to insure the contents of your safety deposit box against theft," he added.

"My boxes were the only ones broken into, correct?"

"I understand how that may seem—"

"How did they find out which boxes I owned?" Petrenko asked.

"I couldn't say."

Petrenko smiled thinly. "If I were you I would figure out a way that I could say."

Brown frowned, clearing his throat. "I don't appreciate threats—"

"No, please don't mistake this for a threat. Somehow these criminals knew which boxes I owned. I would like to know how."

"Maybe they received the information from you," Brown answered stiffly.

"That is not possible. Who at this bank would have access to my box numbers?"

Brown's color paled as he realized the information was stored in a database that almost any of the employees could access. "I don't know," he said.

Petrenko nodded to himself, understanding Brown's reaction. In his pocket he had a hypodermic needle filled with enough digoxin to induce a fatal heart attack. When injected into a person's gums, it is nearly impossible for a medical examiner to find the puncture mark and rule the death anything other than a heart attack. This was not new to him. He had used digoxin before in the Soviet Union on state prisoners, knew the effect it had on the victim, how much noise would be made and how long it would take before death. Of course, the two cops outside would find this man's death suspicious, but let them prove otherwise. Petrenko stared at Brown and tried to decide whether to keep playing this game or use the necessary force to make this man talk. After he extracted the information he needed, the digoxin would be used.

"I don't understand your complaint," Brown added, his lips pulling his mouth into a haughty frown. "According to your statement to the police, your boxes were empty at the time of the robbery."

Petrenko nodded visibly this time. His hand slid into his pocket, feeling the hypodermic needle. In a second he could be standing next to this bank manager, his hand against the man's throat. He would let Brown know what would happen if he didn't start telling the truth. Then, afterwards, he would apply just enough pressure to the man's throat to make him start to scream. As soon as his mouth opened wide enough, the hypodermic needle would be used. Petrenko had little doubt that this man had worked with Raymond Lombardo, providing Lombardo with his box numbers and arranging for the security system to fail. While he knew that there was nothing Brown could tell him to help him get back his possessions, he needed to know if anyone else inside the bank was involved because one way or another they were all going to pay for it.

"This is a waste of my time," Petrenko remarked. He stood up, started towards the door, stopped. "I want a copy of my contract."

The time it took for Brown to turn towards the copy machine located behind him would be all Petrenko needed. He stood patiently, bracing himself, feeling the point of the hypodermic needle. Brown started to get out of his chair. There was a rap on the door, which simultaneously opened, and the *zhid* cop walked in.

"Craig, I'm sorry to interrupt you, but I have a few more questions," Resnick said, all the while looking impassively at Petrenko.

"That's quite all right, Detective. I believe you know Viktor

Petrenko. He will be leaving right after I make him a copy of some paperwork."

While Brown made the copy, Resnick noticed Petrenko remove a hand from his pants pocket, his fist clenching and unclenching. Petrenko took the paper from the bank manager, and when he turned to leave, Resnick nodded to him.

"Be seeing you around, Viktor."

Petrenko nodded back, his eyes as dull as stone.

Dan sat up front with Peyton, Carol in the back with Wendy. At one time they had been close friends, but after Peyton struck it rich they drifted apart. Dan knew it was mostly because of his own pettiness. He had worked as hard as Peyton over the years and it pissed him off that Peyton had made it and he hadn't. The last year and a half being out of work, he had ignored the occasional phone calls from Peyton until they stopped entirely. This was the first time Dan had seen him in over two years, but they were quickly settling into their old friendship. There was none of the usual awkwardness that comes with someone you haven't seen in years. While they drove to Connecticut in Peyton's new Lexus SUV, Dan told him about the book and articles he was intending to write and then his plan to start a business examining outsourced software for potential backdoors.

"That's a fucking great idea," Peyton said.

"What I like about it is it can be started with very little capital," Dan said. "A hundred thousand, and I think I could get this going."

"Maybe I can help you out. Let's talk later, okay, man? Call me next week."

"Sure." Dan paused, added, "As long as you don't string me along like you did with Gordon and his Texas open-pit barbecue."

Dan had meant the comment as a joke, but as soon as it came out he knew it was more pettiness rearing its ugly head. He wanted to kick himself. Peyton gave a pained, almost apologetic smile.

"Yeah, well, I guess I deserved that." Lowering his voice to a conspiratorial whisper he added, "I'll explain about that later, okay, man?"

"Forget it. You don't have to. Me, I don't think I would've wanted to go into business with Gordon either."

"It's not that." Peyton checked the rearview mirror, saw that Carol and Wendy were engaged in a heated conversation. Keeping his voice low, he said, "I would've given Gordon the money as a gift, but Wendy didn't want me to. She was afraid Gordon would be over to the house all the time if we started a business together. As it was, she wanted me to wean him away from us. Shit, man, I wanted to help him out, but there was nothing I could do without pissing off the wife."

"I was joking more than anything else."

Peyton didn't bother saying *bullshit*, but the look he gave Dan indicated as much. "Do you have any idea what Gordon was doing in Lynn?" he asked.

"No idea. All I can think of is he knew I had finished a contract with that bank. He must've gotten it in his head that if they hired me there was a chance they'd hire him."

"That makes no sense."

"Yeah, I know, but we're talking about Gordon."

As they drove, Peyton remarked how weird life was going to be without Gordon around. After all, he had known Gordon almost half his life. There was a note of remorse in Peyton's voice. At one point he seemed to choke up. Dan felt nothing, but he played along and pretended to be equally affected by Gordon's passing.

How in the world could he be expected to feel anything?

After what Gordon did to those two women?

The way Gordon screwed him?

And he did screw him. All he asked of the guy was to keep his mouth shut for ten minutes. Don't do anything crazy for ten lousy minutes. He couldn't do it, though. He had to turn the robbery into shit.

As much as he'd like to, Dan couldn't blame Joel for the way he was acting. He couldn't blame Shrini either. He knew trying to get Shrini's cut from Joel was pointless, and he knew trying to talk Shrini out of it was just as pointless. The damn thing was going to end up with one or the other of them dead. All he could hope for was when the dust settled he'd somehow be left out of it. Thinking about that exhausted him. He closed his eyes, sat back and listened to Peyton reminisce about all the good times with Gordon.

The funeral service was scheduled to take place at the grave site. When they arrived at the grave, there were only a handful of people standing around. Aside from the minister and the cemetery workers, there were six mourners, all elderly. Although Dan had never met Gordon's parents he had heard enough stories about them to be able to pick them out. Gordon's father was a tall man in his eighties, his mother short, plump, exuding both a cheeriness and sadness at the same time. Even though Gordon was their only child, his father had written him out of his will years ago simply because he didn't feel his son measured up. Gordon had told Dan that if his old man died first, he was sure his mom would write him back into the will, but he thought there was little chance of that happening. In fact, Gordon was convinced his old man would outlive him. Although Gordon never talked about it, Dan knew the reason he signed up for the Vietnam War was to try to win his father's approval, since the senior Carmichael had been a decorated war hero during World War II. Likewise the reason he later went to Yale. Neither of them helped. According to his father, Yale wasn't the same as Harvard and the Vietnam War was a national disgrace.

As they approached the grave, Gordon's father stared at them disapprovingly before looking away, his face set in a harsh scowl. Peyton introduced himself. Gordon's father stood silently, his scowl deepening.

"I am so sorry for your loss," Peyton said.

The senior Carmichael nodded grimly. Dry-eyed, he commented that he never understood how a grown man could waste his life doing something as frivolous as playing with computers. Gordon's mother touched Dan's arm, her eyes moistening with tears. She thanked Dan for being there.

The service was short. The minister didn't have much to say about Gordon, mostly talked about how his death would affect his parents. Near the end of the service, Dan could feel someone staring at him. He turned and spotted a man sitting in a late-model Buick. The guy was definitely staring at him and, as Dan stared back, he couldn't help feeling that he had seen this man before. Then he remembered where.

Somehow he kept himself under control and nodded to the detective who returned his nod. He forced himself to face forward. The minister's words blurred together into a monotonous hum. As he swallowed, he could feel a fuzziness coating his throat, then a coldness pushing hard into his skull. A shadow fell over his eyes and the world started to slip sideways on him.

I'm going to pass out right here, Dan thought. *Well, fuck it, let them think I was overcome with grief.*

But he knew the cop wouldn't think that.

The moment passed. Gripping the seat of his chair with both hands, he kept himself upright. While his heart was beating wildly, he knew he was no longer going to pass out. He just had to think this through. It made perfect sense for that cop to come here. Why should he have expected anything different? And as far as that cop now connecting him to Gordon, so what? It didn't matter. They had already pinned the robbery and shootings on Raymond Lombardo. So now he just had to stay calm...

"Are you okay?"

He turned to Carol. "I don't know, I was just thinking about Gordon," he said. "I'll be okay."

Carol took hold of his hand and squeezed it.

The service ended. He didn't want to walk back to Peyton's SUV and have to pass that cop. Instead, he wandered over to the minister and engaged him in small talk. He was trying to steel himself for what was coming when he felt a tap on his shoulder.

"Dan Wilson?"

Dan turned, forcing a confused smile as he looked back at the cop. "I thought you looked familiar. Detective...?"

"Alex Resnick."

"That's right."

Carol was looking on. Dan introduced her to Resnick and told her he had met Resnick the other day when he met with Brown, that the detective was investigating the bank robbery. "Anything I can help you with?" he asked.

"This is quite a coincidence," Resnick said. "I didn't expect to see you here."

"Small world, huh? Gordon and I were good friends. We worked off and on together for almost twenty years."

"I saw his obituary had him as an engineer. So he was a computer programmer like you?"

"Software engineer, that's right."

Resnick glanced around. "Doesn't look like he had many other friends."

"Connecticut is a fair hike from Boston."

"I'm sure plenty of people from his community theater would've come if the funeral were closer," Peyton's wife, Wendy, volunteered.

Resnick raised an eyebrow as he turned to her. "Community theater? Was Gordon an actor?"

"No, nothing like that. He was some sort of makeup guru."

"No kidding?"

"He's been doing community theater for years."

"I saw on the news you caught the guy behind the robbery," Dan said.

"It looks that way."

"That's a relief. At least the guy will pay for what he did." Dan paused. "Did he tell you yet how he broke the security system?"

Resnick shook his head.

"I'm still studying the software and I think I'm close to figuring it out," Dan said. "As I thought, a backdoor was added. A pretty clever one, actually. I need a little more time to finish things up. Maybe another day. With some luck I'll be able to meet with Craig Brown again on Monday."

Resnick smiled thinly. "That was quick."

"Not really. I'm pretty good at what I do."

Peyton put a hand around Dan's shoulder. "This guy's being modest. He's one of the best."

Resnick looked past them towards Gordon's parents. "I don't want to hold you guys up," he said. Looking at Carol, he asked if he could reach her at the same number Dan had given him.

"I'd hope so since I'm living at home with my husband." Carol moved closer to Dan, her grip tightening on his arm.

Resnick took a notepad and pen from his inside jacket pocket and handed it to Peyton, asking if he could write down his and his wife's names, along with a phone number and address in case he needed to contact them. After Peyton handed him back the notepad, Resnick excused himself, telling them he needed to have a few words with Gordon's parents.

On their way back to the SUV, Peyton and Wendy commented on the police showing up at the funeral. Dan couldn't pay attention to what they were saying. All he could think about was the glint in Resnick's eyes when Wendy mentioned that Gordon used to do makeup for a community theater. The way Carol gripped his arm, he had a sick feeling she had noticed that glint also.

26

Resnick didn't believe in coincidences. Fate he believed in, and he had no doubt that it was fate that sent him to Carmichael's funeral. As soon as he spotted Dan Wilson, he knew the guy was involved somehow and when he heard about Carmichael's community theater work, he started to get an idea how.

Resnick couldn't help shaking his head as it occurred to him that Wilson had forced the bank to pay him thirty-two grand to find a backdoor that he had snuck in himself. No kidding he found it so quickly.

As he drove back to Massachusetts, Resnick realized what it was about the robbery videotape that had been bothering him. In his mind he played back the scene of the second victim, Mary O'Donnell, being kicked over on to her back. Concentrating, he slowed it down, seeing it play out frame by frame. As if a pause button had been hit, the scene froze on the gunman's foot being raised. Then a close-up of the sneaker the gunman wore. Then on the logo.

Fuck...

In his mind's eye he could see the logo as clear as day. The one star logo used by Converse. He had Carmichael's report memorized.

Victim at time of death was wearing Grateful Dead T-shirt, khaki-colored short pants, white Converse basketball sneakers...

Resnick pulled the Buick over to the access lane and called the Lynn Memorial Hospital using his cell phone. He'd been contacting the hospital regularly, keeping up with Mary O'Donnell's progress, and knew she was now expected to recover. He was put on hold for several minutes and then transferred to a Dr. Carl Warner. O'Donnell was now alert and able to talk, but since Resnick still had a three-hour drive to get back to Lynn he wouldn't be able to see her until the next day. Even then, Dr. Warner didn't want Resnick to spend more than five minutes with her. Resnick agreed to Warner's request and arranged a time when he could see her.

He swung back on to the highway. Images from the robbery videotape popped into his mind. He could picture the person who had masqueraded as Raymond Lombardo stopping after the robbery to take off his ski mask. There was no question that the person had posed for the camera, and Dan Wilson would've known where the security cameras were located. He was about the same height as Lombardo and had a similar body type, maybe thirty pounds lighter, but that could've been taken care of by some padding under the overalls. The makeup job was first rate, especially the nose and jaw. There was no reason that couldn't have been Dan Wilson.

So Wilson had fixed the software so it would break. If he could've done that, he could have also hacked into the bank's records and discovered who owned which safety deposit boxes. He had to have done some homework, found out who Petrenko was and then come up with his plan. Break into Petrenko's boxes and frame Raymond Lombardo for the robbery. It was damn clever. Wilson must've guessed that Petrenko wouldn't be able to report what was stolen from him; likewise, that the FBI and police wouldn't give up on the Lombardo frame unless they were forced to.

As Resnick thought over the planning that went into the robbery, he found himself grudgingly admiring it. None of them were professionals, probably all of them software geeks. And they pulled this off. At least almost. Wilson couldn't have anticipated the sequence of events that led to the shootings. If that hadn't happened – if they had just ripped off Petrenko and framed Lombardo – Resnick could almost just shake Wilson's hand and tell him good job. Almost. But that's not what happened. Margaret Williams ended up brutally murdered and Mary O'Donnell badly injured. There was a price that had to be paid, not just by Gordon Carmichael, but by Dan Wilson and the other people involved, even if they'd had no idea Carmichael would flip out the way he did. As far as Carmichael went, he pretty much got what he deserved...

Resnick tried to think through what must have happened outside the bank. Carmichael had to have cut through the shrubs before they had him take his overalls off, that had to be why there was no plant debris found on him. Then after collecting his ski mask and gun, they shot him with the same gun he had used inside the bank. They must have had him take off his ski mask first, otherwise fibers from the mask would've been left in his bullet wound.

A thought stopped Resnick. What if they shot him first and then took his overalls off? If they did, they screwed up. The lack of any blood on his body or clothes would be sufficient proof that he had been wearing something else at the time he was shot. Both that and the Converse sneaker could be enough circumstantial evidence to tie Carmichael to the robbery and shootings.

Resnick found Kathleen Liciano's card in his wallet and called her cell phone. When she picked up, she seemed surprised to hear from him.

"I'm sorry to bother you like this," Resnick said, "but do you remember if any blood was found on Gordon Carmichael's body or clothing?"

"No, none. The only traces I found were on his face and neck." She paused. "I would've expected blood to have sprayed on him, especially with the blood patterns I found on the pavement near his body. Why are you asking about this?"

"I'm working on an idea. Any chance you can meet me at your office in three hours?"

"You're talking eight o'clock on a Saturday night?"

"I know, I'm sorry. I'll owe you."

"I'll make a deal," she said, her voice softer. "Take me out for a few drinks afterwards."

Resnick, taken off guard, hesitated for a second and then agreed to the deal.

They had spent almost two hours in Kathleen Liciano's office going over videotapes, photos and other evidence and were now sitting in a martini bar off Newbury Street. Liciano wore tight black Capri pants and a matching short-sleeved polo shirt. Resnick felt disheveled in the same gray suit he had worn all day. Their drinks were brought over. Resnick had ordered a scotch and soda, Liciano a vodka martini.

Resnick took a sip of his drink. He felt awkward as he looked at Liciano. When he met her days earlier her hair had been pulled up and her expression serious and businesslike. Now, as she sat across from him, her brown hair flowed past her shoulders and she was smiling with a slight playfulness. Relaxed, her almond-shaped eyes half closed, she was stunning. He also realized that she was at least ten years younger than him. He took another sip of his drink and found himself looking away from her.

He asked, "Any way we can prove the sneakers the shooter wore in the videotape were the same ones Carmichael had on?"

Liciano fished an olive out of her martini and popped it into her mouth, her eyes thoughtful while she chewed. "I think all we can prove is that they're the same brand," she said. "If the videotape showed the sneaker's tread, then maybe."

"I should still be able to build a circumstantial case against Carmichael," Resnick said. "We've got the same brand of sneakers, unexplained absence of blood on his body and clothes and your computer analysis showing the shooter being the same weight and height. It will then be a matter of convincing the courts to give me access to his phone records."

"What then?"

"If I find any calls to Dan Wilson, I can start building a circumstantial case against him. Right now I have no hard evidence linking Wilson to anything. But if I can get the courts to allow me to dig into his phone and bank records I'll find something."

Resnick could tell that his embarrassment was amusing her. He felt a hotness in his face and knew he was blushing, which made him feel even more embarrassed. Staring at his drink, he muttered, "There's no question in my mind that Wilson's behind this bank robbery. I now have to prove it."

"Alex, why don't you look at me?"

Slowly, self-consciously, he looked at her. A smoldering intensity burned in her eyes. Her lips parted in an amused smile.

"Are you always this shy with women?" she asked.

"Kathleen—"

"Kat."

"Kat," he said. The name made him smile. It was so appropriate given the shape of her eyes and her sleek feline characteristics. "I find you amazingly beautiful," he admitted. "I want to be here with you, but I really shouldn't."

Her eyes dulled. She nodded knowingly. "You're married," she said.

"Divorced. I've still got some issues I need to work through before I can date again."

Her features relaxed, the intensity burning in her eyes again. She sipped her vodka martini and licked her lips. They were gorgeous lips. Resnick couldn't take his eyes off of them.

"As long as you're divorced, we should be able to work through your issues together," she said.

"It's complicated."

"Do you still have feelings for your ex?"

"It's not really like that. I care about her, I probably always will. But I don't see her or talk with her." He lowered his gaze back to his drink. "Anyway, she remarried years ago."

"Years ago?"

Resnick found himself nodding.

"Alex, how long ago did you divorce?"

He had to sit back and think about it before realizing it had been eight years. When he told Liciano, his answer sounded odd even to him.

"You haven't dated at all since then?"

Slowly, he shook his head, both embarrassed and humiliated. It hadn't hit him until that moment that it had been that long. Eight years of simply going through the day-to-day motions of existing, but not really living.

"Alex, tell me what's going on with you."

He raised his gaze back to hers and felt himself swallowed up by her eyes. They were still burning with the same intensity as before, but now there was a sadness there too, an empathy. God, he wanted to tell her, but how could he? How could he tell her about his boy? How could he talk about Brian out loud and admit that his boy was really gone?

Resnick shook his head, lines along his jaw hardening with resolve. "It's too complicated to talk about right now," he said.

As the two of them sat staring at each other, Resnick's attempt to smile turned to glumness. The din from the music and other conversations faded into the background while he stared into her eyes. At that moment she was the only other person who existed in the universe. He wanted to open up to her, but how could he?

She seemed to sense his helplessness. "Alex," she said. "I don't usually ask guys out. To be honest, you're the first." She stopped to sip her drink. As she lowered it, there was more of a warmth in her eyes than a heat. "I know you feel the same attraction I feel. I also know you're a good person with a good heart. I want to get to know you better. For tonight, let's just be friends. We can talk about the Red Sox or movies or whatever. But when things get less complicated and you're able to tell me what's going on with you, give me a call, okay?"

Resnick nodded. He finished his drink, signaled to the waitress that he'd like another. "I just need more time," he said, his words sounding false to him. He breathed in deeply, exhaled, then sat back and tried to relax and simply admire how beautiful Kat Liciano was. "How about them Red Sox?" Resnick said, breaking into an easy smile.

One of the wise guys patted down Petrenko while another of "Uncle Pete" Stellini's men blocked Yuri Tolkov and told him he could wait where he was. Yuri raised an eyebrow. Petrenko nodded to him, indicating for him not to worry about it. Petrenko was then brought back to the same room as the other day. Stellini sat by himself, his lips compressed like he had a bad case of gas. He grunted and pushed himself forward, extending a large beefy hand to Petrenko.

"Viktor, sit down, let me show you something."

Petrenko sat down, crossed his legs and picked up a photo that Stellini had slid towards him. The photo showed Raymond Lombardo on a golf course, a big grin on his face as he joked around with a couple of companions. In the photo he was clean-shaven, his hair dyed yellow.

Petrenko looked up from the photo. "So?" he said.

"That was taken by some newspaper jerk-off who's been following Ray around," Stellini said. "He swears he took that picture same time that bank got hit." Stellini picked up a stack of papers and waved them toward Petrenko. "These are affidavits. Over twenty of them. All from people who saw Ray at that golf course. One of the affidavits is from a judge. All genuine, none of these people were paid off or leaned on."

Petrenko blinked several times as he stared at Stellini. "What does this have to do with returning my property?" he asked.

"I'm trying to tell you. Ray had nothin' to do with that bank job. The FBI screwed up with their frame. All this is going to be in the papers tomorrow and they're going to look like fuckin' idiots."

"What about my property?"

"Jesus, you're a stubborn fuck." Reaching into his pants pocket, Stellini took out a wad of bills and tossed them in front of Petrenko. "Forty-two hundred left of the twenty grand you gave me," Stellini said. "The rest was spread around trying to find out who hit that bank. I'm not taking a single dime out of it. You know what I found out? Zero. Nada. Nobody knows nothing."

Petrenko's eyes grew distant as he stared at the money. He looked up at Stellini, his eyes as cold and lifeless as chunks of ice. "I told you I need those items," he said.

"You got wax in your ears or somethin'? I told you I don't know nothin' about that bank. Nobody fuckin' knows, okay?" Red-faced, Stellini pointed a large sausage-shaped finger at Petrenko. "I know you're some kinda tough guy. But what you got, a dozen people workin' for you? You cause any trouble, we'll bury you all by morning and nobody ever knows the difference. Now get the fuck outa here!"

Two of Stellini's wise guys started to move towards Petrenko. He knew he could take care of them if he had to, but he was beginning to have doubts about Raymond Lombardo's involvement. Maybe the FBI did manufacture the video of Lombardo outside the bank. Maybe they were even behind the bank robbery. Petrenko knew there were high-level government officials who would do anything to get their hands on the computer disks and videotapes that he was keeping in his safety deposit boxes. If they had found out about his boxes, then maybe…

Both wise guys were stopped in their tracks by the look Petrenko gave them, their hard smirks drying up on their faces. Petrenko nodded curtly to Stellini, stood up and left the room. When he saw Yuri, he told him in Russian that things were not good. "I am afraid we might need to relocate to Europe."

During the ride back to Lynn, Petrenko tried to sort out what his next steps were going to be. He still had connections in his home city of Volgograd and could set up operations there. As far as funds, he had maybe one hundred and sixty thousand that was liquid. That would be all he could take. He would have no choice but to leave Yuri behind and entrust him with selling off his other holdings.

When he arrived home, he was surprised to find a message on his answering machine. His number was unlisted, and usually his associates would call only on his cell phone.

The message stated that for a hundred thousand dollars Petrenko would be told how to get back his stolen belongings. The person added that he would call back on Sunday at ten in the morning. Petrenko stood rubbing his knuckles as he replayed the message. The second time around he had no trouble detecting that the caller was of Indian descent.

27

Dan's mind raced as he played back the events at the cemetery. He tried to slow down his thoughts and concentrate on what was said, trying to detect any nuances from the way the cop had looked at him and any changes of inflection in his voice. He couldn't help cringing every time he thought about Wendy telling that cop about Gordon's community theater work. Of all the times for Wendy to have to open her big mouth...

The central air was on, but Dan had still sweated through the boxers and undershirt he wore to bed. He pushed himself up and squinted at the alarm clock. Four seventeen. At least two more hours before he'd have an excuse to get out of bed. He knew there wasn't a chance in hell he was going to get any sleep.

Carol was on her side with her back to him. She had been sleeping fitfully through most of the night. He knew the cop showing up at the cemetery had affected her too. Thank

God Lombardo had been arrested! But even so she must still have her doubts. Not enough so she'd come right out and say anything, but they were there. During the ride back, he could feel her studying him. A few times he caught glimpses of her in the rearview mirror and saw the way she was biting her lip and how pale her skin had become. He knew she was beginning to wonder about that picture of Raymond Lombardo outside the bank with his ski mask off. They'd been married seventeen years and had known each other twenty. Maybe she'd seen something in that picture she'd been in denial about, at least until she had seen that cop at the cemetery. When they had gotten home he had buried himself in his office, claiming he had work to do to finish his contract.

He tried to think through everything that had happened and every conversation he had. Even if that cop did suspect something, there was no evidence against him. Nothing that could link him to the changes he'd made to the bank's security software, or him breaking into their databases or really anything involved with the robbery. He'd made sure there were no records of him purchasing those drills, or the safety deposit boxes he and Shrini had practiced on, or the overalls and the ski masks. All of it had been hidden under a labyrinth of untraceable Internet transactions. There was nothing for that cop to find.

Of course he could be tied to Joel, and if Joel had been careless enough to keep those guns or not hide the money well enough...

Fuck it. He was making too much of this. What could that cop possibly know? That he and Gordon were friends? What did that prove? That Gordon used to do make up for a community theater? Knowing that was still a long way from suspecting that Dan had been made up to look like Raymond

Lombardo. And even if the cop did suspect that, what could he prove? Dan's mind buzzed as he wondered whether the FBI had any advanced imaging software that could identify him from the security tape. He would have to try to research that, but he doubted the security cameras could provide enough resolution for something like that to be feasible. Still…

Enough already! He had been worrying himself sick over this for hours now. Forget it. No more. There was nothing to tie him to the robbery. Hell, there was nothing to even tie Gordon to it. All they had was Gordon's body being found outside the bank and… and that nobody knew what he was doing there. That still didn't put him inside the bank. They had nothing, and more important, there was nothing for them to find.

Dan took a deep breath and exhaled slowly through his nose. It was funny how the mind worked. After the robbery all he could think about were the victims and the damage that was done to them, now all he could think about was self-preservation. He decided that was normal. It didn't make him a bad person. He never would've gone through with the robbery if he had any idea people were going to be hurt. How could he have expected Gordon to do what he did?

How could any rational person have expected that?

But all that was in the past. There was nothing he could do now except move forward and do what was best for him and his family. He had to somehow forgive himself, but for now he needed to empty his mind and relax, at least before the pressure inside his head exploded.

He looked over at Carol and studied the outline her hips made under the sheets. They were so slender, her waist seemingly thin enough for him to wrap both hands around. At forty-four she still had a better body than most thirty-year-olds – hell, forget that, most twenty-year-olds. He touched her hip lightly. He didn't want to wake her. He just wanted to have some sort of physical connection to her, to somehow make himself feel like there was still a reason for hope.

He gently rested his hand on her hip. She made a grunting noise in her sleep and angrily pushed his hand away. He lay paralyzed for a moment, feeling as empty as he had ever felt. Then he just started laughing. He couldn't help himself.

Par for the fucking course, he thought.

Later, when he heard the thud of the Sunday paper against his driveway, he decided he'd been in bed about as long as he could stand. Carol was tossing restlessly, but she was still mostly asleep. Moving quietly, he got out of bed, put on a robe and went outside to get the paper. When he saw the front page, he stood frozen for a long moment not knowing what to do next. Then, resigned to the situation, he headed back inside.

Petrenko let the phone ring six times before he picked up. He placed his hand over the mouthpiece and listened silently.

"Hello, hello?"

It was the same voice from the answering machine. Petrenko didn't bother saying anything.

The pitch of the caller's voice rose in confusion as he tried again. "Hello, is anybody there?"

Petrenko answered softly, "You have items that belong to me, correct?"

"I don't have them." There was a hesitation, then, "But I know who does."

"And why should I believe you?"

The caller told him the numbers of his safety deposit boxes. "You had mostly packets of hundred-dollar bills rubber-banded together. Also videotapes and computer disks. Will you pay me a hundred thousand dollars or do I hang up?"

"Of course I will pay you. What time?"

"Tomorrow—"

"That is not convenient for me. Why not today?"

"Because I said tomorrow. Be at the Middlesex Diner in Burlington at eleven-thirty. If you are not there on time I will leave, and believe me, you will not hear from me ever again. Wait by the cashier and make sure you have the money with you."

"How will I know you?"

"You won't. But I know you and that is all that matters."

The caller hung up. Petrenko, feeling more relaxed than he had felt in days, placed the phone down. He stood for a long moment rubbing his thumb over the hard calluses that had built up over his knuckles.

If the caller hadn't known about the safety deposit box numbers, Petrenko could've considered paying him off – or, if not paying him off, at least letting him live. But now that was impossible. The caller's knowledge, both about the safety deposit box numbers and what was taken from them, meant that he must have been part of the robbery. Which meant he had to be paid back by means other than money.

Petrenko couldn't keep from smiling, thinking that this person must have been double-crossed after the robbery. Well, if he was double-crossed once, he could be double-crossed again.

Resnick was surprised to see that it was after ten o'clock. This was the first morning since he was told about Brian needing a new heart valve that he had been able to stay in bed past six. That was over ten years ago. Now he found himself lounging around, partly thinking about the robbery and what his next steps with Dan Wilson were going to be and partly drifting into daydreams about Kathleen Liciano. He kept thinking of how she looked sitting in the bar: the expression in her almond-shaped eyes, the way her hair fell past her shoulders, the softness of her lips and the way they parted slightly when she smiled. Thinking of her, he found himself longing to see her again. Then, clenching his teeth hard enough to hurt his jaw, he made a decision. She was too young to have all his emotional baggage dumped on her. He'd call her later and let her know that he was afraid things were never going to get less complicated for him.

He pushed himself out of bed, put on running shorts and a T-shirt, did his ten minutes of stretching and went out for a five-mile run to try to clear his head. When he got back he took a quick shower and then made some salami and scrambled eggs for lunch. It was almost twelve before he headed out to the hospital. On his way, he stopped off at a drug store for a newspaper. When he spotted the single-word headline, '*Framed?*', on the front page, it took a moment for it to register. Scanning down the page, he saw the two pictures side by side: Raymond Lombardo outside the bank with his ski mask off, and at a golf course clean-shaven with his hair cut short and dyed yellow.

According to the accompanying article, the photographer who took the golf course picture swore it was taken at the same time that the bank robbery had happened. The article also stated that there were over two dozen people who supported the photographer's claim, all of them filling out affidavits saying they had seen Lombardo at the golf course with one of the affidavits coming from a Massachusetts Superior Court judge. The gist of the article was that the videotape was a fake and that Lombardo was being framed, possibly by the FBI.

Resnick put down the paper and first tried calling Hadley at his home before reaching him at the station.

"What do you want?" Hadley asked brusquely.

"Nothing really. I thought maybe you'd want me to come in."

"Didn't I assign you to watch Viktor Petrenko?"

"Yeah, you did, but after what was in the paper—"

"Look, I'm with the district attorney right now. If you want to put in any overtime today, keep watching Petrenko."

Hadley hung up. Resnick stared at his cell phone, wondering what the hell was going on. Shaking his head, he slipped the phone back into his pocket, paid for the paper and headed off to the hospital.

When Mary O'Donnell's eyes closed, Resnick couldn't help thinking she had passed on. Holding her hand and feeling the coldness of her skin, that was all he could think of though logically he realised this was the effect of the morphine. She reminded him of the way his mom had been during her last few hours. His mom was only fifty-two when she died. She had been brought to the hospital after her stroke and had the same shrunken look to her face. The same heaviness in her eyelids. The same frailness.

"Mrs. O'Donnell," Resnick said. "Are you awake?"

Mary O'Donnell's eyes fluttered open. "I'm so tired," she

forced out, her voice barely above a whisper. The whole middle of her body was thickly bandaged. Even with the morphine drip, Resnick knew she was in a great deal of pain.

"I know," Resnick said. "I'd just like to ask you a few questions. Do you remember anything about the man who shot you?"

"He talked about Brazil."

"What was that?"

"He was talking stuff about Brazil. I couldn't understand him. Also something about the New Jersey Shore." She stopped for a moment to catch her breath. "One of the beaches there."

"Which beach?"

"Asb—" She coughed weakly. The effort seemed to wipe her out. When she could, she whispered, "Asbury Park."

"Did you see anything that could help us identify him?"

She closed her eyes again. Resnick thought she had drifted off. He was about to leave when she whispered something too low for him to make out.

"What was that?" he asked. He moved closer to her.

"His sneaker…"

"We know, he was wearing Converse basketball sneakers."

"Not that. Green paint on the bottom."

That seemed to take all the strength she had. Resnick lowered her hand, placing it gently to her side.

"You've been a great help," he told her. He was about to say more, but realized she was drifting off, her breathing growing shallower.

"Don't worry," he said, more to himself that to her. "They're not getting away with this."

Later, when he was walking across the parking lot to his car, his cell phone rang. It was Hadley.

"Alex," Hadley said, his voice sounding so tired that Resnick could picture his pale blue unhappy eyes drooping with exhaustion. "Why don't you come in after all."

Dan knew there was no getting around Carol seeing the newspaper and reading about Raymond Lombardo. If she didn't read it in the paper she'd see it later on the news. All he could do was prepare himself for what was coming and to try to act as oblivious as possible when she called him on it.

From the corner of his eye he saw her picking up the front section. He was sitting at the kitchen table drinking his coffee and pretending to read the sports page. Carol stood by the refrigerator, holding the paper in one hand while pouring a glass of orange juice with the other. All at once her body went rigid. While reading the front page, her eyes narrowed into thin slits and her mouth compressed into a small tight circle. Muscles clenching along her jaw formed hard lines above and below her lips. She looked worn out, almost like she had aged twenty years.

In an odd, barely recognizable voice, she asked, "Did you read this?"

He peered at the paper, feigning mild interest in what she was showing him. "Yeah, pretty wild, huh?" he said. "Sounds kind of far-fetched to me."

"Far-fetched? What do you mean far-fetched?"

"That he wasn't the guy who robbed that bank."

"How can you say that? With all of those people claiming they saw him at the golf course? And that picture?"

"The guy's mafia. I'm sure he knows how to buy witnesses."

"A judge?"

"Why not? They can be bought like anyone else."

"What about the picture?"

"You're kidding, right?" Patiently, as if talking to a child, he explained how with digital cameras any picture can be faked. "Why are you so interested in this?"

Dan had asked the question with such naivety that it stunned Carol. She stepped back like she'd been slapped, her jaw dropping open.

"D-Do you think Gordon was involved?" she asked.

"Involved in what?"

"What happened in that bank."

"*Gordon?* Come on."

"Why else would he be there?" She looked away from him, almost as if she were afraid he would answer. Or worse, that she'd see the answer in his face. She said, "Maybe he made someone up to look like that mafia person."

She was so damned intuitive. Why'd she have to be so fucking intuitive?

He rolled his eyes to emphasise that she was talking nonsense. It took every ounce of control he had to sit there and act as if this were a joke. As if she were pulling his leg or something. Inside he was dying.

"If Gordon was that good he would've been working on Broadway," he said, praying that his tone sounded as unconcerned as he wanted it to.

Yeah, you're right, darling, Gordon should've been doing makeup at the Schubert and I should be up there right now on the same fucking stage doing Hamlet with the performance I'm giving.

Jesus, is she buying it?

*

"Dan, if there's anything you need to..."

The question died in her throat. Her mouth moved silently as if she were chewing gum, but she couldn't finish the question. As much as she wanted to, she couldn't ask whether he was involved. Oh God, he was grateful for that. He knew she was desperately trying to convince herself that she was being crazy. His insides felt like they'd been turned into an icy sludge, but he sat there trying to give the impression that he had no idea what she was really asking, all the while feeling he'd go insane if he had to sit there another minute.

Susie wandered into the kitchen. She seemed to sense something was wrong. As she looked from Carol to Dan, her features became pinched.

"Hi, Princess," Dan said.

"What's wrong?" she asked, her voice flattening into a monotone.

"Nothing, Princess. Your mom saw something in the paper that she found interesting, that's all."

The look Carol gave him was damning, but she didn't say anything. She walked over to Susie and kissed her on the forehead.

"Darling, what can I make you for breakfast? French toast? Pancakes? Eggs?" she asked while using her daughter to shield her eyes from her husband. How he ever managed to just sit there smiling and pretending nothing was wrong was beyond him. Somehow he did it, but God only knew how.

"I just want cereal," Susie said, peeking suspiciously at her father as she tried to figure out what was going on.

"I better get some work done," Dan said, excusing himself.

When he got to his study he collapsed into his chair. His hands were shaking, his heart pounding as if it were going to break. He had an image of all the lies he had been telling Carol, one piled on top of another, each larger than the one before, each making the tower more and more unstable as it leaned on the verge of collapse. If any more were added, they would come crashing down on him. Somehow he had to get out from under their shadow. He had to stop the lies.

How?

In a couple of days this would blow over. Carol would bury her suspicions and sooner or later forget about them. The cops had no real reason to suspect him. Or Gordon for that matter. There was no reason for this to change anything. He just had to stay calm. Focus on his articles, his book proposal, his business idea…

But how was he going to survive the next couple of days?

Sitting there realizing the futility of the situation, he lowered his face into his hands and wept like a baby.

Kenneth Hadley sat upright behind his desk with his doughy hands folded in front of him, his pale blue eyes looking miserable. Agent Donald Spitzer sat to his side and for once his long face looked more grim than dour. Resnick pulled up a chair.

Hadley said, "The district attorney wants us to drop all charges against Raymond Lombardo and release him."

"That's about what I would've expected—"

"That son of a bitch manufactured those witnesses," Spitzer interrupted through clenched teeth. "Same with that picture."

"I don't think so," Resnick said.

"You don't think so? What kind of bullshit is that? Of course he did!"

"Alex, we're still going with the theory that Lombardo is behind the bank robbery," Hadley said. "Today's newspaper article hasn't changed that. Agent Spitzer, along with Stillwall and Hollings, are going to look into Lombardo's witnesses, also that photographer, and see what type of connection they might have with him. If we can get the court's assistance, we'll also check their bank accounts and see if we can spot any unexplained transfers."

"What did you have me come in for?"

Hadley's round face seemed to deflate as he stared at his detective. Sighing, he said, "I was wondering if you have any other theories?"

"Possibly one."

Hadley's face tinged pink. "Would you care to share it?" he asked, barely keeping his annoyance in check.

"Not without a chance to dig into it more."

"Do you have anything to make it more than a theory?"

"Not at this point."

"Was your following of Viktor Petrenko at all productive?"

"Not really."

"Why don't you spend the next few days exploring your theory then."

"A complete waste of time," Spitzer offered, his mouth settling into something bitter.

"What about Walt?" Resnick asked, ignoring the FBI agent.

"I was just about to suggest he help you with this."

Resnick nodded, told Hadley he'd let him know if his theory developed into anything more substantive and left. Without

Hadley mentioning it, he understood that the district attorney must be pressuring him to investigate other alternatives to the bank robbery.

If Spitzer hadn't been sitting there, Resnick might have let on that he had Carmichael made as the shooter. Before going to Hadley's office, he had stopped off at the evidence room and examined Carmichael's sneakers. Sure enough, there were spots of green paint on the bottom of them. If he checked Carmichael's apartment he'd probably find that one of the rooms had been painted the same shade of green.

The problem was he didn't trust Spitzer. He had no doubt the guy would screw things up with Dan Wilson. There was more to it than that, though. He didn't even have a circumstantial case yet against Wilson. No real evidence of any kind. He had to find something concrete first, something he could use to force Wilson to hand over the items that were stolen. He couldn't risk Wilson's name showing up in the papers before that. Resnick knew full well what Petrenko would do to Wilson's family if that happened. He pictured the way Wilson's wife looked at the cemetery. At the time he sensed that she suspected something, but that was about it. She wasn't involved in this, and shit, they probably had kids. Petrenko would take care of all of them. No, he had to try to nail Petrenko first.

He thought over what his next steps were going to be. All he knew for sure was that tomorrow was going to be one hell of a day.

28

Craig Brown called at nine fifteen to ask Dan whether he had made any progress.

"It's only been a few days, but yeah, I was going to call you later. I have it figured out—"

"Can you be at the bank at ten thirty?"

"Sure."

Brown hung up. Dan couldn't help feeling taken aback by the bank manager's abruptness. He sat for a moment wondering about it before giving up. His mind was just too fuzzy to think properly right then.

He hadn't slept the night before. That made two nights now. Physically he felt like crap, almost as if his head were filled with sawdust. Even after four cups of coffee he could barely focus on anything.

Carol was still in bed. He had waited until three in the morning the other night to join her knowing she'd be too groggy and out of it to want to talk about anything, let alone Gordon being involved in a bank robbery.

From three until six thirty he lay wide awake. The whole time his mind raced with different images, some making sense, some completely crazy.

God, he just needed to get through this. A few more days maybe and he'd be able to put this mess behind him. Pretend the robbery had never happened and then just focus on starting over fresh. Just a few days...

He gathered up his papers and headed over to the bank. Traffic was lighter than normal, even for the summer. What normally would've been an hour's drive took forty minutes. Still, it was a tough ride for him. He had trouble keeping his eyes open, both from being bone-tired and also the way the morning sun hit him. By the time he got to Lynn he felt wiped out. He used the extra twenty minutes to stop off for a couple of donuts and a fifth cup of coffee. All the liquid in him made him slosh when he moved, but the sugar and extra caffeine helped to clear his thinking. He had even been able to work out what he was going to say to Brown.

Craig Brown met him in the bank's lobby and escorted him quickly back to his office. From the way the bank manager acted Dan knew something was up and it came as no surprise that the detective from the other day was waiting in the office. Next to him sat another cop, at least that was Dan's guess based on the cheap suit the guy wore and his short, almost military-style haircut. He was younger than Resnick, bigger, but not in good shape. Kind of flabby. Dan nodded to Resnick and then held out his hand to the other cop.

"I don't believe we've met," Dan said.

That seemed to catch the cop by surprise. He glanced over at Resnick who sat stony-faced. "Detective Maguire, Lynn Police," he murmured.

After shaking hands with Maguire, Dan spread out computer listings on Brown's desk and explained why the security software had failed. As he talked, Resnick took out a sheet of paper from a folder he was carrying and held it up so he could look at Dan and the paper at the same time. He didn't say anything, but kept looking back and forth between Dan and the paper. Maguire got up and stood behind Resnick so he could do the same. While Dan found it distracting, he was just too damned tired to think much of it.

"You're right," Maguire said to his partner, interrupting Dan's explanation.

"Yeah, I thought so," Resnick said. "Craig, why don't you come over here. I'd like your opinion on this. Mr. Wilson, if you could, move your head a little to the right."

Dan stood frozen while the bank manager got up and walked over to the two cops. "What do you think," Resnick asked. "Is that Mr. Wilson or not?"

Brown gave Dan an icy stare. "I believe it is," he said.

Resnick nodded. "Mr. Wilson, let me show you what we've been looking at."

He turned the paper around so that Dan could see it was the same photograph from the newspaper. The one that was supposed to look like Raymond Lombardo after taking off his ski mask.

"That's you under all that fake hair and makeup," Resnick said.

"You're kidding, right? This is some kind of joke?"

Resnick ignored him, turned to the bank manager and asked if he could give them some privacy.

"Craig, this is crazy. That's not me," Dan said.

Brown gave Dan one last icy stare before looking away and leaving the office.

Resnick stared dispassionately at Dan. "Before you say a word, we know your friend, Gordon Carmichael, was involved in the bank robbery. We have physical evidence identifying him as the man who shot Margaret Williams and Mary O'Donnell."

"Gordon did what? Jesus Christ, I don't believe—"

"Your act's not going to work with me," Resnick said. "You might as well skip it and just sit still and listen to what I have to say."

"Go ahead, 'cause I have no idea what you're talking about."

Resnick turned to Maguire and shook his head sadly. "He doesn't listen, does he?" Then to Wilson, "If you insist on playing this game, go right ahead. It doesn't change anything. We both know what happened. You came up with a way to sabotage the bank's security software."

"How could I have done that? I never had access to the software—"

Resnick turned again to Maguire. "There he goes again. He actually thinks he's going to convince us we're wrong."

"Pathetic," Maguire said.

This was the very moment Dan had been terrified of for months. The fear of this happening had been gnawing at him ever since he came up with the idea of robbing the bank. All the worry and stress he'd put himself under and now that the moment had arrived he felt none of the panic he would've expected. Instead only a calmness. He had a clarity of thought that he hadn't had in a long time. None of the fuzziness he'd been suffering. Maybe it was the exhaustion, maybe he just didn't care any more. Whatever the reason, nothing the cops were saying affected him.

"Fine. I'll just keep my mouth shut then," he said.

"Probably a good idea," Maguire agreed.

"I have to hand it to you," Resnick said. "The robbery was clever. You're obviously a bright guy. Just as you figured out how to rig that software, you also broke into the bank's records and found out who owned the safety deposit boxes. Somehow you figured out who Petrenko was. It was pure genius ripping him off and framing Raymond Lombardo. But where you screwed up was shooting Carmichael and leaving his body at the scene. If you hadn't done that I never would've suspected you."

"No question, you would've gotten away scot-free," Maguire added.

"My guess, you weren't the one to actually shoot him," Resnick said. "One of your buddies leveled an assault rifle on Carmichael right before he shot those two women. I'd have to think he was the guy who shot your friend. Anything to say yet?"

Dan shook his head.

"You might like to know what really happened with Carmichael," Resnick went on. "The best I can tell he was only talking harmless nonsense to Margaret Williams. Stuff about Brazil and Asbury Park Beach in New Jersey. The problem was one of your buddies molested her a few minutes before Carmichael wandered over."

"Your fat buddy," Maguire said. "The short little fucker wearing the running suit."

"You know who we're talking about, right?" Resnick asked. He waited patiently for Dan to answer him. When he didn't, Resnick continued. "Ms. Williams probably thought Carmichael was the guy who shoved his hand up her skirt. The whole thing was just bad luck. You still have nothing to say?"

Dan shook his head, shrugging.

Resnick breathed in deeply and let it out through his mouth.

He hadn't expected Wilson to have the nerve to sit there as calmly as he was. He had been betting that this would crack him and was beginning to wonder how badly he had misjudged the guy.

"Here's the deal," Resnick said. "I don't think you're a bad guy. I saw the way you reacted after the shootings."

Maguire added, "It's on videotape, buddy. We can show it to you if you'd like."

Resnick waited, got no reaction. He continued, "To me, it looked like you were in shock when you ran into the lobby and saw those two women. My guess, you never expected anyone to get hurt. You thought you'd just rip off a very bad guy and frame another bad guy. The problem is people did get hurt. Because of that I can't let you get away with this."

Resnick took two photos from his folder and flung them in front of Dan. They were both crime-scene photos. One of them showed Margaret Williams lying dead in a pool of blood. The other showed Mary O'Donnell with her stomach blown out and her intestines showing through a gaping hole in her middle. Dan looked at them and then back up at Resnick.

"Why don't we get this over with," Resnick said. "You'll feel better afterwards."

"There's nothing to get over," Dan said, his voice flat. "First you try to frame one person with a fake videotape and when that doesn't work you try this."

Maguire's mouth opened into a bare-fanged grin. "Can you believe the balls on this guy?" he asked Resnick.

"Go ahead if you'd like, arrest me," Dan offered. "You can't prove any of this because none of it happened."

Maguire stood up, his hand reaching for his cuffs. "What do you say, we bring this asshole in?"

Dan held both hands out so he could be cuffed. "I'm not saying another word without a lawyer."

Resnick stopped his partner. "Let's give the guy a chance," he said. Then to Dan, "You don't have anything to hide, right?"

"Not a thing."

"Then you wouldn't mind if we searched your house?"

"Knock yourself out," Dan said.

29

Shrini arrived at the Middlesex Diner shortly before eleven. After driving around the parking lot so he could look for Petrenko and satisfy himself that the Russian wasn't there, he parked and hobbled to the diner's entrance. He still hadn't gotten used to the crutches. It was slow going and by the time he got to the cashier's station he was winded. He knew it was partly due to the adrenaline pumping through him. This was a bold move he was making, but to succeed in life you have to make bold moves. Dan could act meekly if he wanted, but *he* sure wasn't going to!

One of the waitresses showed him to a table and he ordered coffee and an egg-white omelet. He checked his watch. It was seven past eleven. The numbers seven and eleven struck him. They were a good sign. The strutting peacock was going to crap out, not him.

The anticipation wore on him while he waited. His food was brought over and he nibbled at it, every minute or so straining his neck to look out the window. He checked his watch. Eleven twenty-eight. He told Petrenko what would happen if he wasn't there on time and he meant it! His fingers tapped the table as he waited. It was now eleven thirty-two. He started to get up but indecision slowed him. Crossing his arms, he decided to give Petrenko ten more minutes.

When those ten minutes vanished he got up and paid the cashier. He took a step towards the door and froze. He couldn't walk away. It wasn't just the money. He had to make sure that peacock got paid back. His face flushed as he told the waitress he'd like to sit back at the table and have another cup of coffee.

At twelve thirty he gave up. Petrenko wasn't coming. For some reason he must've thought Shrini's call was a crank. Dejected, he gathered up his crutches and hobbled towards the diner's entrance. The steps leading out were tricky. He had to hold the crutches with one hand while he held the railing with the other, all the while hopping on one foot.

When he got to the bottom of the steps, he readjusted the crutches under him. He took several steps to the curb and then stopped to position one of the crutches more comfortably under his armpit. Right before the blow to the kidneys he sensed the two men behind him, but he didn't have time to react. The blow paralyzed him. For several seconds he couldn't breathe. His knees buckled, hot tears flooding his eyes.

They grabbed him from both sides. A car swung around, the trunk popping open. He was tossed into the trunk. This all happened within five seconds from the time he was hit. He tried to struggle and claw his way forward. Something hit him hard on the side of the head. Then blackness.

Pain brought him back to semi-consciousness. Every part of him seemed to throb with pain. While he wavered in his semi-conscious state, he had the sensation of spikes being driven into his broken ankle. Every few seconds there would be a dull thud followed by a jolt of pain shooting through him. One horrific jolt knocked him back into consciousness. His eyes opened to catch Petrenko swinging back a golf club. He started to scream as Petrenko drove the club into his unprotected ankle. The pain exploded inside him. At some level he knew his eyes were open, but the room flickered on and off into darkness. Sort of like a light bulb crackling on the edge of blowing out. Barely, he maintained consciousness.

"Our guest has woken," Petrenko announced.

Behind Petrenko stood three other Russians, all looking on with mild amusement. Shrini's arms were pulled tight over his head, his feet dangling, barely touching the floor. Something cold and hard bit into his wrists and he realized he was handcuffed, probably to a pipe. He looked down and saw that his injured ankle had swollen to the size of a large eggplant, its color an unnatural deep, darkish blue. The sight of it made him light-headed. As his eyes started to roll up in his head, Petrenko grabbed him by his hair, jerked his head up and slapped him hard across the face.

"No, I do not think so," he said. "For now you're staying awake."

When Shrini's eyes could focus again, he saw the corners of Petrenko's lips turn up into a dull smile while his eyes remained vacant. Then Petrenko's hand wrapped into a fist, and in a blur, threw a quick jab catching Shrini hard in the ribs.

Time seemed to hold still as he tried to gasp in air. For a long moment he didn't think he'd be able to, not with the way his stomach muscles were convulsing. Then somehow he started breathing again. Labored, but he was breathing.

"No more," Shrini tried to say.

Petrenko tapped him again in the ribs. A sharp, jagged pain ripped through him.

"Please," Shrini forced out, tears streaming down his face. "Don't hit me again."

"No?" Petrenko asked. "And why not?"

"Believe me, I'll tell you everything. Just don't hit me again."

"You'll tell me everything, huh?" Then in a low, menacing voice, "Where are my belongings that you stole?"

"New Hampshire." Shrini gave him Joel's name and address, his words spilling out of him.

"Everything of mine is there?"

Shrini nodded.

"Why?"

"He took it all. There was nothing we could do."

"Who else was part of this?"

Shrini shook his head. "This peacock has everything of yours. Isn't he enough?"

Petrenko picked up the golf club, settled into a golf stance, and slowly brought the head of the club back.

"Fore!" he hollered good-naturedly. One of the Russians behind him snickered.

In a breathless, frantic burst, Shrini told him all about Dan.

"That makes three of you," Petrenko said. "What about the other three?"

"There were only two others."

Petrenko eyed him suspiciously. "The newspapers claimed there were six of you."

"They're wrong. There were only five. The other two are dead."

Petrenko raised an eyebrow in disbelief. "Is that so?"

"Kasner killed them both." Shrini stopped, the pain

throbbing through his battered ankle choking off his words. When he could, he added, "The person shot outside the bank was one of us."

"Who helped you from inside the bank?"

Shrini gave Petrenko a confused look.

"Don't act dumb now. Someone inside the bank helped you."

Shrini shook his head.

"No? Then how did you find out which safety deposit boxes I owned?"

"My friend hacked—"

Petrenko tapped him on the ankle with the golf club. "Names!" he demanded.

"Dan Wilson hacked into the bank's database," Shrini said, grimacing as tears welled up in his eyes.

"And the security system?"

"He rigged the software so it would be disabled during the robbery."

"This bank manager, Craig Brown, wasn't involved?" Petrenko asked with some disappointment.

"No."

Petrenko stroked his chin, considering what was said. He had to admire the execution of the bank robbery. This Dan Wilson could be useful and for a moment he thought about forcing Wilson to work for him, but decided against it. The man had tried once to steal from him; he couldn't be trusted. More importantly, a message had to be sent. Wilson and his family had to be taken care of and it would have to be bloody. First, though, he would retrieve his belongings and take care of this *zhid* up in New Hampshire. After that, he'd take his time with Wilson and his family.

He told Shrini that he was going to go on a ride with them. "If you make any noise or do anything to upset me I will leave pieces of you along the highway."

Shrini nodded weakly.

The handcuffs were taken off and Shrini was thrown on to his stomach and hogtied. Yuri Tolkov started to push a soiled rag into his mouth, but Petrenko stopped him. In Russian he told Yuri that he didn't want to risk Shrini choking to death during the ride. "He might be useful for now. Later we'll dispose of him."

Two of the Russians carried Shrini to a blue BMW sedan that had been stolen hours earlier and dumped him into the trunk.

30

The two detectives were in his basement. Resnick had already taken down several of the ceiling tiles so he could look in the space above them. Now he was walking around the room tapping on the wood paneling. The younger detective was sweating heavily as he searched through boxes that had been stacked in a corner.

Dan told Resnick that there were no hidden compartments. "If that's what you're looking for," he added.

Resnick didn't bother acknowledging him; he simply kept up with his tapping.

Dan checked his watch. It was two thirty-five. They'd been searching the house for almost three hours now and still had the garage and shed to go through. So far he'd been lucky – both Carol and the kids were out – but how much longer was his luck going to hold?

With that thought, a car pulled into the driveway. He knew

it had to be Carol. Without saying a word, he went up the basement steps and reached the front door at the same time as his wife.

"You have someone over?" she asked.

"Let's talk outside."

As he led her outside, her face grew pale and drawn. She didn't bother looking at him, instead she stared at Resnick's Buick and the way it was parked so it had Dan's car blocked in.

"The police are here, aren't they?" she asked.

"This is nothing to worry about—"

"They think you were involved in that robbery," she said. The look she gave him stung worse than if she had slapped him. "They're searching the house right now."

"It doesn't mean anything—"

"What do you mean it doesn't mean anything? They've been going through my dresser drawers, going through everything I own! I'm going to have to wash all my clothes."

She stopped. Her face scrunched up as if she were about to start bawling. "Have our children been home?" she asked.

Dan shook his head.

"What if they had been?"

"They haven't, okay? Look, this will all be over soon." He tried to meet her eyes, but had to lower his gaze. "They're only doing this because I worked on the security system."

"You have to tell me the truth," she said, her voice dropping so it was barely above a whisper. "Look at me."

He forced himself to meet her eyes.

"Were you and Gordon involved in the robbery?"

"This is ridiculous. How could you even ask me that?"

"For the sake of our children you have to tell me the truth. Dan, please, tell me the truth!"

"I've already told you the truth. How many times do I have to say it? Jesus Christ. I'm a software engineer, not a criminal. This is all just nuts."

Her mouth started to move, but she swallowed back whatever she was going to say. Nodding slightly, she looked away from him and went inside.

"Where are they now?" she asked.

He indicated towards the basement. As if on cue, rustling noises came from there. She turned towards the basement door, took a few steps and stopped. As she stood frozen her body seemed to shrink inward. She looked so frail and tired that it brought a lump to Dan's throat. Almost as if she were moving in molasses, she started again. Dan followed her down the stairs.

Resnick gave her a short nod when he saw her. The other detective tried to say something innocuous and turned away when he saw the look Carol gave him, his voice trailing off into an unintelligible mumble. Carol stood silently with her arms folded tightly across her chest. Dan stood off to the side and watched.

When they were done in the basement, they next searched Dan's workroom, then the garage and finally the shed. When they were done, Resnick walked the backyard searching for any possible hiding places.

"Are you satisfied yet?" Dan asked.

"No, not yet," Resnick said. "Do you rent any storage space?"

Carol's reaction gave the answer away. "Go ahead," Dan told her. "It doesn't matter. Tell them about our storage locker."

She bit her lip as she looked at Resnick. "Two years ago we rented storage space in Andover," she said.

"What for?"

"To hold some extra furniture. At the time we were thinking of buying a bigger house."

"Why didn't you?"

"Because the company I was working for shut their doors," Dan said. "We thought we were going to make millions. We didn't."

Resnick gave Dan a hard look. "I'd like to see that locker."

"No problem, I'll take you there."

Dan reached over to squeeze Carol's hand. She pulled away and turned her head so she wouldn't have to look at him.

Maguire moved alongside Dan. "You can't blame her," he said.

When they got to their cars, Resnick suggested Dan ride with them. "In case we find something, your wife won't have to pay to have your car towed back."

"Very thoughtful of you," Dan said, "but I think I'll take my chances."

Dan got in his car and waited until Resnick pulled his Buick out.

A blue BMW drove past Joel Kasner's house. It continued another hundred yards before pulling over to the side of the road. Petrenko got out of the front passenger seat, stretched, looked around and was satisfied with the location. Nobody was going to hear the gunshots. Still, this would have to be quick – ten minutes at the most. No matter how isolated the location appeared he didn't want to risk a local cop stumbling upon them. If that happened, the cop would have to be taken care of and he'd just as soon make this as clean a job as possible.

He cracked open the magazine of his 9mm Beretta, checked that it was loaded and slid the magazine back in place. Yuri got out from the driver's side while two other Russians emerged from the back. Yuri moved past them and took a bolt-action ten-round rifle from the backseat. The other two Russians carried sub-compact snub-nosed pistols.

Shrini was taken out of the trunk and cut free. They gave him a minute to rub the cramps out of his legs and arms. Then Yuri and one of the other Russians dragged him to his feet.

"You are going to do precisely as I say," Petrenko said, moving so he was less than a foot from Shrini. He showed Shrini his Beretta. "If you fail to do so I will put one of these bullets in your head."

"I need water," Shrini said, his voice raspy, barely a croak.

"Later."

"No, you had me in a hot car trunk for over two hours."

Petrenko put the barrel of his gun against Shrini's ear. "I said later."

"Go ahead. I'll die anyway without water."

Petrenko, annoyed, barked out a command in Russian. One of his men searched the backseat and brought out a bottle of water. Shrini emptied it in seconds, his hands shaking while he held the bottle to his mouth. Half of the water ended up going down his shirt.

"That is the last time you disobey me," Petrenko said, trying to maintain his patience. "Now you will walk to your friend's front door—"

"He is not my friend."

Petrenko put a hand up to his face and shook his head. Slowly, as he fought the impulse to blow Shrini's brains out, he continued, "You will walk up to his door and call for him."

"How am I supposed to walk? I don't have my crutches, and look what you did to my foot."

"You'll find a way."

Shrini took several hops and collapsed on to the ground. "I can't do it," he cried.

"Then crawl." Petrenko aimed his gun at Shrini's head. "I have lost patience with you."

Shrini made a decision then. If he was going to die, he'd just as soon see that peacock die first. He crawled. When he got to the front door, he pulled himself up into a standing position. One of the Russians positioned himself by a window. Petrenko and Yuri moved so they were on one side of the door, the other Russian stood on the opposite side.

"Now," Petrenko ordered.

Shrini started pounding on the door. "Peacock, open up!"

There was some noise from inside the house. To Shrini it sounded like someone was running up and down a staircase. The Russian standing by the window nodded at Petrenko, then aimed and fired. The ricochet from the glass took off the tip of his nose. Then a shot fired from inside the house took off the rest of his face.

Petrenko stared blankly at the dead man's body before realizing what had happened – that the window had been installed with one-way bullet-proof glass. His face slowly transformed into something not quite human as he knocked Shrini aside and tried kicking down the door. The steel-reinforced door held, his knee didn't. Grabbing his injured knee he barked out orders to Yuri and the other man to get the car. Both turned and ran towards the road, both men keeping low to the ground so they wouldn't be targets from inside the house. Petrenko watched them disappear behind some bushes. As he started to straighten up, Shrini grabbed him from behind, his forearm pushing hard into Petrenko's throat.

In the position Petrenko was in all he could do was flail harmlessly. There was no way he could break Shrini's chokehold. The strength of this person surprised him. As the world started to darken on him he fell to one knee, then the other and finally on to his stomach. As his head was pushed to one side he saw Shrini's leg stretched out and realized that Shrini was lying crisscrossed on top of him, probably so he could brace himself.

Petrenko still had his gun. He moved his arm slightly from his side and pointed the gun where he expected Shrini's injured ankle to be and then started firing until he heard the sound of a bullet hitting bone. There was a muffled scream. The grip around Petrenko's throat loosened enough for him to break free. Gasping for air, he lifted his gun arm and shot Shrini two times in the eye.

Yuri arrived with the BMW. Petrenko pushed himself to his feet. Coughing, his face a deep purple, he ordered Yuri out of the car. "You," he commanded the other man, "drive through that wall!"

The man looked at the house and then at the rifle barrel Yuri had trained on him. He shifted over to the driver's seat, revved the engine and floored the gas, aiming the BMW to the left of the front door.

The car made it halfway through the house, both front wheels blowing out on impact. The Russian, though, trapped by the front airbag, was easily picked off by Joel with a single shot from his AK-47.

The car had knocked a large hole through the wall. Yuri charged through it, firing his rifle. Joel hit him once in the shoulder and again in the chest, but before Yuri went down he got off a round hitting Joel in the hand. The bullet blew off two of his fingers and sent his AK-47 clattering across the floor.

"*Motherfucking cunt*," Joel swore as he stared at the bloody stumps where his fingers had been. When he looked up he saw Petrenko through the hole. The Russian fired once at Joel, hitting him in the thigh and sending him falling on to his back.

"You fucking *zhid*," Petrenko swore. "You're going to steal from me?"

He squeezed his body through the opening in the wall. As Petrenko made his way forward his injured knee seized up. When he recovered he found that Joel, still lying on his back, had a forty-five caliber pistol aimed at him.

"I was carrying two guns, asshole."

There were three gunshots, all rapid-fire. Petrenko looked with mild surprise at the three red dots spaced out along his chest. Then he fell over dead.

Joel looked down and saw he was bleeding badly from his thigh. *Commie son of a bitch hit an artery*. He took off his shirt, and using his teeth, ripped off a strip of fabric. Wrapping it above his wound and pulling as tight as he could, he tied his makeshift tourniquet. He sat for a moment, trying to build up the strength to stand. He got halfway to his feet and then blacked out.

The two detectives found nothing in Dan's storage locker. Resnick told his partner to meet him at the car, waited until he left and then pulled Dan aside.

"I can't let you get away with this," Resnick said.

Dan didn't bother responding. As Resnick looked at him,

the muscles along his jaw hardened until his face looked carved out of stone.

"I'm going to keep searching until I find something. Even if I don't find any concrete evidence I have to make you pay for this. I can't let you skate with one woman dead and another critically wounded." Resnick paused, sucked in his breath. "Do you have any idea what type of animal Petrenko is?"

"I never heard of this Petrenko—"

"Let me educate you then," Resnick said, giving Dan a cold stare. "He used to torture people for the KGB. Over the years we've found bodies dumped in the ocean that have been skinned head to toe. There's no doubt in my mind Petrenko did them personally, but he's smart and I've never been able to tie him to any of them. If I arrest you and get your name in the papers, he'll go after your family. Even if we assign a police detail to protect them, he'll get them. The guy is as relentless as he is sadistic."

Dan's color drained a few shades. "I don't appreciate this type of threat, Detective."

"It's not a threat. I'm telling you what will happen for a fact." Resnick looked away as he rubbed his jaw. "I know he had other items besides money in those boxes. I know him well enough to know that. My guess is those items would send him away to prison for the rest of his miserable life."

Raising his gaze to meet Dan's eyes, he added, "If I were you and I cared at all about my family, I'd make sure those items ended up in my hands."

Resnick gave Dan a short nod and left.

When Dan got back to his car he sat paralyzed for a long moment. Then he took out his cell phone and called Joel. The phone rang until the answering machine picked up. He hung up and tried again. This time after the fifth ring someone picked up.

"Joel, are you there?"

"Yeah, you woke me. Who's talking?"

"Dan. We got to meet."

"Yeah, okay." There was a long pause. "You come here now, I'll split everything with you."

The phone went dead on him. Dan had no clue what was behind Joel's change of heart and wondered whether this was some sort of setup. In the end he decided he had no choice. He put away his cell phone and headed for New Hampshire.

31

It was a little after seven when Dan pulled up in Joel's driveway. The scene outside the house looked like something from a battlefield. With the summer winding down and the days getting shorter, the evening's dusk added to the eeriness of the scene. Dan couldn't quite comprehend why a car would be sticking halfway out of Joel's house until he spotted the two bodies.

He walked slowly up the path to the front door and saw that one of the dead bodies was Shrini. He felt nothing seeing his friend lying there dead with a large gaping hole where his eye should've been. He rang the bell and stood mutely until he heard Joel weakly call out for him to come in through the hole in the wall.

Dan walked past another dead body and around the back end of the BMW before squeezing through the opening between the wall and the car. Inside he saw two more dead bodies and then caught sight of Joel propped up in a sitting position. Joel looked white as a sheet, a large puddle of blood underneath him. From what Dan could tell, blood seemed to be spurting out of his leg.

As Dan moved into the room he stared transfixed at one of the dead bodies, realizing it was Viktor Petrenko.

"Hey, pal." Joel tried to smile. "Here's the deal. I'll give you half of what I got. First bury these bodies, clean up in here, then take me to the hospital."

"I can't do that, Joel. I'm sorry, but I don't trust you any more."

Joel's half-hearted smile disappeared. He lifted his gun and aimed it at Dan. "You trust me to blow your head off if you don't do what I say?"

"Do what you have to, Joel."

Joel's eyes glazed over for a moment and then softened back to something more human. "*Motherfucker*," he swore. "All right, I can't blame you. What will it take?"

"I have to get my money first."

"You give me your word you help me afterwards?"

"You've got my word."

Joel made his decision, nodded slowly. "You try fucking me, you're dead, understand?"

"Whatever you say, Joel."

"End of my shooting range, you shovel off a foot of dirt. You'll find a safe there. Combination two, twelve, two. You're going to take only half, right?"

"That's all."

"Then hurry up. It's going to take a while to bury these bodies."

Dan went down to the basement, found a shovel and dug out enough dirt to expose the safe. He opened it, took out the duffel bag that he had used in the robbery, then wiped off whatever fingerprints he might've left.

When he got back upstairs, Joel asked what he was doing with the bag. "I thought you were only going to take half," he demanded.

Dan ignored him and kept walking.

"*Motherfucker!* We had a deal!"

A bullet whistled past Dan's ear. When he turned around he could tell from the expression on Joel's face that the shot had not been meant as a warning shot. The only reason he missed was because his eyes were clouding up and he probably couldn't see straight.

"You gave me your word," Joel insisted. His body swayed back and forth. He wasn't going to be able to keep himself propped up much longer.

"Joel, you're bleeding out. No matter what I do you're going to be dead soon."

As Dan squeezed through the opening in the wall, he heard another shot fired, but had the feeling that this one missed wildly. Walking towards his car, he heard one last *Motherfucker* yelled out, Joel's voice now feeble, barely recognizable.

During the ride home he thought about what his next steps were going to be. He no longer had to worry about Petrenko. Eventually the cops were going to find out about what happened at Joel's house, but what would that prove? Even if they could now tie Shrini and Joel to the robbery they still had nothing to tie him to it… except his cell phone call to Joel. What could they prove from that? They still had no real evidence. Maybe they'd make him go through a trial, but he'd get through it.

He got home after nine. The house seemed quiet. Too quiet. He found Carol sitting alone in the kitchen, her face worn out, her eyes red and puffy as if she'd been crying.

"Where are the kids?" Dan asked.

"At friends' houses." She faced him. "That rash you had. That was the same day as the robbery. You got that from the makeup."

"I told you how I got that—"

"Quit lying to me, Dan. You've been lying to me for months. All those meetings with Shrini and Gordon were so you could plan the robbery. Joel was involved too, wasn't he? I remember that phone call you were so afraid of me overhearing."

"Carol, please—"

"Quit lying to me, Dan. I can't stand it."

Dan sat down across from her. He couldn't bear to look at all the pain in her eyes. All he could do was bury his face in his hands. "We were going to lose the house. We were going to lose everything we had."

"So you robbed a bank. You killed a girl. Dan, she was only twenty!"

"Twenty-three," Dan corrected her.

Carol's jaw dropped as she stared at him.

"No one was supposed to get hurt," Dan said quickly. "Gordon went nuts. There was nothing I could do."

They sat in silence. Dan couldn't break it. All he could do was wait for Carol to say something.

Finally, she did. "Get out. I never want you anywhere near me or my children ever again."

"Carol, I love you."

"I might still love you too, Dan. I'm not sure right now. But I can't have you around my children."

"Please, I had to do what I did." He forced himself to look at her. "I'm going blind."

"What?"

"I have retinitis pigmentosa. Another year or so and I'll be completely blind."

"My God! Why didn't you tell me this before?"

"You had enough to worry about as it was. If I had a job I would've had long-term disability to protect you and the kids. But without it what was I going to do? Have all of you end up in the streets?"

"We would've managed somehow."

"How? On welfare? In a project somewhere?"

"We would've managed," she repeated stubbornly. "Dan, it's too late now to fix things. There's nothing you can do except leave." She paused. "I won't tell the police what I know, but you have to leave."

Dan stared at her helplessly. As much as he didn't want to admit it, he knew there was no point arguing with her.

"Let me at least give you the money," he said.

"No, don't you dare even try."

"Jesus, Carol—"

"Just leave, please."

"What are you going to tell the kids?"

"I'll think of something."

Dan tried to think of some way to change her mind but knew in his heart there was nothing he could do. He got up, walked slowly, stopped once to look back at his wife and then left.

Resnick hated the way things were left. He had nothing concrete to charge Wilson with and he wasn't going to risk having the guy's wife and kids massacred as some sort of ploy. He was stuck and he hated being stuck.

He lifted a finger to the bartender, indicating another bourbon was in order. As he downed the shot, he made a decision. He got off his barstool, threw twenty bucks down and left the bar.

He didn't have any real plan as he drove to Wilson's house, but somehow he was going to get through to the guy. If it meant dragging him to Mary O'Donnell's bedside, he was going to get through to him.

When he got to Wilson's house his wife answered the door. He felt a tug at his heart when he saw lines creasing her face that hadn't been there only hours earlier. She told him her husband wasn't home and she didn't expect him to come home any time in the future.

"Why is that?" he asked.

"Something personal between the two of us. Nothing I care to discuss."

Resnick hesitated, then asked if he could come in.

"I really have nothing to say to you."

"Please, just give me a few minutes."

"Fine, a few minutes."

She tried to smile as she stepped aside. Or maybe she was trying to keep from crying. Resnick couldn't tell which it was.

He stood in the living room, waited for her to take a seat on a sectional sofa, and then took a seat kitty-corner to her.

"This looks like an expensive house. Pretty expensive neighborhood also."

Carol didn't respond.

Resnick felt another tug at his heart while he watched her sitting with her hands clasped tight together, struggling to keep her composure. "When your husband lost his job, things must've gotten difficult financially," he said.

She nodded, bit her lip. "I found a job. Dan got himself a contract. We did okay."

"His contract pay anywhere near what his salary used to?"

She shook her head.

Resnick took a deep breath and let the air out slowly. He hated what he was doing but he had no choice. He handed her the same crime-scene photos of Mary O'Donnell and Margaret Williams that he had shown Dan earlier. Her face went white as she looked at them.

Resnick said. "I know your husband planned the robbery. He's responsible for what happened to those two women."

"I can't tell you anything," she said, her voice coming out in short gasps.

"Mrs. Wilson, I know you had nothing to do with this, but I need your help."

She broke out sobbing, her face becoming a mask of pain and hopelessness. Blindly, she stood up, her shoulders rising up and down rhythmically with her sobs. Then she held out her arms.

Awkwardly, he stood up. He knew this wasn't right. He was trying to put her husband away, for Chrissakes. But what was he going to do, just let her stand there and bawl?

She fell into him, her head hard against his chest as she sobbed.

Damn, this is just not right, he thought. He put one arm around her and patted her back.

He understood fully what she was going through. She had just lost her husband, the father of her children – really her whole way of life. As he held her, felt the smallness of her body and her tears soaking through his shirt, he started thinking of his own losses. His beautiful wife, Carrie, and that heart-wrenching smile that she had. All those years wasted in his self-imposed isolation. And Brian...

It was the first time he had truly let himself think about losing Brian – actually admit to himself that he was never going to see his boy again – and the thought overwhelmed him.

Brian was gone.

There was no way of ever bringing him back.

His boy was really gone...

As the realization forced itself upon him, the pain became so unbearable he didn't think he could live. It was as if his heart were going to explode. All of the pain came crashing down like a tidal wave, catching him in its currents, tossing him about in a dizzying fury. God, how could he survive this? Survive knowing his boy was really gone. That he'd never hold his Brian again. Never see his boy again. How in the world was that possible?

Resnick realized he was sobbing also and that he was holding Carol even tighter than she was holding him.

Dan drove until he was bleary-eyed, until he couldn't focus any more, and then stopped at the first roadside motel he came to. Where was he, Ohio? Indiana? He had no idea. All he knew was that he was exhausted.

The desk clerk asked him if he had any bags. Dan couldn't help laughing when he told him only one. The clerk looked at him as if he were crazy. Fine, let him.

When he got to his room, he dumped the contents of the duffel bag on to his bed. Packets of hundred-dollar bills covered the bedspread, some of them spilling on to the floor. He guessed he had over a million dollars. There were a bunch of silk bags among the money. He emptied out dozens of diamonds from them.

All that money lying in front of him. All those diamonds glistening under the dim light from a sixty-watt bulb.

He tried to figure out what he was going to do with all of that money. Finally, he came to the conclusion that he didn't have a clue.

Not a fucking clue.

www.serpentstail.com

Visit serpentstail.com today to browse and buy our books, and to sign up for exclusive news and previews of our books, interviews with our authors and forthcoming events.

| NEWS | cut to the literary chase with all the latest news about our books and authors |

| EVENTS | advance information on forthcoming events, author readings, exhibitions and book festivals |

| EXTRACTS | read first chapters, short stories, bite-sized extracts |

| EXCLUSIVES | pre-publication offers, discounted books, competitions |

| BROWSE AND BUY | browse our full catalogue and shop securely |

FREE POSTAGE & PACKING ON ALL ORDERS...
WORLDWIDE

Follow us on Twitter • Find us on Facebook